KILL ALL ANGELS

ROBERT BROCKWAY

KILL
ALL
ANGELS

TITAN BOOKS

Kill All Angels
Print edition ISBN: 9781783298013
E-book edition ISBN: 9781783298020

Published by Titan Books
A division of Titan Publishing Group Ltd
144 Southwark Street, London SE1 0UP

First Titan edition: December 2017
2 4 6 8 10 9 7 5 3 1

A CIP catalogue record for this title is available from the British Library.

Printed and bound by CPI Group (UK) Ltd, Croydon, CR0 4YY

This book is dedicated to you, the reader.
I spent years digging this shaky tunnel down into
the most diseased and horrible pits of my soul,
then asked you to come visit. You said, "yes."
That was very stupid, and you'll almost certainly
die down here, but thank you.

ONE

Carey. 1984. Los Angeles, California. Chinatown.

Ever heard the noise fingernails make when they're digging into steel? No? Oh, well, when you're on the other side of it—the screeching muffled but somehow also amplified by all that metal between you—it's almost pretty. Sounds like whales singing.

"We ain't got much time before those things get through that door," I said, wrapping my belt around the interior hinge and cinching it tight. It wasn't a great barricade, but it would hold for a few minutes. "And you've seen what they'll do to us when that happens, so listen close, I'm only going to explain this once. No questions. None of that 'oh no, that's crazy, I don't believe it' garbage. After the shit you've seen in the last ten minutes, you lost the right to be skeptical."

The kid's eyes were the size of hubcaps. Couldn't do much more than nod.

"Let me start from the top. There are angels—you haven't seen those yet—but they look like little stars, just burning in the air right in front of you. They make a sound like the ocean in a storm, if a thousand people were drowning in it. They do something to people. They treat us like a math problem. They pick out all our little quirks and problems, every redundant or unnecessary bit, and they solve us. Usually when that happens, there's a boom and a shudder and the person is just gone. No idea what happens to them."

The door shook with a sound like a garbage truck hitting a telephone pole. The kid shivered. I went on.

"But sometimes a solve doesn't go quite right, and the person doesn't disappear. There's something left over, like a remainder to that math problem. When that happens, the person pukes up a bunch of black shit that takes on a life of its own—that's what those tar men that burned your friends to a crisp are. And the shell of the human being left over becomes this unkillable pyscho—that's what the Chinese girl with the silver hair is, and that's why she ate part of your girlfriend back at Madame Wong's."

The kid clearly wanted to cry, but was trying not to for my benefit.

"Oh, also the Empty Ones—that's what we call those shells—do something to people, too. They take away bits of their humanity, until all that's left are those faceless punks out there calling for your blood. There's your rundown. You cool?"

"Y-yeah," the kid said. "Super cool."

There has never, in history, been a person less cool.

He was a little guy. 120 pounds and 5'4" on a good day. None of that muscle. He had the build of a man who survives solely on government cheese and instant noodles. There was a streak of light blue through his spiked blond hair, and he had some wispy facial fuzz that would require a second puberty to qualify as a mustache. He was wearing skintight blue jeans, fashionably torn, of course, and a faded T-shirt for a band called Red Wedding. Never heard of them. Made a mental note to check them out afterward, in his honor.

"All right," I said, and clapped the kid on the shoulder reassuringly. "So here's the plan: when I say go, you're gonna take this broom and run out the door swinging."

"What? Like hell!" The kid tried to cringe back from me, but there wasn't much room in the walk-in freezer. He just kind of cowered around the frozen peas.

"Listen, kid, remember earlier? When I said 'you know what they're gonna do to us?' I didn't mean you. They're not gonna do a damn thing to you. They don't care about you. You're an object. You're not even an obstacle. The only thing they want is me. The only reason your friends died—and I am so sorry to say this—is because they were in the way. They were in between those things, and me. I'm what they want, and what I'm really doing here is asking you for a favor. I need you. I need you to save my life."

"Save you? How?"

"You go out that door swinging, and maybe it throws them off their game for just a few seconds. A few seconds for me to run. They'll all chase after me, but they won't spare you a second glance. Those few seconds are all you can buy me, but it's better than nothing. I'm hurt, and I was never all that fast to start with, so I probably won't make it far, but I've gotta try. Please, kid. Just a few seconds of broom swinging and maybe some yelling, if you're feeling up to it. That's all I'm asking from you, and then you turn around and you run like hell and forget about all this. Except for the part where you're a hero. My hero."

"They'll kill me, they'll—"

"They wouldn't piss on you if you were on fire. You're a gnat. You're not even something worth swatting away. As long as you don't actually hit one of them, they'll forget about you the second they see me."

"I don't hit 'em?"

"No, kid. It wouldn't do a damn thing if you hit one anyway. Just swing that broom around, make a big show."

The kid swallowed hard. Had an Adam's apple like a kneecap. He bit his lip and nodded.

I gave him the broom. He wielded it like Excalibur.

I opened the door, and he charged out screaming, swinging it in broad strokes like a battleaxe.

The Chinese girl with the silver hair—that's Jie, more on her later—punched straight through his chest. Sent his heart splattering into the wall. It almost hit me, as I ran for the window.

I tucked into a ball just as I hit the glass, and didn't even try to break my fall.

My name is Carey, and I wasn't always an asshole.

Well, I wasn't always *this much* of an asshole.

Let me tell you about how I got here, and maybe you'll understand.

TWO

Kaitlyn. 2013. Just off the I-10, outside Quartzsite, Arizona.

A few years ago I had an ex-boyfriend who was into the Asian spirituality stuff. It didn't seem to matter what kind of Asian: Buddhist, Shinto, some Hindu and yoga thrown in there—he was like spiritual fusion cuisine. Very Californian.

He wore his hair up in a frizzy little man bun, and had an eyebrow ring. Jackie gave me so much shit for dating him, but Jesus Christ, you should've seen his abs. Like a cobblestone street. And he could bend himself into a human pretzel, which was occasionally interesting. Plus he was always nice to me. A total dipshit, of course, but a nice one.

He tried to get me to meditate a few times. He said it was all about feeling your skin, really concentrating on the boundary between you and the world. Then feeling that skin get thinner and thinner until there was nothing separating you from everything else. I could never get it. I just wound up getting stupid thoughts stuck in my head: the lyrics to a silly pop song or something. He'd spend twenty minutes contemplating nirvana; I'd spend twenty minutes endlessly repeating the chorus to "Night Moves." It wasn't spiritually helpful.

Still, I didn't have any better ideas on how to start. I sat cross-legged in the sand, trying to ignore the highway sounds coming over the bluff, the sun burning my skin, the particles of grit slowly grinding their way into my underwear.

I am not Kaitlyn. I am just this body. I am not this body. I am nothing.

An ant or something was crawling over my right ankle. Somewhere behind and above me, a tiny bird chirped. A dozen little itches sprang up all over my body. I could feel my hairs waving in the breeze. If the whole idea of meditation was to lose your sense of self-awareness, it wasn't working. I was becoming, if anything, hyper-aware.

Way to totally fuck up Zen, Kaitlyn.

Maybe I need to go about this the completely opposite way. Get lost in my thoughts until I forget myself. Okay, so, what to think about?

Counting sheep? That's for when you can't fall asleep. Baseball? No, that's sex. And that's for guys. Plus I know jack about baseball. Uh . . .

Name all the Pokémon?

I wonder if I could still do that. It's been years since I last played that game.

Nobody achieved nirvana by naming Pokémon, Kaitlyn. Jesus Christ!

I'd better figure out a way to get Zen, fast.

That's probably the least Zen thought you can have.

I could sense Carey's and Jackie's eyes on me, already losing patience. We'd been burning road between Mexico and L.A., when I made them pull the car over like I had to throw up, then just got out and sat in the dirt. They probably wouldn't give me much quiet time. To be honest, I'm surprised they let me have any. After all, I was the one with "the big idea"—and now here we are, parked on the side of a highway in the Arizona desert, the two of them drinking warm Tecate in the Camry while I sit in a pile of hot sand and totally fail to commune with the divine.

Trust me, I basically told them, *I totally have this angel thing on lock. I'll kill 'em all and have us done in time for happy hour.*

In truth, I didn't have a plan; I had a feeling. I felt that if I could just find and take one more angel, I could stop all of this. I did not have any more *helpful* feelings, like how to find one, or what to do afterward.

When Carey heard "find one more angel," he said, "Let's go to L.A." That's about as much as he'd share, but I wasn't exactly an open book myself these days. I bit my tongue when he and Jackie asked what, exactly, happened back in Mexico. I looked the other way when they inquired about my "plan." I pointed behind them and shouted *"what in god's name is that?!"* when they had the gall to ask about the last time I slept.

Days, weeks, more? Exhausted but never tired. That's not normal, that's inhuman—

And let's just put a stop to that thought-stream, shall we?

Meditating. That's what we're doing.

I couldn't empty out my head. I just kept going back to that moment in Mexico, when I stepped sideways and blinked out of existence. Replaying it in my head. Trying to figure out exactly what I did. I know I felt something like a draft, coming from nowhere. Only it wasn't warm, or cold, or even wind—just a faint influx of otherness. Something not here, or of here. I focused in on the draft, let it wash over me, and then I was gone. To a place that wasn't anything. I couldn't actually see it, in the conventional sense. But it was like standing in a foggy hall of mirrors, where each mirror reflected a reality that was slightly different than my own. I followed the mental image. Pictured the hall, imagined the mirrors.

What do you see?

Well, this one makes me look fat. That one makes my face looks long. Hey, this one makes me look short, and the other one kind of wobbles from side to side like—

This isn't going to work.

I sighed.

Pikachu.

Bulbasaur.

Charizard.

Squirtle.

Blasto—

THREE

Jackie. 2013. Just off the I-10, outside Quartzsite, Arizona.

"What about you?" Carey said, and gestured with his beer can toward Kaitlyn, sitting crisscross applesauce in a dry riverbed. "You go in for all this Hindu voodoo Jazzercise bullshit?"

"None of that was even slightly right," I said.

I drained the last of my Tecate, which was now room temperature, provided that room was a hot trunk in the Arizona sunshine. I tossed the can on the floor in the backseat. Carey crumpled his and tossed it in the ditch running beside the shoulder. It landed next to a wadded up ball of aluminum foil with two bites of burrito inside, a few crumpled-up napkins, and six other half-crushed Tecate cans.

"Can you not litter?" I said to him.

Carey burped as loud as he could.

"What, am I ruining this pristine vista?" He swept his arm grandly over the sand, sand, more sand, handful of stunted bushes, and white girl quickly turning red.

"You're such a dick," I said. I cracked open another beer. Tasted like somebody had made tea out of cigarette butts.

"How long is she going to be out there?" he asked.

"No idea," I said. "How long does it take to master bizarre teleportation powers stolen from an evil ball of light?"

"Like twenty minutes, tops." Carey laughed. "Hey Jackie, you know what we could do to pass the time?"

"Fuck by the side of an active highway, in the backseat of this stolen 1996 Toyota Camry, on top of all the Red Bull cans and fast food wrappers, in like, 103-degree heat?"

Carey tapped his nose.

"I'll pass. I'd rather juggle the balls of a rabid grizzly."

"Well, our other option is watching Sitting Bull here contemplate her—whoa, what the hell?"

I followed his gaze to Kaitlyn. But there was no Kaitlyn. She was gone. I looked around: nothing but flat, featureless desert as far as the eye could see. What? There was nowhere to—she couldn't even *duck* without us seeing her out there.

"Holy shit! Did you see where she went?" I grabbed Carey's forearm, all loose flesh over wiry muscle.

He looked down at my hand.

"No, but I know what we can do to pass the time while we wait for her to—"

FOUR

Kaitlyn. 2013. Just off the I-10, outside Quartzsite, Arizona.

Snorlax.

Goldeen.

Cubone.

Uh . . .

Mew.

Mew . . . two?

It was getting cold. Or at least not so sweltering hot anymore. How long had I been out here doing this? I opened my eyes and saw nothing but black.

What? No way it got this dark this quickly.

I rubbed my eyes. No help. I put my hand on the ground to push myself up, but there was no ground there. There was no up. There was no self to push. I could feel my body, was aware of its position in space, but I clearly wasn't in the desert anymore. I wasn't in anything. Just floating in a kind of dark, temperature-less amniotic fluid. I stared hard, trying to make out what was around me. In the distance, dim pinpricks of light struggled to resolve, then faded again. At first I thought they were faint, but as time went on it seemed more like they were just distant. I thought about moving closer to them. Pictured myself kicking my feet, swimming through—what? water? space?—toward the lights. I couldn't tell if it was working.

Great. I meditated myself into the cosmic kiddie pool and now I have to just wait for an adult to come fish me out.

I felt the draft again. A foreign presence gently tickling my skin and raising the fine hairs on my forearms.

I'm going about this wrong. I'm still thinking physically. Trying to kick my feet. Picturing myself struggling through space, like that's what this place was. Adjust your thinking, Kaitlyn.

I am not here. This is not a "here." If I am not in this place—if this isn't a place at all—then I am not pinned to a single location. I do not need to move. I simply need to exist elsewhere.

The blackness flashed, and instantly came alive with burning white stars. I couldn't tell their exact distance or scale, relative to me. But I got the feeling they were small— around my own size. Which meant they were close, all bunched together in the space immediately surrounding me. I reached out to touch one—

No, that's physicality again.

I made myself more aware of the orb nearest me. Inside of the light, something moved. Patterns like circuit boards. They expanded, contracted, changed shape. There was something wrong about the way the lines joined together. They met in impossible places, formed junctures that I couldn't comprehend. It made me feel cold inside, and nauseous—the first feelings since I wound up here. I became dimly aware of a sound. Loud static and high-pitched squeals. Like a busy highway, if every other car was screeching to a halt. These weren't stars.

They were angels.

Thousands of them. I looked further into the dark, and saw that they marched on into infinity. Forever, until their light was too faint to see. Not thousands—millions, billions.

I am not here. I am not actually surrounded by countless balls of fatal light that want nothing more than to simplify my code and nullify my internal existence. This is not happening. I'm just going to slooowly picture myself existing back where I was. Or you know what? Even farther away than that, so far I can't even see the lights.

And just like that, they were gone. Everything was gone, even the blackness. Surrounding me was pure absence. A non-place. Colorless. Toneless.

And then, before me, something like a cube appeared. It was comprised of multiple thin, square layers, stacked one atop another. I got the sense I was supposed to do something with it. I tried to reach out to touch it, but I had no physical body.

Huh. Okay, let's try another tack.

I thought about it spinning, and it spun.

Cool.

I thought about it getting closer, and it did. I focused in on the bottom layer, and it burst out of the cube, expanding until the non-place around me filled with stars, nebula, and planets. A thick cloud of brown dust swooped toward me. I tried to shield myself by reflex, but there was no point. I wasn't here. My viewpoint swirled about in its depths, turning listlessly, and then it was gone. The cloud vanished into the distance. As it pulled away, I could see that the dust wasn't entirely brown—when far enough removed, it took on colors and made patterns. Sweeping orange melted into dull crimson faded into dark purple. Stars engulfed me, burning the air beside me one second, then shrinking away until they were just pinpricks of light.

Oof. Enough of that.

It wasn't vertigo, exactly, but the rapid sense of expansion left me feeling shaky and fragile. I focused on pulling the universe back together. It shrank, compacted into a shimmering plane, and slotted itself into the cube. Another layer began to pull out from the mass, but I mentally pushed it back in.

I didn't need another demonstration. I got the message: Each of these thin cross-sections was a universe, carefully fit together to form a whole of something else: the cube.

Okay, so . . . what's the point?

One by one, tiny pins of light stabbed through the bottommost layer of the cube. They were cold and featureless. I heard the dull roar of static when I focused in on one.

These were the angels I had seen earlier.

The next highest layer lit up: a pattern of angels almost, but not quite identical to those below it. And the next, and so on. Each layer's layout of angels slightly different than the one below, slowly forming a three-dimensional pattern. Taken alone, in the seemingly flat planes, the angels were just isolated balls of light. When taken altogether, each layer building upon the other, another picture became clear: Sprawled throughout the universal cube was a mass of slowly writhing tentacles, made of pure, white, screaming light. An infinity of angels, each a separate being in their own universe, linked together throughout dimensions into a single, massive creature.

A word popped into my mind: "Siphonophora." I'd learned it on a fifth-grade field trip to the Monterey Bay Aquarium.

"Who knows what this is?" the man with the big calves and the ponytail asked us.

A bunch of kids yelled out "jellyfish!"

Ponytail laughed.

"You'd think that, but no! This is a Portuguese man o' war, and it's not actually a jellyfish, but something we call a siphonophore." He gestured toward the tank, and we all dutifully peered into the scratched glass to watch the gelatinous stringy blob undulate through the blue. "That means it's not one big creature, but many smaller ones joined together into a single community that works together so closely, they can't even live apart!"

I just nodded and let the information immediately slip out of my little kid brain. I wanted to see the otters. I could give a damn about jellyfish—unless they had little whiskers and held hands so they didn't drift apart while they slept, jellyfish had *nothing* on otters. But all the information came flooding back now, looking at the disembodied spray of white tubes inhabiting the universal cube.

Not inhabiting. Infecting.

They were my thoughts, but they felt forced. Just like the Siphonophora memory, come to think of it. I'm the one thinking these things, but not the one t*elling* me to think them.

This wasn't a random happening. This was a presentation.

Something was showing this to me. I became aware of a presence out here with me in the non-space. Nothing visible or substantial, but I could still feel its bulk. Or weight, or . . . I don't know. I only knew that it was indefinably, immeasurably vast. I felt like krill, drifting in the ocean, waiting for a whale to come by and feed.

Infected, came the thought again.

It was true: The siphonophore wasn't just living in the cube, like a goldfish in a bowl. It was spreading through it. Where the tentacles of light passed through, the cube became wan and still. The siphonophore was careful not to occupy one space for too long, or return to it too frequently, giving the cube just enough time to regenerate before sucking the life out of it again. It wasn't a natural inhabitant of the universal collective. It was a parasite. A colony that passed through every observable dimension, each single creature linking the energy it stole to the others.

If I had a body to shiver, I would have.

It was bad enough, thinking the angels were some race of otherworldly beings with evil intent. I, perhaps arrogantly, felt I could fight that somehow—but this? A whole universe is small to this thing. It spans every possible reality, twisting through the very core of existence. What could I do to this? Kill one angel—kill a thousand, a million—it wouldn't even register to the whole. I'm nothing against this. I'm helpless.

The link is not just their strength, it's also their weakness.

That thing again, thinking my thoughts for me.

What are you?

No response. Just that mental image of the whale again, drifting in space—slow, oblivious, eternal.

Why are you out here?

I felt the presence shift. It drew closer to the cube, and the siphonophore flared an angry, bare-bulb white.

Pain. Massive, incommunicable agony on a scale beyond comprehension. I felt shredded by it, like every atom of my body had been torn apart and flung in all directions with incredible force. But of course, I wasn't really here. I had no body. When my mind recovered from the shock, I put it together.

The cube, the . . . the collection of universes and dimensions or whatever. Reality. That's your home?

Nothing.

And the parasite, it kicked you out of there. Took over. Right?

Nothing.

Great. Now I'm getting the cold shoulder from a cosmic whale.

I don't get it. I don't get how to help you. I want to, I really do. That's my home in there somewhere. It's so small and utterly meaningless to things like you, I'm sure, but it's all I've got and they're killing it. If I can help, like you seem to think, you have to tell me how.

A layer slid out from the cube and wrapped itself around me. I had the sensation of falling from a great height, while simultaneously drowning in the deepest ocean, crushed by billions of tons of liquid force. Then the expansion stopped, and I found myself parked in the field of angels again. Frozen lights scattered through blackness.

For a very long time—or perhaps no time at all, it was hard to tell in here—nothing happened. Then my point of view shifted closer to the nearest angel. Closer again. Even closer, until I was practically inside of the thing. All I could see was furious screeching white, impossible angles, and sharp lines that twisted round and intersected themselves. I couldn't take it. I tried to cover my eyes, pictured my hand coming up before my face. I brushed against the angel— maybe not my physical body, but my presence—and it recoiled. Thin brown cracks spread out from the point of contact, networking like veins or lightning strikes. They branched off and multiplied until the entire ball of light was overtaken. I'd seen something similar once before, when I'd been inside the angels, just before I shattered them. But it didn't break apart this time, it just splintered and splintered until there was no surface left untainted.

The corrupted angel floated there inert, dull mud against the blanket of black. My point of view pulled back dramatically. I thanked god I didn't have a stomach here, so I couldn't puke in the space between dimensions. From my new angle, I was looking at an extreme close-up of the cube, at the point where two layers met. The inert angel I had just touched overlapped slightly with a still-brilliantly white one on the next layer. Slowly, the color began to seep from the brown orb to the white one, until it, too, was riddled with cracks. My point of view pulled out again, and again—each time showing me the same thing: cracks spreading from angel to angel, snaking up the tube of light until it was light no more. Fully outside the cube now, I could see the cracks spreading like a disease, from one tentacle to the next, poisoning the nest until the whole siphonophore was the color of a dead tree. When the last light diminished, the tentacles disintegrated entirely, dissolving into dust and disseminating into space.

That was the end of the show.

Nothing happened for a while.

I don't know how to describe the feeling of an impossibly gigantic, creation-spanning creature waiting on a response from you. It was the sinking sensation you get after you've been pulled over, while you're waiting for the cop to get out of his car and walk up to your window. But obviously multiplied by a number so large that it probably doesn't technically exist.

Yeah, okay, yes.

I thought to myself, assuming the entity would pick it up.

I get it. The link is how I bring them down. I don't kill the next angel entirely, I just like . . . poison it somehow and let it spread. Right?

Nothing. It doesn't like rhetorical questions, I guess.

So why me? I'm a freak, I get that. But what makes me different from the freaks that came before me? Why couldn't they help you?

Bacteria. Or cells, or . . . something microscopic. A squiggly thing with two weird appendages snaking out. They reached toward a spiky blob. The thing and the blob fought. The blob won. The squiggly thing died. The scene repeated—this time there were three weird appendages on the squiggly thing. Fighting. Death. And again and again and again—more appendages, different shapes, the results always the same (death and death and death)—but there was progress made each time, until finally, the squiggly thing wrapped itself around the spiky blob, and absorbed it.

I'm like an . . . immune response? You're just what, changing us a little bit each time, and then throwing us at the parasite until one of us finally wins?

No response.

That's messed up.

A quaver.

We're not bacteria.

A wobble.

FUCK. YOU.

The entirety of the non-space groaned, wavered, and abruptly transformed into the face of an extremely ugly, beaten-up old man with beer breath.

"Gah!" I yelled, and pushed the face away.

"What?! Jesus fuckin' hell, Kaitlyn!" Carey said, falling backward out of the Camry's passenger door and onto the warm asphalt of the I-10, still searing in the Arizona sun.

"What happened? Where am I? How long was I gone?"

"I don't know, like thirty seconds?" Carey said. "We just noticed you were missing and were about to go look for you—"

"*I* was about to go look for you," Jackie corrected.

"I was gonna go too! I was just heading to the car first for a search-and-rescue burrito . . ."

"Then you just sorta popped up here in the backseat," Jackie finished.

"It was only thirty seconds? It felt like days, maybe even weeks. . . ."

"Where the hell did you go?" Carey asked, pushing himself into a squatting position outside the car. He surreptitiously snuck a hand into the backseat. He rummaged around in the burrito bag without breaking eye contact.

"Outer space at first, and then this un-place beyond space where the universal cube was. . . ."

Jackie looked at me like you look at your grandma when she can't remember your name. Carey was still feigning concern as he stole and unwrapped his burrito. Still giving me the knit-eyebrow "I'm listening" expression, even as he took the first bite.

"It's hard to explain," I said, pushing myself upright and scooting back up against the far door. I pulled my knees up and buried my face between them. The sun was stupidly bright, after spending so much time in the dark and the non-space. "I think I used my power again. Like I felt this draft of energy, so I followed it out, and something was waiting for me. . . ."

"The angels?" Jackie ventured.

"No, like a . . . a presence. I don't know. It was massive.

I got this kind of mental image of a sorta whale . . . like . . . thing, floating out in space."

"And what did the space whale tell you to do, Kaitlyn?" Carey asked, still maintaining his fake concern, but obviously stifling laughter.

"God damn it, it made more sense while it was happening." I looked to Jackie for understanding, but she was still giving me the "maybe it's time for a nursing home" face. "It was real! It happened! And it told me what the angels are, and how to kill them. I think I even understand what I am now."

Carey, mouth too full of burrito to talk, just rotated his wrist, indicating I should keep going.

"The angels aren't just here, in our reality. They're in every reality, and they're linked between them. They're their own creatures here, but they're also part of this one massive colony so complex that it's a whole *different* creature that exists across entire dimensions. And that colony-creature is sucking the life out of everything, everywhere. The angels solve life where they find it, and use the leftover energy to feed the rest of the colony, taking as much as they can without destroying the entire food source. It's a massive parasite using the whole of existence as a host. That's why the . . . *the space whale* . . . needs me. It can't live here with the parasite."

Neither Jackie nor Carey responded.

"I think, based on this sort of layered cube of universes that the entity showed me, that I finally get what it was I actually did back in Mexico. What I did just now. People like me, the mutations, we take some of an angel's power when we kill it. I'm not teleporting from place to place; I'm stepping between dimensions like the angels do."

"This is a super helpful space whale," Carey said, not bothering to suppress the laughter this time.

"Are you sure this wasn't like, a dream, or a hallucination or something, K?" Jackie shoved Carey out of the way and knelt on the seat across from me. She put her hands on my knees and stared right into my eyes.

"No—or maybe yes, but it doesn't matter. It's still true."

Jackie bit her lip.

"What, you've seen angels that solve people like math problems, and tar men that melt your skin, and immortal B-list celebrity psychos, and you're drawing the line *here*? *This* is the thing that's too absurd to believe?"

Jackie peered back over her shoulder at Carey, who was squatting on the side of the highway powering through a cold burrito so hard he was eating bits of the aluminum foil. He shrugged.

"I guess not? I don't know, K. This whole deal—going back to L.A. at all, much less going there to look for the angels and the faceless dudes—it doesn't seem very . . . *not* stupid."

"Well, you don't have to come," I snapped.

Right, Kaitlyn. This is Jackie's fault. She doesn't believe in your magic space whale and doesn't want to die fighting an inter-dimensional parasite. She's being totally unreasonable.

"No really, you don't though," I said, and put my hands over hers. "And I don't mean that in an angry way, or a hurt way—you *really* don't have to come. It's so risky. I told you before: Nobody will blame you for bailing. We'll still be okay. I'll be okay. You can get out of this and just go be safe."

"Aw," Carey said, wadding up his empty aluminum foil into a ball and tossing it blindly over his shoulder. "Thank you!"

"Not you, asshole," I said. "I was just talking about Jackie.

You got me into this crap, you're damn well seeing it through to the end."

Carey laughed. "I don't care why you're doing it, I'm on board as long as we're killing angels and their little butt-buddies."

"I'm on board because it's you, K. Not because the space whale told you to, or because I think it's a good idea to go picking fights with light bulbs that disintegrate people. I'm on board because I'm always on board with you and your stupid, stupid plans."

I smiled at Jackie.

"That's not me, Jackie," I said. "You're always the one with the dumb ideas, and I'm always along for the ride."

"Yeah, well . . ." She backed out of the car ass-first, and Carey made a big show of watching. "Turnabout is fair play."

She held out her hand to help me up, and I took it.

FIVE

Carey. 1981. Valencia, California. Six Flags Magic Mountain amusement park.

I smashed the pedal to the floor and ducked down just as the lip of the go-kart caught the Empty One in the shin, nearly shearing his leg off at the ankle. He didn't make a sound. His creepy little half smile never even faltered as he crumpled over the cockpit and rolled across my back.

"Ha, that's one for me!" I yelled to Randall, who was coming around the loop just opposite me on the track.

"Check again, Speed Racer," he yelled, flipping me the bird.

I looked over my shoulder and saw a hand, white-finger-clutching the roll bar.

Did I cut off that guy's arms too? Awesome.

Then a face popped up just behind the hand, still smiling at me like I was a precocious child misbehaving at a library.

Shit.

The Empty One had latched onto the kart at the last second, his legs and lower torso dragging on the track as I whipped through the corners. He brought his other hand around the side of the open cockpit and grabbed my arm.

His grip sent blue bolts of pain zipping through my neck. He bore down so hard he impaled himself on the shoulder-spikes of my leather jacket, but showed no sign of letting up. My kart veered wildly, nearly tipping over at the big bend where the track doubled back. I wedged my knees into the steering wheel, keeping my foot down fast on the gas pedal—if I slowed down enough for him to get any leverage, he'd take my head clean off—and tried to pry him loose. It was like being caught in a bear trap. I beat on his face as best I could from the awkward angle, poked at his eyes, pulled at his fingers. Nothing. He just kept smiling quietly.

I took the S-curve way too fast. The kart teetered on one side, then the other, then crashed down flat and weaved across the straightaway. I was coming up on a bend where the track nearly met itself, and could see Randall hauling ass down the opposite side. He saw the pained expression on my face, and started to yell something, but I cut him off.

"Let's play chicken, pussy!" I hollered.

I didn't have time to explain what I wanted him to do, but I've known Randall most of my life. He will always play chicken, he will never swerve, and he really, *really* hates being called a pussy.

At the last wide straight just before the double back, I heel-toed the gas and brake, then wrenched the wheel hard to full lock. The centrifugal force threw the Empty One wide like a yo-yo, but his grip didn't weaken. The extra pressure digging into my flesh nearly made me black out. I hit the gas again and went squealing back the way I'd come—in a head-on collision course with Randall, just coming around the S curves behind me. I could see it on his face—teeth gritted, eyes down, hands planted on the wheel—he was all in. I aimed my kart straight for his and evened out.

Foot planted. Searing pokers digging into the meat of my shoulder. Biting my cheek to keep from screaming. Seconds from impact.

And then I slammed on the brakes.

Three things happened simultaneously:

The Empty One was thrown up and forward over the pivot point where he gripped the roll bar, doing a sort of one-armed handstand directly above my head. Second, the nose of my kart took a steep dive, scraping against the asphalt. Third, I was thrown forward in my seat and laid flat against the tiny dashboard.

Randall, true to his nature, didn't swerve or slow in the slightest. The wheels of his kart hit the downward-angled nose of my own, sending him airborne right above my cockpit. His kart caught the inverted Empty One straight in the nose, evenly dispersing most of his face across the track.

My kart slid to a sideways stop. There was a pained screech and the crash of metal on rubber somewhere behind me. Then the patter of bloody rain and the thump of a limp body on asphalt. I looked at my shoulder. Four long jagged tears in the leather where his fingers had been. Blood was already flowing down my elbow, tracking along the bottom of my hand, and running in a solid rivulet from the tip of my pinky. I considered signing my name on the bastard's mangled body. But there was no time.

I shimmied out of the go-kart and jogged over to check on Randall. His wheels had left long black snake tracks straight into the dividing wall, which was thankfully made of stacks of old tires. He'd caught one to the face, but he was up and moving. I mean, not very well, but movement is a good sign. He was staggering around the track like a cruise-ship drunk in a rough storm. I caught up to him and snapped my fingers in front of his eyes. They focused, but only after about ten seconds.

"Hey, shake it off, man," I said, pulling his arm over my shoulder and carry-walking him toward the exit gate. "That'll put the Empty One down for a few minutes, but not out, and the others won't be far behind."

"I didn't swerve," he said, his voice thick and warbling like Stallone at the end of *Rocky*. "Pussy."

I laughed.

"You did not," I agreed, and pushed through the turnstile first. I pulled him after me, and went to hook his arm again, but he shook me off.

Randall took a few uneasy steps, but his balance held. He poked at his face.

"Is it bad?"

He had a discernible tire track running sideways across one cheek and his nose was bent hard to the right.

I smiled at him.

"Massive improvement," I said.

Who's the pretty one now, buddy?

"If you can walk, you can run. Let's get out of here before—"

"I pull your tongues from your heads and stick them up each other's assholes?" a female voice interjected.

A short Chinese girl with a bright silver bob was sitting on a park bench in between rides at the far end of the courtyard. She had her legs crossed at the knee. She was wearing black leggings and half of a torn yellow T-shirt with the word HULKAMANIA zigzagging across the front. Big bangle earrings, heavy makeup, black lipstick, glitter on the cheeks. She jiggled one of her bright red, six-inch heels absentmindedly. Behind her, a spattering of punk rockers and new-wave kids. I tried to make out their faces and came away with a headache for my troubles.

Unnoticeables.

Which made her another Empty One.

"Listen, baby," I said, stepping out in front of Randall so he could see the hand I held behind my back. "If you wanna throw me some quick head behind the merry-go-round, that's cool, but I go first. Your friends have to wait their turn. I don't do sloppy seconds."

Behind my back, I extended my index and middle fingers, scissoring them back and forth in the universal "running" motion. Then I pointed to my left, toward the gate of the nearest ride: one of those roller coasters where your feet hang out the bottom. Then I held up five fingers.

"Aw, hell," I said. "Who am I kidding? Of *course* I do sloppy seconds!"

"Ugh." The Chinese girl scowled down at her own long pink nails. "You people are always so crass."

Four fingers.

"Me?" I laughed. "You said hello by threatening to make us toss each other's salads."

Three fingers.

"That's a fair point." She quirked her head sideways, and her bitchy valley-girl accent dropped away. Her voice was flat and toneless. "I have to work on those inconsistencies. Thank you."

Two fingers.

She turned her head toward the faceless kids idling behind her.

"Gut them," she said. "Rape them first. Or after. Or during. Your call."

One finger.

I bolted.

From behind me I heard Randall yell: "What? God damn it!"

I checked to see if he was following. He was, but he'd started late and wasn't exactly in peak condition. The Unnoticeables would close ground on him fast.

"Some warning would be nice!" he yelled, staggering into and knocking over a trash can.

"I gave you a countdown!" I said. "I made the running motion, pointed toward the roller coaster, then counted out five seconds!"

"I didn't see any of that! I have, like, half of a concussion, asshole!"

I made the entrance to the ride first, slid to a stop, and grabbed the security gate. I rattled it most of the way shut, then waited for Randall to sprint through. I slammed it closed as he lunged past me and ate shit on the concrete just beyond the threshold. The Unnoticeables came running full force into the security fence, not even trying to slow before body checking it. I was thrown back on my ass beside Randall. I helped him up and dragged him unsteadily through the turnstiles. I shoved him into the nearest seat of the coaster, ran back to the kiosk and hit the start button—thank god for big red buttons labeled START; I would literally be dead dozens of times over if this world wasn't idiot proofed just for folks like me—and booked it back as the cart lurched into motion. I jogged up alongside it and hopped into the last seat right before it left the station. I looked back at the station—at the Unnoticeables standing dumbfounded on the edges of the tracks—and laughed.

"Haha, eat shit!" I hollered, flipping them the hardest

bird I could manage with one hand, while securing my harness with the other.

"Uh, Carey?" Randall called out from five rows in front of me.

"Yeah?"

"Isn't this thing just going to go around the track and wind up right back there at the same station in, like, two minutes?"

FUCK.

"Yeah," I said, as casually as possible, "but this gives us two minutes to think, right?"

Dead silence.

Randall wasn't buying it.

"Hey man, we're coming up to the first drop, get your seat belt on!" I shouted.

"My what?" Randall started to say, but we were already dropping, and it turned into an unintelligible scream.

Randall was lifted halfway out of the cart, his right arm hooked through the unbuckled harness, holding onto the underside of the seat in front of him with just his toes. He was making frightened walrus sounds and slapping about uselessly with his other arm, trying to find purchase. The coaster went into a sharp banking left, sending Randall flying wide and to the right. He hung on to the harness, but his feet slipped out and he flapped alongside the cart like a wind sock.

"Hold on!" I shouted.

Well, that was a stupid thing to say.

He responded with a series of terrified yelps. The cart banked back right and Randall's legs were thrown into the seat behind him. He wrapped around it as best he could and held on in the fetal position.

"Hang in there, man! There's only one more curve and a

loop before it hits another climb and slows down!"

"One more curve and a WHAT?"

Oh, right.

The curve was no problem. The loop didn't go as smoothly. Randall's legs came loose at the peak, when we went fully inverted, and he hung there for a split second—dangling from nothing but one arm hooked into a loose harness—before momentum caught up with him and he slammed crotch-first into the divider between the seats.

"Are you all right?" I asked him.

Randall was alternating between "Jesus" and "fuck" so rapidly they became one word: Jesusfuck. But he managed to crawl back into his seat and buckle the harness as the cart began its next ascent.

This was the big drop. The flagship moment of the ride. The cart climbed slowly, probably more slowly than it needed to. A few agonizing extra moments to appreciate the tension before the big release. The track was angled to the side, to let riders really appreciate the scale of what they were about to go through: Beyond the peak the track dropped straight off for what looked like hundreds of feet, then bottomed out quickly and shot back up a small rise—likely to maximize G-forces and trick the rider into feeling like they were going airborne.

It looked intense. If we even made it that far.

Standing on the ground below the lowest point of the dip, when it was no more than six or seven feet off the ground, were three Unnoticeables, staring patiently up at us. I was suddenly acutely aware that my feet were dangling, unprotected, in the open air where the cart's floor should have been. I struggled with my harness, but my body weight was shifted backward from the climb, and there was too much pressure on the buckle to let it release.

"Randall . . ."

"Jesusfuck Jesus fuck fuckJesus—" came his mantra.

"There's a bunch of Unnoticeables waiting for us at the bottom of the next drop. I think they're going to try to grab our legs."

"And what do you want me to do about that?!" He turned as far around as his harness would let him and stared at me from the corners of his eyes.

I gave him a big, exaggerated shrug.

And then we fell.

Quicksilver backflips in my stomach. Blood to my head. My vision faintly red at the edges. Wind roaring in my ears like the ocean in a storm. I tried to pull my legs up, but the velocity had them pinned back beneath my seat. We were approaching the bottom. The Unnoticeables jockeyed for position. You can't make out their facial features—not really. It doesn't seem unusual to you at the time. Each one just seems like an entirely forgettable person. A face in the crowd. But you can tell expressions. And the ones at the bottom were grinning like a bunch of hyenas watching a zebra stumble. I braced myself as far back in my chair as I could, and I noticed Randall . . . doing the exact opposite. He was leaning forward in his seat, wriggling his hips so he could get his legs as low as possible.

"What the fuck are you doing?" I yelled, but I could feel the wind rip the words from my mouth and fling them backward. No way he heard me.

Randall dropped his leg low and back. The cart rocketed into the dip. One Unnoticeable shoved another out of the way and jumped up, arms open to catch Randall's leg. At the absolute limit of our velocity—with all the mass of the free-falling cart behind it—Randall swung his foot forward in a huge football punt, and caught the airborne Unnoticeable right beneath the chin.

His *fucking head came clean off* and went spinning through the air, pinwheeling blood.

I've forgotten my first kiss. I remember losing my virginity, but I couldn't tell you her name. I know my dad left me and Mom at some point, and she said I was inconsolable—I cried for hours. I don't recall a minute of it. But I swear to god, until my dying day, I will remember every millisecond of that beautiful bastard of a kick, and I will weep tears of glory.

"WA-HOOOO!" Randall screamed, understandably. "DID YOU SEE THAT SHIT?!"

"YOU ARE A MAJESTIC BEAST!" I yelled back.

"HOLY SHIT I THINK I BROKE MY LEG!" he responded, then pulled his knee up to his chest and huddled in pain.

Whatever happened to us from here on out, it was worth it. All of it. All of our past mistakes had only served to make us the people we were today—the people that just roller-punted a monster punk's head clean off his shoulders.

I was almost at peace with what was waiting for us when the cart pulled back into the station—when the remaining Unnoticeables would tear us apart with their bare hands. Then the cart came to a jarring halt, whiplashing me with my own harness. My chin hit my chest and I bit the tip of my tongue. I tasted blood.

We were only halfway through the roller coaster's run, just cresting the small peak that came after the big dip.

Was there an emergency stop on this thing?

Haha, did those stupid assholes pull it?!

I mean, I knew the Empty Ones generally pulled their Unnoticeables from the dregs of humanity: junkies, hobos, punks, drifters, vagrants—people that wouldn't be missed. But I guess I never stopped to appreciate that it meant they couldn't exactly recruit the best and brightest. The Unnoticeables could've just waited for us at the station and had us literally delivered to them in a nice tidy package, but instead they pulled the e-brake with our cart on a hill. They'd have to climb up here to get us.

"Randall, unbuckle!" I said, loosing my own harness and clambering over the seats toward him.

He struggled with his harness, adrenaline making his hands shaky and disconnected. I reached over his shoulder and pulled the clip free, then jumped over the next two rows to the front of the cart. I heard the slip of rubber on plastic, and a scream. I looked back and found Randall crumpled between rows of seats, head down and legs in the air. I monkeyed back over to help him get upright, but he screamed again when I pulled on his leg.

"I wasn't kidding, it's fucking broken!" he yelled.

"Well, how was I supposed to know?" I said, yanking on his arms.

"Because I shouted it at the top of my lungs like five seconds ago?"

"Well yeah, but I figured you were just being a little wimp," I said. "You know, like usual."

That should do it.

Randall slapped my hands and pulled himself up the rest of the way. It was a cool night, but thick drops of sweat were beading on his forehead. His cheeks were flushed, but the rest of his skin was pale. Sheer spite for me would only get him so far. I hoped it was far enough.

"Come on," I said, making my way back to the front of the cart and slipping down onto the tracks. "We've got a good lead, but they're probably climbing up already."

Randall eased himself gently down from the nose of the cart onto the single thick beam that made up the track. It was a few feet wide at its thickest, with two thinner slats running down the bottom of each side. We couldn't walk on it, but we could straddle the thicker rise and push off the slats with our hands and feet, sort of crotch-gliding like a stair railing. Downhill would be easy enough, uphill would be a bitch. Especially for Randall with his bum leg.

"If those dipshits on the ground actually are climbing up already, we can slide down this next dip and climb off. We might be able to get out of here before they even realize we're gone."

It was a weak plan, but the alternative was either waiting for them to get a clue and turn the cart back on, crushing us or knocking us off to our deaths, or slowly groin-mounting an entire roller coaster and—I don't know, starting a new life up there at the top? There wasn't much of an alternative, was the point.

"Okay," Randall said, barely a noise.

I could practically hear his teeth grinding from here.

The problem wasn't getting momentum—the track was greased with some sort of industrial lubricant—it was controlling it so I didn't go veering off to one side, or slowing it so I didn't friction-burn my own testicles off. If it was hard for me, it must've been unbearable for Randall. But I'd called him a wimp earlier; he'd die before complaining now. We crotch-slid as low as the track went before it hit the next rise. But it was still about fifteen feet off the ground.

"All right," I said, swinging my legs over and lowering myself onto the metal support beams. "Here's the easy part."

Randall's barely constrained yelps of pain did not agree with me. I made the climb fine, and jumped the last few feet so I could assist Randall. He tried to kick me away, but only twice, so I knew he really wanted my help. I eased him down to the ground, and tried to offer him my arm. He shook his head silently, and started to walk. He took tiny little paces, shuffling forward a few inches at a time.

"Listen, man—" I blocked his way. "I'm sorry I called you a wimp. I was just trying to piss you off so you'd get moving quicker. But we are not going to make it with you waddling around like a sick penguin. You have to take my hand."

"Say it," Randall said. He clenched his jaw, crossed his arms, and glared at me.

"C'mon man, we do not have time for—"

"Bullshit. It's a few seconds. Say it."

I sighed.

"You're the baddest motherfucker since Shaft."

Randall nodded once, curtly, and threw his arm around my shoulder. I took the weight off his bad leg, and together we did an impromptu three-man race for the perimeter fence.

The good news was: We made it way before the Unnoticeables!

The bad news was: It was a fence.

The implications of that didn't really occur to either of us until we stood at the bottom of it, gaping up at the barbed wire atop the chain-link. It was only ten feet high. It may as well have been a thousand for Randall.

"Okay," I said, hoping that if I just talked fast enough and kept moving my momentum would stumble me onto a plan. "I'm gonna climb up first and throw my jacket, then come back down and boost you up."

"Sure," Randall said, "or you can just think happy thoughts and we'll both fucking fly out of here on our magic fairy dust."

"Well, what then? What's your plan?" I snapped.

"I don't know!" He lowered himself back against the fence. "We look for another opening, or we stay and fight. I took one of the bastard's heads off with one leg. I still got three more limbs; by math that means I can take at least three. You got four on you—then we start head-butting."

I laughed, despite everything.

We both thought hard for a minute, but it wasn't exactly a strength for either of us.

"All right," he finally ceded. "Start climbing."

I slid out of my jacket and looped it around my neck, holding it in place with my teeth. I hooked my Chucks into the chain-links and started up. The climb was easy enough, but wrangling the jacket up and over the barbed wire with one hand was way more awkward than I'd thought. It took me a few swings to get it to catch, but it caught wrong—most of the fabric on this side of the fence—and I had to wrench it free and start again.

"Carey," Randall warned.

I looked down at him. He was staring up at the roller coaster. I could see five dark shapes crotch-sliding into the dip.

"I'm moving!" I said, and flipped the jacket over again.

Didn't catch. Caught wrong. Didn't catch. Didn't catch.

"Fuck!"

"Any time now," Randall said.

I didn't need to look to figure out that they had made the lowest point by now and started climbing down.

I wadded up my jacket and threw again, starting wide and releasing at the top: it floated up and over, folded in on itself, seemed about to fall back toward me . . . and then the sleeve caught a barb and it settled over the bulk of the barbed wire just like a tablecloth.

I jumped down immediately, without looking, and nearly drop-kicked Randall in the face. I glanced back at the roller coaster—one of the Unnoticeables had just made the jump to the ground, another right behind him, three more still sliding down the dip.

I ducked down in the front of the fence, looped my hands together, and lowered them between my legs. Randall set his good foot in them, groaned at the pain as his weight momentarily shifted to his busted leg, but then pushed up into the saddle. I heaved upward as hard as I could, right when he jumped, and he caught the links high, just below the crest. He pulled himself up the last few feet, tried to throw his body over the jacket-covered barbs, but didn't make it. He just hung there.

"Get moving!" I yelled.

"I can't get the leverage," he said. "Come up here and pull me over from the other side."

"You goddamned wimp!" I said.

"No seriously," he answered, not playing the game. "It's not happening. Get up here."

I scrambled up the fence like a squirrel on coke. Randall was right—getting over the hump was harder than it looked. The barbed wire bulged out on either side, and there was no place to grab. You had to reach over the hump to the far side of the fence, and that meant momentarily balancing on both legs while you stretched for purchase. I went for it, and got a grip. I tried to pull myself over, but my legs flipped up above my head. I snatched at my jacket, but it gave way and I fell the full ten feet down the far side, straight onto my back. The air went out of me. I wheezed like a career smoker and watched little Christmas lights flash across my field of vision. Randall was saying something, but I couldn't make out the words. Could only focus on vainly gasping for air like a landed fish.

"You all right?!" he said, when I could finally focus enough to understand him.

My breath came thin and ragged. I barely got to my feet.

"Yeff," I said, trying to say "yes," but merely panting out the last half syllable.

Weak as I was, I immediately looped my fingers through the chain-link and started climbing. I didn't even make it off the ground before I fell. I got up and tried again, not doing much better.

"Carey," Randall said, and something in his voice stopped me. He was climbing down.

"What the hell are you doing?" I said.

He lowered himself the last few feet and dropped to the ground, managing to put most of his weight on his good leg.

I stopped and looked at him, the diamond patterns of the chain-link casting shadowy X's across his face.

"You got to go," Randall said.

"Bullshit!" I said, and slapped the fence. "Just give me a second, I'll get over there—"

He just gestured backward with his head. I looked over his shoulder and saw that all five of the Unnoticeables had made it to the ground now and were jogging in his direction. Maybe a hundred feet away. They'd get to him way before I could.

"Well then fuck it, let's go with your plan. I'll climb back over there and we'll kick their asses."

"Oh yeah? Let's see you do it, then."

I jumped up as high as I could and seized the fence, but I couldn't support myself. I slipped down and kicked dirt at Randall in frustration.

"You fuckin' wimp." He laughed.

"No way," I said. "We aren't going out like this."

"*We're* not," he agreed.

Fifty feet now. Probably less.

"Tell them I died how I lived," Randall said, twisting on a wry smile. "Punting some chump's head clean off his body."

He turned away from me, and hobbled out to meet the crowd.

Three of the Unnoticeables broke off, surrounding him, but keeping their distance for now. The other two cut Randall a wide berth and kept right on running toward the fence. They leapt up and hit it high, then started climbing. They didn't need a jacket-bridge; they didn't care. They just wrapped their fists around the barbs and started pulling. The one closest to me got his loose blouse-shirt thing caught up in the tangles, so I guess '80s fashion did one thing right. The other one was only a bit farther away, and though I could see his hands shredding as he pulled himself through, it wasn't slowing him down much.

One of the three surrounding Randall lunged. Randall danced to the side and clocked him hard. The Unnoticeable went down, but Randall stumbled on the follow-through and limped a bit. The other two saw it—saw him favoring that leg. One charged before Randall could recover, while the other circled around and kicked out his knee. Randall went down with a scream, then all three were on him, and the screaming stopped.

The Unnoticeable climbing the fence nearest me had his chest and arms through the barbed wire already. Thin streams of blood poured from multiple cuts across his face and torso, but he was still steadily wriggling through. Even the blouse-wearing bastard was shimmying out of his fancy top and starting to make headway.

Where Randall had stood, I could see three silhouetted shapes flailing at a dark lump on the ground that offered no resistance.

Shit.

Torn Blouse Guy was almost through now, his black leather pants shielding his lower half from the worst of the barbs. The other one was just kicking his boot free from the tangles and getting ready to jump.

Fuck.

The silhouettes bashed and wailed, tore and gouged. The lump did not move. Did not cry out.

The Unnoticeables dropped from the fence to either side of me.

I ran.

I ran like the miserable fucking coward that I am, and I have deserved every single thing that has happened to me since.

SIX

Kaitlyn. 2013. Los Angeles, California. West L.A.

Have you ever gone on a vacation or something for a few weeks, then came back to your own house and found it smelled kind of funny? Maybe not bad, necessarily, but it's a noticeable odor. It takes you a few hours to get used to it, and then you won't smell it again until you leave for another good length of time.

My apartment smelled of pretzels and tequila. To my recollection, I hadn't had either in here in a long time. I had no idea where the smell came from, but it was strangely comforting. Every time I smelled it and thought *what the hell is that?* my mind filled in the answer: home.

I took in my belongings with fresh eyes. I memorized every inch of them, all too aware they could be taken away again in an instant. My mismatched thrift store mugs, still set out to dry on the kitchen towel by the sink. My pile o' jeans, hunched in the hallway between the living room and bedroom. My ceramic owl toothbrush holder. My gargantuan, extravagantly comfortable bed.

It filled every inch of my room with memory foam

goodness. My big, pillowy down comforter was bundled up into a little Kaitlyn nest in the far corner. I kicked off my shoes, crawled into my favorite part of every day, pulled the door shut behind me, and made myself into the smallest ball possible. I did nothing but breathe bed-smell and value every inch of its contact with my body. Weeks of scratchy motel sheets, formless airy pillows, strangers fucking overhead or fighting next door, and now, to be back in my most private den of comfort, I just couldn't help it.

I started crying.

It began as a happy cry, my body overwhelmed by pure endorphins. Then it became one of relief, as all the binding stress wrapped around me began to loosen. Then it took a wrong turn and became a deep, wracking sob of stupid self pity.

Why the hell am I involved in this? Why me? I just wanted to race cars and see movie sets and—

No, that's not even it. I didn't want those things. Jackie wanted those things for me. I wanted to . . . I wanted to . . .

Okay, so I don't know what I wanted to do. I wasn't happy waiting tables in Barstow, where everybody knew every inch of your business; I wasn't happy waiting tables in L.A., where everybody follows up the question "what do you do?" with the question "okay, but what do you *really* do?" I went along with Jackie when she moved to L.A. because she was my only friend—my only connection to any living thing, really—and that made *her* home. Then came L.A. and improv classes and yoga and Jackie shining with the light of purpose fulfilled while I sat there like a lump. Wondering what was for me.

And now, I had my answer.

Marco, the former teen heartthrob that wanted to eat

my insides. Faceless goons that did his twisted bidding. Hulking black monsters that melted flesh like butter. Static-screaming angels that simplified the algorithms of humanity just to keep an uncaring universe turning.

Jackie was meant to live a hip and bohemian life in Los Angeles, networking with minor celebrities and doing sketch comedy. I was meant to battle a multidimensional parasite and its attendant cult at the expense of my self and, most likely, my life.

I feel like I got the slightly shorter end of the stick here, Jackie.

And with that, the tears shut off like a switch.

I'm being stupid. Selfish. Sullen. Like a kid that doesn't get what they want at Christmas so they start yelling at Grandma. That's not me, and it's not helping.

I wiped my runny mascara on my bedsheets.

Why not? I don't sleep anymore. Won't be needing my comfort nest ever again.

I sat up and stared blankly out my window, looking down toward the bottom of the hill—the bodega and the taco cart, the Mexican family that ran the donut shop sitting on their stoop, laughing and barbecuing.

Not for you. Not anymore.

I giggled bitterly to myself.

There was a knock at my door. From the other side, Jackie said, "K? You all right in there? It sounded like you were crying. . . ."

I leaned over to twist the knob, and let the door creak open on its own. When it did, Jackie saw the streaked, puffy mess of my face and frowned. She didn't come in from the hallway. There was literally not an inch of standing space in my bedroom—it was fully consumed by the massive bed—so to "come in" would be de facto cuddling, and I guess she wasn't up for a snuggle. Instead, she awkwardly sat at the border of my mattress and twisted to face me.

"What's up?" she said.

I laughed.

"That's such an inadequate question, Jackie."

"I know, I'm sorry," she said. She looked at me with platitudinous eyes.

"And that's such an inadequate response."

"Look, I know what you're going through but there's no need to take it out on—"

"You . . . *know what I'm going through*?" I barked out an ugly laugh. "Nobody has *ever* known what I'm going through. *I* don't know what I'm going through."

"But you have friends who are here for you. . . ."

"Oh, cool," I said, giving Jackie a big thumbs-up. "The power of friendship will surely see me through any challenge!"

I expected her to snap back at me, but instead she mimed spreading out a rainbow with her hands and sang the old "The More You Know" PSA jingle.

I laughed, earnestly this time, and that shut me right down. Even when I'm being a total bitch, Jackie makes me laugh.

"I'm sorry," I said, and scooted across the bed toward her. "I'm just so . . . I don't know if tired is the right word. Weary, maybe. I've been running on nothing but momentum for weeks now, and this is the first time I've had to stop, even for a second. Everything caught up to me."

"I get it, K." She wrapped her arm around my back and laid her head on my shoulder. "If you'd asked me what the weirdest, scariest thing in the world was two months ago, I probably would've said Danzig. Now it's like we're trapped in a nightmare world. I wish I could say something comforting to you but . . . well, we saw how that worked out just now."

"It's okay," I said. "It helps to know somebody else is as screwed as I am."

"Ha, well, I'm not quite there yet. I haven't started hallucinating space whales."

I pulled away from her so I could see her face.

"What do you mean, hallucinate?" I asked.

"What do you mean, what do I mean?" She pulled away a little herself.

"You think I hallucinated all of that? Jackie, that was real. It was showing me something . . ."

"You still think that? K, I figured if we got you out of the sun, got you someplace to unwind, you'd reset back to normal. . . ."

"I am normal! Or as close as I get anymore. Jackie, it's seriously important that you believe me about this."

"So you're still going to follow through with this crazy fucking plan?" she said, and pushed off from the bed. She frowned down at me from the hallway. "You're still going after another angel?"

"It's the only way to—"

"Fuck that!" Jackie's voice cracked when she yelled. "Look around, there's nobody here! Marco is dead. His little cult scattered to the wind. Nobody is looking for us. We won. We're out! Let's just go back to living."

"It's not over. Marco was nothing to these things—less than nothing. There are so many more and they'll never stop, unless we stop them."

"Ease up on this 'we,' stuff, K. Back in Mexico, I told you I was with you until the end. Well, here it is: the end. I'm with you. I'm *not* with you starting it all up again because you got heatstroke while meditating in the desert and talked to Shamu the fucking astronaut."

I tried to rev up my anger, but I'd already started and stopped too many times. I couldn't muster the energy.

"I'm not going to keep begging you to stay," I said, my voice flat.

"Nobody asked you to—no, you know what?" Jackie ran her hands through her hair, blew out all her breath. "We're tired, we're stressed, we shouldn't be doing this right now. I love you, K. I do. We've got some shit to talk about, though, all right? And I think we both need a little time to be normal first."

I smiled weakly.

"So, I'm going to go and check in on my parents. They're used to me disappearing for a while, and even occasionally maxing out Dad's credit card—but they generally expect a visit afterward and some kind of explanation. Plus, I just really need to go to a nice, big house right now, sit on a couch that costs more than my car, eat some overpriced Whole Foods kale chips, and watch like sixteen hours of reality TV."

I nodded. Jackie's parents had followed her from Barstow (yes, they were that kind of parents), where they'd owned like half the town. They lived in an intimidating mansion out in Brentwood. I could sure understand wanting to be there, instead of here.

"Hey, say something?" Jackie said. She reached out and touched me on the shoulder.

"Something," I said. It didn't even get a chuckle. "No, seriously. That's good. You take a break, Jackie. You deserve it. In fact, I'm going to see if I can convince Carey to take off for a while so I can have a ridiculously long shower without worrying about him peeking through the keyhole."

"Okay, I'll be back tomorrow—probably kinda late. Promise me you two won't do anything . . . space-whale related until then?"

"I promise," I said.

She squeezed my shoulder, and I squeezed her hand, then she turned to leave. I could hear Carey snoring out on the living room couch. I was thinking of ways to wake him up politely, when Jackie slammed the door behind her as hard as she could.

You're the best, girl.

"Whu fuggin' Jeezis." Carey flailed and mumbled in sleep-addled confusion.

I'd been sharing hotel rooms with the guy for weeks. I knew he'd drop right back to sleep in a matter of seconds unless I moved fast. I jumped up from the bed and hit the ground running. I slid into the living room—socks coasting across smooth wood—and screamed, "CAREY! EMERGENCY!"

He made more half-conscious noises of concern.

I stepped forward and slapped him across the back of the head.

"What?! Damn it, I'm up. What?"

"We're out of alcohol."

His eyes went wide.

"No, you had all those bottles above the fridge before," he pleaded.

"Yeah, but you drained them all before we left, remember? Except for the flavored vodka. You poured that down the sink."

"That's right. Did you ever thank me for that?"

I rolled my eyes at him.

"Look, I'll front you some cash for beer if you do something for me."

"Okay, but we'll have to stick to oral unless you have a condom," he said, with total sincerity.

"Not even if you looked like Christian Bale and smelled like freshly baked cookies," I said. "I'll throw down for the beer if you stay gone for a few hours. I need some alone time."

"Ah, I gotcha," he said, and winked. "You want me to pick up replacement batteries too, for the ones you run down?"

"Jesus, shut up. The offer is going once, going twice . . ."

"Hey! I didn't say no! I'll go," he said, stumbling to his feet. He held his hand out in front of me like an expectant toddler.

I went to the cabinet by the back door and pulled down my lucky cat bank. I forget what he's called. I think it's a Japanese thing—little cartoon kitty smiling with one paw in the air. I unscrewed his head and brought the body over to Carey. I showed him the inside, filled with quarters.

"Seriously? Change?" he asked.

"Seriously? Like you're too proud?" I countered. "It's my laundry money. More than enough."

"All right, all right," he said, and took the cat bank from me.

He headed for the door, then paused with his hand on the knob. He turned back toward me.

"You gonna leave this unlocked for me to 'accidentally' walk in on something?"

I flipped him off. He laughed, and stepped out. He left the door open. I sighed and closed it behind him, then set every lock I had. Just to be safe, I double-checked the back door and all the windows, too. I stood in the middle of my quiet living room, all alone and with nothing to do for the first time in as long as I could remember.

So. . . what now?

I thought about watching TV, playing internet, reading a book—it all seemed so trivial.

Shower first, I guess, then I'll figure it out from there . . .

I headed to the bathroom, paused at the door, and glanced down at the storage containers that supported my bed. The middle one held socks, underwear, a clothes steamer, various odds and ends, and my vibrator. Since Carey had put the idea in my head already, it had been— Jesus, *months.*

I showered until the hot water ran out, toweled myself off, and crawled into my nest naked. I came twice, and only stopped there because I figured I should eat something. I slipped into my ratty pajamas—pilled fleece sweats and a baggy, hole-riddled Guns N' Roses T-shirt left over from an ex-boyfriend—and plundered my kitchen. Nothing in the fridge would be good, for sure, and I didn't even wanna trust the freezer in case there had been a power outage or something while I was gone. But the pantry held two cans of SpaghettiOs, and that sounded strangely appealing. My go-to comfort food. I should have been starving, but faced with the reality of eating, I just . . . wasn't. The front door rattled hard, and I heard a thump.

"Aw, damn it," Carey yelled, from outside.

There was never a *good* time for Carey, but I'd enjoyed the hell out of my recuperation period and was okay with the idea of company. I padded over to the door and flicked the locks open. Carey took one look at my ensemble and dropped all pretense at lusting after me. He pushed past and made straight for the kitchen. I could hear him shoving things aside to make room for the beer, then the sound of cardboard tearing, and the pop-hiss of a can being opened. He came out holding two beers—one open, one not. He sat down at my tiny dining room table and drained one of the cans completely, his knobby Adam's apple bobbing up and down with every chug. When it was empty he set it down on the table, cracked the next one, and took a sip.

Only when he finished that one did he get up, grab two more, and set one in front of me. I raised my eyebrows at him. He waggled his at me. I shrugged and pulled the tab. We sat like that for another few minutes without saying anything.

"You enjoy your alone time?" he finally said, with feigned interest.

I shrugged.

"So . . . universe cubes and space whales, huh?" Carey said. I could hear the laugh in it.

"Damn it, it wasn't an *actual* cube, or an *actual* whale. I said it was more like a metaphor for . . . uh . . ."

I gave up. I knew I'd lost Carey at "metaphor."

He sat quietly, sipping his beer and staring out the back door. There was nothing interesting out there: two mismatched thrift store folding chairs, an IKEA table, and an old Persian rug growing mold spots. The little patio was completely fenced in against the access path that ran behind the building.

"Okay, you don't believe me," I tried again. "That's fine, but—"

"I didn't say that." He looked me straight in the eye. "I believe you. I've seen what you can do since taking that first angel. You're connected to something bigger, that's obvious. I wasn't thinking about whether or not to believe your story. I was thinking about how to find another angel."

"R-really?" After my conversation with Jackie, I just figured it was going to be Kaitlyn against the rest of the rational world. "Any ideas?"

"Just one, and I'll be honest: It's fucking terrible."

I laughed. He didn't.

"No, really," Carey elaborated, no mirth to his tone. "It's bad. It's dangerous, morally bankrupt, and something I find personally fucking detestable. If I had any other leads whatsoever, no matter how bad they were, I would jump on them like a hobo on a pint of Mad Dog before pursuing this one."

"Wow, uh . . . what is it?"

"I can't say yet." Carey saw me start to protest and held his hand up. "That's how bad it is. If I told you about it, you'd stop me, and then we'd be nowhere. I just need you to say it. Say you're absolutely sure that the only way forward is to find another angel as soon as possible."

I chewed on my lip.

Was I sure about the visions? Really sure? Jackie could be right. It could be heatstroke or sleep deprivation or something. I didn't think I was feeling the effects of several weeks of restless nights, but maybe it was taking some hidden toll. . . .

No.

I can feel it in my chest: a sort of fullness, puffing me up when I should be deflating. I've never felt that before, but I know what it is: purpose. This is right. The vision is real.

"I'm absolutely sure," I said.

"Fuck," Carey said.

He pushed back from the table and went to the kitchen. He banged around in the fridge, and emerged with two beers in each hand and one tucked in his waistband.

"I'll be back later tonight," he said. "But if I'm not, assume I died horribly and never stop running."

"You're being dramatic," I said.

"I'm really not," he said, and stomped out the door.

I got up and got myself another beer, too.

SEVEN

Carey. 1981. Valencia, California.

I woke up feeling like I'd smoked two packs of cigarettes and tried to run a marathon. Spiderwebs of pain were tangled all through my back and chest. I tried to sit up, gasped, sucked in breath, caught a bunch of spit, and started coughing. I passed out.

I woke up again, feeling like I'd smoked six packs of cigarettes and tried to swim the English Channel. I took it slow this time. I eased myself into a sitting position, and took in my surroundings. I guess I'd broken into a construction site and crawled into a big cross section of pipe to sleep it off.

Jesus. How much did I drink last night? And of what, jet fuel?

I looked around for Randall, thinking at least I could slap him awake and make myself feel better by making him feel worse.

Then it came back to me.

I didn't sob, or scream, or punch the concrete and bust up my knuckles. I just went flat and cold, like somebody had popped my top and left me open in the fridge all night.

Stop. Don't do that. Not yet. You lost him once before, remember? The Unnoticeables took him in New York, and you got him back. This is just grounds for another awesome rescue mission, full of punches and shenanigans. Another chapter in the Carey and Randall story. Four years of fucking up monsters and still going strong. . . .

I tried to crawl out of the pipe. It took way longer than it should have. I thought I'd just knocked the wind out of myself last night, but it was plain that my ribs were fucking shattered. I hobbled instead of walked. It felt like stitches covering every inch of my lungs. I was winded after three steps, but I pushed on. I had to get back to Six Flags, see if they left a trail I could follow to wherever they'd taken Randall.

It took me hours to hike up the small bluff that I must've sprinted down last night. I couldn't even muster the strength to push aside the scrub, so I kept getting caught up in small bushes and skinny little trees that I should've been able to plow right through. Halfway up, I looked to my left and saw a neat paved path snaking up the hill straight to the gates. It wasn't the first time I've called myself an asshole, but it was certainly the hardest.

The sun was almost directly overhead by the time I reached the perimeter fence of the amusement park. I was shivering and sweating at the same time. It felt like I was trying to breathe through lungs filled with gravel. The inside of my leather jacket was soaking wet; it pooled in the elbows where I had my arms crossed against my chest, trying to hold my ribs in place. But I made it. I made it to the top of the bluff. I made it to the fence. I made it to the spot where Randall fell, and now I could track him down.

I didn't need to go far.

He was still lying right there where he fell, limbs

shattered, face a bloody Halloween mask. I didn't need to check if he had a pulse or any of that shit. His head was twisted nearly backward. I looped my fingers through the chain-link. It started as a dramatic gesture, reaching toward my fallen friend, but then I was just trying to hold myself upright. I wanted to climb the fence and drag him out of there, bury him somewhere he'd like—like beneath the floorboards of the girl's restroom at the Whiskey a Go Go. I wanted to at least grab something to remember him by like his . . .

Huh. I guess Randall wasn't much for material things. I couldn't think of a single thing he owned that would mean shit to either of us.

But he deserved better than this. He deserved better than to be left mangled beneath a roller coaster at fucking Six Flags. He deserved *at least* Disneyland.

I couldn't even give him that. I turned and looked back down the way I'd come. A steep, dusty hillside littered with roots and other pitfalls. I couldn't do it again, not on the way down. I hobbled over to the side entrance, where the path intersected the fence. A sallow-chested teenager was sitting on a little wooden stool just outside the gate. He saw me walking the fence line and frantically whispered something into his walkie-talkie. It didn't look like he got a response, so he just sat there, quietly panicking while I approached him, surely looking like some desperate murderous junkie who'd do anything to pay for his next fix. I got within speaking distance and he cleared his throat like six times.

"S-sir the park is closed this week for renovations," he began, but I just waved him off.

His mouth snapped shut like a ventriloquist dummy. He

watched, mute, as I staggered onto the paved path, and began slowly, achingly limping down it. After a few dozen steps, I stopped, turned back to the kid, and raised both middle fingers. I held them there for a full minute while he stared at me, unwilling or unable to speak. Then I turned and walked away.

That's how I left my best friend. Sprawled out under a roller coaster, corpse baking in the California sun, his eulogy just two shaky middle fingers extended as far as they could go.

It took me ten minutes, two bribes, and six threats in four different languages to convince the cab driver to pick me up. I didn't have any money for the bribes, and I don't speak four languages. I can swear in sixteen.

He was Czechoslovakian or something. I got drunk on Long Island once with some Russian motherfuckers that I'm pretty sure were close enough to Czechs. They taught me, and I'm remembering phonetically here, *"lee-zat moj pika!"*

I screamed that at the cabbie a few times, and he opened the door.

I think it means "lick my pussy."

He didn't say a word during the rest of the very long trip from Valencia to the west hills of Los Angeles. But he watched me through the mirror more than he watched the road. He pulled to a stop outside of Matt and Safety Pins' place.

We called her Safety Pins because, when we met her, she'd had safety pins stabbed through her ears in place of earrings. She'd always been more about the grand gesture than the authenticity. We called him Matt because he was a black punk, and you didn't need help to remember a black punk. There were, like . . . four of them. In the world.

The two had made good since me and Randall last saw them in New York. She'd come out here to be an actress, or a model, or a singer, or whatever it is professionally beautiful people do. Matt, the awkward goon, did the only thing he could do: He dropped everything and followed her. What were his other options? A little shit like that doesn't get a girl that looks like Safety Pins every day. He dug in like a lamprey and rode her all the way to Hollywood. For her part, she didn't seem to mind. She genuinely seemed to love the chump, even though his ambitious L.A. plan was apparently to get work at a record store and smoke weed literally every second he wasn't working.

Safety Pins, not surprisingly, had an equally beautiful, and therefore rich, family. She and Matt were staying in her uncle's second home. It was all boxy, with floor-to-ceiling glass looking down on L.A. like a judgmental god. It had a kidney-shaped pool with plastic blue water. A little one-bedroom poolhouse/guest quarters that Randall and I crashed at when we arrived in town. Took them two days to notice us in there, but they gave us permission to stay after a few beers and gentle reminders about who kept them from being melted by tar men back in NYC.

The cabbie didn't like me stepping out of the taxi without paying him. He leapt out the driver's side and crab-walked around the front of the car—trying to cover every direction I might run at once. The dickhead couldn't see I wasn't in any shape to run anywhere. I was barely on my feet. I hadn't caught more than a glimpse of myself while he was staring me down through the rearview mirror, but I knew I looked like death's pale, sickly cousin. We argued for a few minutes across a language gulf so vast it was practically a sea. The only thing either of us understood was how much each wanted the other to go fuck themselves.

Matt finally came out the door with a short-short fuzzy girl's bathrobe cinched around his waist. He ran toward us waving his arms, trying to keep the peace. A few more minutes of swearing, threatening, and bartering and my fare was established. Matt went back inside to get the cash to pay for it, while the cabbie and I exchanged evil eyes and taught each other rude gestures. When Matt settled up the tab, the driver got back in his fish-reeking taxi and peeled out, holding two fingers in a wide open "V" out the window.

"Lick my pussy!" I yelled at the quickly disappearing cab, and turned back to a clearly pissed-off Matt, who was waiting for an explanation.

"All of my ribs are broken. Randall's dead. Get me a beer," I said.

I pushed past him, into the main house where Randall and I hadn't been allowed until now, and curled up on a gargantuan white leather sectional that probably cost more than my freedom.

Matt ran in after me, spouting a million questions.

"All of my ribs are broken. Randall's dead. Get me a beer," was all I would say to him. Finally he gave in, jogged to the kitchen, and returned with two dark-colored bottles.

"What the fuck is this?" I said, craning my head to get a better look at the abomination he'd just handed me.

"It's . . . beer?" Matt settled in on the couch next to me. "Carey, can you please explain what the hell is going on now?"

"This isn't beer," I said. "Beer comes in cans. What the hell is a 'stout'?"

"There are other kinds of beer," Matt said.

I took a sip. It tasted like truck-stop coffee and the way a freshly paved highway smells. I handed it back to Matt and glared at him. He sighed, got to his feet, and returned to the kitchen. He came back holding his own bottle and one dented can of Schlitz. He passed the latter to me, and I popped the tab. I tried to chug it, but my ribs weren't cooperating. Felt like a snake crushing me from the inside. I had to settle for sipping it. This was not a sipping occasion.

"Now explain," Matt said.

I did. I told him the whole thing. Every little bit, including the part where I cut and ran on Randall, leaving him to die. That stupid little ball of pride in my throat tried to keep me from confessing that, but my self-hatred won out. I didn't just admit it; I hammered the point home. I omitted the fact that Randall told me to leave him. I added in a few bits about how girlishly I ran, wrists flailing, crying all the way, while Randall begged me to stay and help. If it wasn't the truth, it's how the truth deserved to be. When I was finished, I waited for Matt to hate me. The bastard couldn't even give me that.

"What the hell else were you supposed to do, man?" he said. "You were hurt. You couldn't have saved him. What's the point in both of you dying? At least this way you can get the fuckers back, right?"

"No!" I heaved back to throw my beer across the room, but it wasn't empty yet. Sipping was messing with my momentum. I reconsidered the dramatic gesture and took another sip instead. "I mean, yeah, they are absolutely going to pay for this. But I should have stayed. He would have stayed for me."

"Randall?" Matt raised an eyebrow. "You sure about that?"

Well, maybe not.

"Yes, no doubt about it," I said.

We drank our beers quietly for a minute.

"But how do we get back at them?" I said.

"I don't know, but—" Matt said, then backtracked. "Wait, 'we'?"

"What? Randall was your friend, too—are you saying you're not with me on this?"

"Hell yes I'm saying that. Why would you think I was? I'm not a fighter, man. Even if what you wanted me to fight was remotely human, they'd still kick my ass."

"We fought them before, in New York—" I tried to remind him, but he cut me off.

"No, dude. *You* fought them. I ran the hell away, remember? I ran right out of the apartment when they busted through the door. Then I ran down the street. Then, for good measure, I ran all the way across the god damn country. I didn't know they'd be here, too."

"Well, now it's time to stop running," I said, trying to bolster myself for an inspirational speech.

"Bullshit," Matt said, instantly. "This is the *best* time for running, and that's exactly what me and Melissa are going to do, the second she gets back."

"You're just going to bail on me now?"

"*Now?* Are you not listening? We bailed the second we found out about all this. We thought you and Randall were just here to get drunk and go to shows and catch some sun. If we had any idea you two were going after these things, we would not have let you stay here. We want no part of any of this. We just want to get high and fuck and be happy, man. That sounds way better than getting butchered in a sewer somewhere."

Now I crumpled my beer can in my fist and whipped it at the TV. Matt jumped to his feet.

"Some of us don't have that fucking option, Matt!" I screamed, and immediately regretted it. Lightning crackled around my back and chest.

He just stared at me, a big dumb sad bear look on his face.

I settled back into the couch.

"But you're right," I said. "You guys do have the option. Take it. You don't have to run anywhere. I'll be gone by tomorrow. Just give me a few hours to rest up."

"No, man, you don't have to—"

"Yeah, I do. If they knew where I was right now, they'd be here already. You two will be safe here. But if I stay any longer, they might find me."

Matt wanted to object further, I could tell. But he didn't. He just looked out the window for a while, instead of at me.

"But you're going to fetch me beers and blankets until then," I said.

He smiled at me.

"Fuck your heartwarming moment," I snapped. "I said *get me a god damn beer.* Go!"

Matt laughed and left for the kitchen.

When Safety Pins came home and found me and Matt completely trashed in the living room—me tucked into a nest of pillows, blankets, empty beer cans, and pizza crusts; Matt laying flat on his back across the coffee table, his head lolling upside down, trying to toss wadded up napkins across the room into some expensive-looking African basket thing—all she said was "do I need to do a liquor run or did you leave me some?"

She should've been mine.

All of her pretension, her poser affectations, her fad-chasing—none of it mattered to me right then, because she didn't yell at us about the mess, or the fact that we were hammered at 5:30 in the evening, she just . . . understood. And she joined right in. And also because she still had some seriously rockin' tits.

I am not a picky man.

We cried. We swore bloody oaths. We told our favorite Randall stories: I related, for probably the twentieth time, the tale of 4th of July, 1975, and how Randall ended up with a penny permanently embedded in his ballsack. Matt told a little story about the time we all went to Coney Island, and he didn't have enough money for lunch. Randall waited until everybody was distracted, then quietly slipped off to buy Matt a couple of chili dogs. He said not to tell anybody. Safety Pins talked about how she'd always found him super hot, and she really admired his fashion—he was so unique, you know? He just didn't give a damn about gender roles and stuff.

I told her she should thank god every day for those tits.

We drank to Randall. Then we drank to him again. Then we drank to old times. Then we drank to Burt Reynolds for some reason. Then we just drank.

I woke up the next morning still feeling like a giant had scraped me off the bottom of his shoe, with the added benefit of a massive hangover. I limped to the bathroom and threw up, nearly passing out from the pain it brought to my ribs. I drank three huge glasses of water, then stole an entire loaf of bread and half a bottle of fine-looking Scotch from the kitchen. I raided the guest house for my few meager belongings, shoved them into my ripped JanSport, and left without saying good-bye.

Matt and Safety Pins would sleep until noon, then get up and be all sad about my disappearance for a few hours.

Then they'd grab Mexican and margaritas at some little hole in the wall that only they knew about, and they'd fuck on their giant round bed, beside their giant square windows looking down on Los Angeles like a postcard. They'd forget, and they'd be fine. Besides, this whole Beverly Hillbillies thing was never my scene. Bastards like me, they don't deserve comfort and affluence. They deserve cold pavement and jeans that haven't been washed in years. They deserved to have to fight off stray dogs for their dinner and beg cash from passersby. They deserved the looks of disdain the real people would give them instead of that cash. They deserved the god damn street. And that's just where I was going.

EIGHT

Carey. 1982. Los Angeles, California. Koreatown.

It doesn't rain in L.A., it pours. The water here doesn't fall in waves of droplets, it's like somebody turned on a million faucets in the sky and they dump a solid stream of vaguely acidic water straight into your face, down the gap between your shirt and back, and into the holes in your duct-taped Chucks. Because rain is so rare in Los Angeles, all the dirt and the grime and the oil just soaks right into the ground. There's a thin film of pollution wrapped over every single surface in L.A., settled into the fine cracks, nestled right into the pores of the city. And then it rains, and all that shit washes up to the surface. You can barely walk down the street without skiing on a layer of grease.

L.A. drivers are bad enough on the average day—pushed to the brink by traffic and heat—then you factor in their total inability to drive in anything but mild sunshine, plus this slurry of crap you could use to lubricate the engine of an aircraft carrier, and it's downright deadly out there for a pedestrian.

I lost "pedestrian" status last year. Now I'm somewhere

between "burden on society" and "scary hobo." If the cars don't slow for pedestrians, they don't even stop for the burdens and the hobos.

At first it wasn't so bad, being on the street in Southern California. It's mostly warm, though some of the nights get colder than you might think. There are plenty of hidden corners in the urban maze to slip away and get some sleep. Occasionally, while begging, you'll luck across some C-list celebrity trying to appease his success-guilt, or some adman trying to impress an aspiring actress, and they'll fork over way too much cash. There are lots of cheap Mexican food places, but beer is kinda expensive. It all seems to balance out.

But after a while, the vibe out here gets to you. It's the gulf between the rich and the poor. It doesn't feel so stark elsewhere. Not even in NYC. Back there, you get the feeling that even the millionaires take the subway or grab a slice at a dingy pizza place every once in a while. But L.A. feels like there are two worlds. There's yours: a sepia-toned sprawl full of rats and cockroaches, where junkies die in the gutters and the street sweepers don't even stop to move them. And then above your shitty world, propped up on great concrete pillars surrounded by spikes and wrapped in barbed wire, there's a shiny and clean place, full of green trees and blue seas and gorgeous girls laughing big, showing teeth that shine like headlights.

It didn't bother me, being a scumbag in New York. It bothers me out here.

But then again, it should bother me. Cowards, fuckups, and failures shouldn't feel cozy and placated; there should be a spot inside them that's raw and red and never stops aching. If there isn't, then you're not human anymore. I nurture my wound whenever I can. I cultivate it when I'm wrapped up in my thin sleeping bag behind the butcher in Koreatown, absorbing all the cold from the pavement through my tailbone. I tend to it by savoring every disgusted look I get when I swoop down on the tables in outdoor restaurants and grab the leftovers before the waiters can get to them. I grow that little wound every day.

But hell, even I need a break once in a while. I heard X was playing at the HK Café in Chinatown. I usually crash further west, but X was worth half a day's walk. Normally, I'd take Daisy for a trip that far, but between the busted brakes, the rain, and her bald tires, the decision was pretty much made for me. It's not that I cared whether I lived or died—please never accuse me of that—just that I'd spend more time crashing than I would riding. I wouldn't make the show in time if I rode. Besides, she'd probably been stowed too long. Downtime doesn't do a motorcycle good. Battery's probably dead, tires even flatter than usual, rats in the airbox again. Walking, it was.

I figured all my old tricks for sneaking into shows still played out West, and if they didn't, well, there's always the punk kids. One of them will trade a ticket, or at least the cost of it, if I go buy them beer. Of that I can be sure: Punk priorities are the same, everywhere you go.

It seemed like a good idea at the time, before the fucking afternoon monsoon hit. By the time I made Chinatown every inch of me had been soaked so thoroughly that I was starting to prune, and that was just the start of my night. I still had to either skirt security or court a clique of underage, sober punks. And the HK looked tougher to slip into than I thought. I'd been there a few times before, back when me and Randa— . . .

I'd been there a few times before.

But back then I'd been a paying customer. I hadn't paid much attention to how easy it would be to sneak in. And the answer was looking like "not very." There was a bouncer/ticket taker out front, beneath the cheap neon sign advertising "genuine Chinese dishes," and a dark red metal door with peeling paint around back that led to the kitchen. But that was it. For sneaking into venues, you generally wanted a side or band entrance—someplace nonemployees, or at least temporary employees, would walk out to smoke, and you could just jog right up, catch the door, say "thanks, man," and slip by like you had business in there. The HK Café was primarily a restaurant: The front door was manned, the back door led straight into a busy kitchen, and that was it. Unless I could distract the bouncer, I wasn't slipping in. I looked around—there were a lot of places I could start fires, but none that wouldn't do more damage than I was comfortable with tonight.

Fine.

Time to play the beer-fairy. But that means standing out here in the grease-trap rain even longer, scouting the crowd for nervous kids with that sad look in their eyes that said they'd struck out at shoulder-tapping. There was a promising group of four young guys with shaved heads, but I didn't know the skinhead protocol out here in L.A. They might be shaky from a lack of quality lager in their system, or they might be shaky because they're itching for an excuse to stomp a hobo. A little flock of new wavers had staked out an awning half a block down while they waited for the doors to open. I was already approaching them when I saw one whip out a little flask and pass it around. They were taken care of. Everybody else looked of age, or already hammered.

Shit.

I bummed around the crowd for another half hour, hoping a good set of sober punks would come along and save me, but no such luck. The doors opened, the crowd filtered inside, the bouncer grabbed his little podium and pulled it in after him, and the doors closed again.

The rain showed no sign of letting up. I settled for trying to find somewhere relatively dry against the club itself, so I could at least listen to muffled guitars filtered through drywall. Looking toward the front, there seemed to be a little gap between the buildings on the right. Not quite an alleyway, but big enough to slide into. I slogged over there, my Chucks so soaked they were actually spraying out more water than they absorbed, and slid into the gap. The light from the streetlamps didn't make it into the little alcove, so I kept my eyes on my feet and my hand on the wall while I pushed in far enough to stay dry. I bumped into a corner where the wall of the HK Café staggered out a bit, so I slid around it, hoping the gutters extended farther back there.

Three Chinese guys were huddled in the far end of the access way, hunched over and smoking. Trying to stay dry like me. One had on a filthy white apron. The other two were dressed nearly identically—a sort of '50s greaser meets Bruce Lee outfit. Tight black jeans, white T-shirt, black mechanic's jacket, slick-backed hair.

There were two options: Either they were with one of the opening bands, or they were in some kind of gang.

The cook turned and caught me looming back there in the dark, looking suspicious as hell. He whispered something in that jumpy little singsong of theirs, and the two others turned to look at me. I could tell by their stance alone, these men did not have rock in their heart. I slipped back around the outcropping and jogged toward the main plaza, but that goddamned L.A. muck sent me sprawling. I hit the ground chin-first, felt a tooth chip. I tried to push myself up, but my hands just slipped away, too. I settled for half-crawling, half-falling toward the end of the alcove. If I could just make it to the main square I would—well, honestly, I would probably still get my ass kicked.

The relationship between the punks and the Chinese is a complicated one. They know there's money to be made from us, hosting shows nobody else will host, selling cheap beer and fried anything to the drunken *gweilo*. But they also know we get out of hand. We trash their venues, we piss on their walls, we disrespect their workers. I mean, not all of us—there are plenty of courteous punks out there (I'm uh . . . not always one of them)—but enough of us cause trouble to strain the relationship. So the Chinese seeing me trespassing in their workers-only zone, well after the doors to the show were closed? That could be enough to set them off.

But at least if I made the main square, they probably wouldn't knife me or anything. Too many potential witnesses.

I hope.

Hey, apparently that's all moot, though, because this fucking California mud-oil is like crawling through half-melted Jell-O. I heard squishy footsteps behind me, then a shoe on my ass, then my face was in the mud. I didn't make it anywhere near the exit. I tried to roll over to show the Chinese guys how utterly harmless I was—you know, lie to them—but they weren't having it. One of them stood behind me—the cook, I assumed, because I was flanked on either side by skinny black jeans and boat shoes. One of them kicked my arm out from under me when I tried to push myself up. Face down in the muck again. Tasted like exhaust fumes, match heads, and dog shit. The one that kicked my arm was now standing on my elbow, pinning it down. The other one put a foot on the back of my head and pressed.

I was facedown in the sucking mud. Nose, mouth, and eyes engulfed in it. I tried to turn my head, to break the seal and breathe, but I couldn't. There was something hard to either side of me, like I'd fallen in the gap between two paving stones. The Chinese greasers either didn't realize I couldn't breathe, or didn't care. They weren't letting up. I struggled with my free hand, grabbed the pant leg of the one pinning my head, but I couldn't get enough leverage to yank it from under him. I could only hold on and squeeze. My other hand spasmed open and closed on nothing. I kicked with my legs, but they slid uselessly in the muck. I pushed out with my tongue, lapping up the filthy slime like it was pudding, but the rain just filled in the gaps as soon as I could make them. I could feel the muck up my nose, slithering into my sinuses, filling the insides of my face and throat with thick, cold grime. My will broke. My lungs seized, trying to suck in air, and I inhaled pure mud. A shock shot through me, like I'd caught a bullet to the chest.

I thought they said drowning doesn't hurt. Maybe that only counts if it's water, because drowning in shit hurts like crazy.

I felt a heavy thump reverberate through the paving stones on either side of my head. Angry birdsong as the Chinese guys panicked, a few more solid bumps, and then the pressure was off my head and arms. I whipped my neck back, coughed, gagged, threw up about a pint of mud and took a long, agonizing breath. It probably hadn't even been a minute, but it felt like I hadn't used my lungs in years.

Like they'd atrophied from neglect, filled up with dust, got eaten through by moths, and now precious air was leaking out through all the cracks and holes. I couldn't do anything, could only lay there, splayed out, sucking oxygen and fighting back the multicolored tide lapping at the edges of my vision. I was distantly aware of the sounds of fighting somewhere behind me. Barking and yelping, swearing in Chinese, meaty *thwacks* of fists on faces.

When I could move, I didn't bother looking back. I speed-crawled the rest of the way down the alcove until my hands slapped brick. I hauled myself to my feet and bolted well into the center of the square before I collapsed again. I fell backward against the concrete base of a light post and stared hard through the charcoal-gray curtain of rain. The access way was just shadow at first. Then something moved back there, coming toward me. A figured emerged—a man, bit on the short and slight side—but I couldn't make out the details. The rain was too heavy, and I still had muck in my eyes. The guy saw me, though, and he approached. I was still too winded to run, could only sit there and hope it wasn't one of the Chinese guys.

He stepped into the circle of light.

It was one of the Chinese guys.

Of course it was. Do you deserve any less, asshole?

But no—it wasn't one of *the* Chinese guys. It was just *a* Chinese guy. This one was wearing torn jeans over filthy long johns, a thick, black leather motorcycle jacket, and a Dead Kennedys T-shirt—the anarchic DK logo scribbled in red on black. His head was shaved, save for a row of six-inch liberty spikes down the center of his skull. He had a thin dusting of beard in that awkward transition phase, like he was still trying to decide whether to grow it out or not. He took a few steps closer to me, paused, and waved way too enthusiastically.

"Hey, man! You here for the show?" he said, all chipper.

"I was," I said. My voice sounded terrible, like I'd been gargling glass. "Couldn't get in. Did you save me from those guys?"

"Sure did!" He smiled, all teeth. "High five!"

"What? I mean . . . sure?" I couldn't get to my feet yet. I held my hand up weakly. He held his hand out too, still five feet away, then walked it over and slapped it against mine. Then he backed up to where he'd been standing.

I put my own hand down, slowly.

"Thank you," I said.

"No problem!" he chirped.

We stared at each other in silence, me gasping torn breaths, him smiling aimlessly.

"No offense," I said, "but this is really weird."

"Oh?" he said, and then his voice went flat and toneless. His face lost all tension. "This is not how humans respond in this situation. I did not know that. It is not a situation I encounter often. I will make a note of it in the future."

Motherfuck.

NINE

Katilyn. 2013. Los Angeles, California. West L.A.

Carey went out to grab dinner around seven. I gave him twenty bucks from my emergency stash. I promised myself I wouldn't be surprised when he came back with ten bucks' worth of food and ten of rotgut. I'd gotten all of my alone-time needs out of the way that afternoon, and with Jackie gone to visit her parents, it felt wrong to have the house to myself again. I guess I had grown used to the motels—to other people not only always being in the same house as you, but the same room. Hogging the television, snoring on the bed, occupying the bathroom for a suspicious length of time without the shower running.

An apartment to myself now felt lifeless, like I was sitting on a couch in a doctor's office, rather than in my own home. I used to spend most nights like this happily—all alone, doors locked, in my rattiest PJs, having a drink or two while playing internet or reading a book. Now I just kept getting up to check the windows to see if Carey was back yet. I paced into the kitchen, verified the nothing in my fridge, more out of habit than desire, and back out into the living room. I straightened some things on my shelf for no particular reason, then down the hallway to my bedroom. I stared at my bed for a longing moment, then turned around and went back to make sure the fridge hadn't suddenly spawned something interesting. I wished for a bag of potato chips, just so I'd feel like I accomplished something after I demolished them. That apathy again: not full, not hungry, not interested. I lifted my curtains and checked the empty street. I picked up an issue of *Cosmo* that Jackie had left over here, and glanced through the comfortingly vapid contents. She had written sarcastic answers to all of the questions in the sex quiz.

> **Does your man like it when you call him naughty names during sex?**
> *No, he cried a little when I called him micro-dick.*
> **Does your man enjoy it when you dress up for him?**
> *I wore his dad's old suit and tried to go down on him but he wasn't into it.*

I smiled at the ghost of Jackie in the room with me for that moment, but it faded quickly. I went back to the fridge. Thought hard about just straight up drinking some mustard, then back to the window, lifted the curtains, checked the empty street.

A pale face stared back at me from the other side of the glass.

I jumped and squeaked like a '50s housewife seeing a mouse. I dropped the curtain, and it fell back across the window.

God damn it, Kaitlyn, how many times do you have to go through something like this before you stop behaving like a frightened schoolgirl?

I took two steps back. There were heavy bars on all the windows and doors—*thanks, history of gang activity in my area!*—but it's not like that made me safe from all of the things that *could* be after me. I patted my right front pocket, feeling for my cell phone. I forgot that we'd ditched them weeks ago for fear of being tracked. I still had that phantom urge to check for it all the time, and a vague feeling that I was forgetting something important when I didn't find it. It was like realizing you've forgotten your keys, all the time.

And stupid Kaitlyn was all "oh, ha ha, who needs a landline?"

Okay, possible scenarios:

Best case, it's just a pervert or a burglar.

Aw, remember when that was the worst case?

It could be an Unnoticeable, just checking the apartment to see if anybody was here before reporting back to its masters. If so, that meant it was alone, that it wouldn't come after me, and that I might be able to take it if it did. But only if I had a weapon.

Worst-case scenario, it's an Empty One. It would be able to pull those bars right off the wall and come in after me, and there's absolutely nothing I could do to stop it.

This is not a terribly comforting list.

Well, what could I do about those things? If it was an Empty One, I might as well put on my one nice dress and try to die looking dignified. Nothing to be done about it. If it was a pervert, burglar, or Unnoticeable, I would need a weapon.

Mental catalogue: I had a telescoping baton under my bed that . . . shit. I lost that when Marco broke in here last time. I still had that sketchy can of mace with the cartoon devil girl on it, but I didn't exactly trust its build quality. Seemed just as likely to explode in my own face as the intended victim's. So, what? Kitchen knives? I'm not really the cooking type. Most of my meals come in Styrofoam containers. I do have some old chef's knives, but they couldn't cut tension.

Think think th—

The doorknob rattled.

Whatever it was, it definitely wanted in.

Ad hoc weapons, then: what can you use to stab or bludgeon? A cast-iron pan? A rolling pin? I don't have either of those and *what am I doing, operating on cartoon logic?!*

I grabbed a small steel lamp from the table beside the couch. It had a good heft to it. Not aluminum or anything, and the square base was especially heavy. The corners were pretty sharp. I ripped the cord out of the wall, tore the shade off, and unscrewed the light bulb. I got a brief vision of me rearing back to strike the invincible pervert only to realize that the cord had caught somewhere, preventing me from swinging. I wrapped the cord around the shaft and looped it back on itself. It formed a kind of textured grip.

All right, asshole. Got myself an IKEA mace. Ready when you are.

A rattling sound from the backyard. There was a little access gate to get down there from the landlord's property above me. I never used it. It had a padlock on the latch that I didn't even have the key to. Whatever the intruder was, it had *just* tried the gate. Now it would have to jump the fence to check the doors. Maybe I could get the drop on it.

I padded to the back and swung the security door open as quietly as I could. It wasn't quite dark yet, but it was getting there. I hadn't turned on the outside lights. A few lemon trees, a tall hedge, and the neighboring apartments, leaving only heavy twilight shading the backyard. I ducked low and stuck to the wall, sliding up to where the intruder would have to step if they wanted to check the back door.

The gate rattled again, louder this time, followed by a weighty *thump*.

They'd jumped the fence. Footsteps crunched down the gravel pathway. Getting louder. Growing closer.

I wrapped both of my hands around the cord-grip. I heaved the lamp back.

A shadowy figure rounded the corner and went to put a foot on the first step. I leapt up with all the force I could muster and put my full body weight into the swing. The base of the lamp connected with a wet crunch and the figure reeled backward. I didn't have a landing plan. With all my weight thrown forward, I stumbled awkwardly down the few stairs from the raised deck to the backyard and skidded to my knees. I instinctively used my hands to brace my fall, and came down hard on the lamp. My knuckles got caught between the metal base and the gravel. I felt my skin tear.

No time for that.

I pushed myself up and readied the lamp-mace again. The figure was dazed, but not down. I took two running steps for another swing, emitting my fiercest war cry— entirely unintentionally, didn't even know I *had* a "war cry"—and brought the lamp around in a fast, wide arc.

The figure put out a hand and caught it without flinching. It twisted, wrenching the lamp out of my grip, and tossed it away like a wadded-up napkin.

Well, I guess we're not dealing with your garden-variety pervert. At least I went out swinging. Literally.

The figure's back was turned to what little light there was left. It was just a silhouette: shorter, slight, but with broad shoulders. Close-cropped or shaved head. Almost certainly a guy.

I kicked for its crotch. My bare foot crumpled into his groin so hard I thought I might've broken some toes. The man just laughed. He reached out and grabbed me by the throat. It happened so fast I didn't even see him move. He was an inch or two shorter than me, and probably around the same weight. He lifted me off the ground with one hand.

An Empty One.

My bare feet kicked wildly. I tried to get some purchase to take the weight off of my neck, but there was nothing. He swung me in toward him, then back out and straight down into the ground. All the air left my lungs in one great rattle. The edges of my vision faded, grew black, and then I was out.

I opened my eyes and saw the underside of my landlord's deck. I felt gravel grabbing at my T-shirt and fleece pants. Pressure on my scalp. I was being dragged by my own hair, still in my own backyard. I must've only been out for a few seconds. I tried to twist away from the Empty One's grip, but I could barely lift my arms. The slightest physical effort sent the blackness seeping back into my vision. I instead focused solely on breathing, and didn't even manage that very well.

The Empty One opened the security door, which I'd left unlocked behind me, and dragged me inside my house. He threw me into the couch so hard it rocked back on two feet, then came down with a *thump* that shook the bones of the house. He closed the door behind him, and turned to face me.

He's so young.

I guess I knew the Empty Ones could be any age when they were taken, but this one was almost a kid. Barely out of his teens, if that. He was Asian, short, slender, wide nose and thin lips above a dark patch of goatee. He had his head shaved nearly bald, just a bit of black stubble showing. He wore a heavy motorcycle jacket, torn jeans, and big clunky Frankenstein boots. He saw me staring at him and his slack, emotionless face split into a sheepish grin. Or a reasonable facsimile thereof. He didn't get the eyes right. They stayed flat.

"What do you got to drink around here?" he asked.

I just stared at him in mute terror.

He went to the kitchen. I took the opportunity to roll off the couch. I wanted to land on the balls of my feet and silently stalk out the back door, hop the fence, and run forever. Instead I fell straight on my face and moaned like a dying cow.

"Hey," he called from the other room. "Don't try to go anywhere, or I'll butcher you, okay?"

He sounded so amiable, like he was asking a good friend to bring him a Coke.

The floorboards reverberated beneath me with every footfall from his heavy boots. He bent and lifted me by the back of my shirt and the seat of my pants, then dropped me unceremoniously back on the couch, facedown.

"You don't have any booze here at all?" he asked, sounding positively heartbroken.

I turned my head so I could see him with one eye, my nose and mouth buried in the couch cushions.

"Mmf," I said.

"Damn," he said. "What about dope? Weed? You look like a weed chick. Probably got one of those medical cards, am I right?"

He laughed and stood up straight to survey the living room.

"Come on, let's smoke up. Take the edge off while we

wait," he said. He clapped his hands, rubbed them together, and held them out toward me.

When I didn't respond, he dropped the human face and let the slack visage take over.

"This does not have to be bad," he said, his voice like a cold wind. "People can have fun, even in bad situations. Let's make this a positive experience."

Jesus fucking Christ, I thought Marco was creepy. What the hell did a thing like this consider fun?

"I don't have anything," I said, barely able to speak above a whisper. "I'm sorry."

Should I tell him about Carey, so he's not surprised and liable to do something nasty? Or would that ruin Carey's element of surprise, and screw us both?

"There's some money in a coffee can above the stove," I said. "You could go out and grab us some drinks if you want."

He actually seemed to think about that for a second.

"No," he finally decided. "You would probably try to run, or do something else stupid in the name of survival. We will just wait."

Wait . . . for what?

"But hey," he said, back to feigning humanity. "Surely you got some music or something, right?"

I pointed at my iPod, charging on the low table that held my TV and Bluetooth speakers. He picked it up and stared at it with open disgust.

"These things are so soulless, man," he said. "I miss vinyl. How do you . . . ?"

He mimed poking at buttons, then tossed it to me. I picked it up slowly. No sudden movements. I powered it on and scrolled through the menu. I paused with my thumb above the wheel.

"What uh . . . what kind of music do you like?" I asked.

He smiled big and said, "Got any punk?"

I did not. We listened to Herman's Hermits instead. He was tunelessly screaming all of the words to "I'm Henry the VIIIth, I Am." It was just starting on the third refrain when somebody knocked on the front door. Well, "knocked"—it sounded more like they were trying to kick it in. The Asian kid hopped up and went for the door. I couldn't see it open from my spot on the couch, and was too terrified to move.

The back door, Kaitlyn! You can make it!

I remembered one of the first times I'd seen Marco. He'd come to the bar I was working at to surprise me. I had barely even thought about running when he closed the ten feet between us in the blink of an eye. The Empty Ones were so fast. I'd never make it.

"Carey!" the kid yelled excitedly. "You ugly son of a bitch! Haha, you got old as shit!"

Carey said something to him I couldn't quite hear, but it was plain that he wasn't nearly as enthused as the kid. And yet he wasn't screaming in panic, either. . . .

The door swung closed. Heavy bootsteps and shuffling Chucks. Carey had a greasy paper bag in one hand and a bottle of whiskey in the other. He saw me frozen there on the couch, all disheveled and shaking, weeds in my hair and bits of gravel on my clothes.

"Jesus Christ, Zang," Carey said, turning to the Asian kid. "What did you do to her?"

"What?" he said, all innocent. Then the façade faded and he continued: "She provoked me. She is not seriously wounded, much less torn in half with her guts strewn in the trees. I thought you would be happy with the progress I've made."

"Happy with . . . ?!" Carey snapped, but then thought for a moment. "Actually, yeah, this is a big improvement over last time."

Zang beamed. He slapped Carey on the shoulder so hard that he dropped the food bag.

"And you brought whiskey!" Zang laughed.

I didn't want to speak yet, lest I risk pissing the thing off. But I gave Carey every ounce of "what the fuck?" my eyes could muster. He saw me, mouthed "sorry," and shrugged. He followed Zang into the kitchen. I heard them bang around in there, looking for something.

"No shot glasses?" Zang said, after a minute of fruitless searching.

"Nope," Carey said. "All she's got are these."

Carey came out first, holding three coffee mugs that I'd picked up in bulk from a Salvation Army store. One said CAMP CADY WILDLIFE ASSOCIATION, one said I'M NOT AS THINK AS YOU DRUNK I AM in Comic Sans, and one just had a picture of a really fat cat on it, stuck in a cat door. Carey set them down, twisted the cap off the whiskey, and slopped a good amount in each mug. Zang grabbed his and downed it, then immediately started pouring more. Carey came over to me with the fat cat mug. I shook my head.

"Take it," he said. "You're gonna need it."

I wanted to slap it across the room and punch him in the nose, but instead I grasped it with shaking hands and took a sip. I winced and gagged, coppery hellfire steaming up my sinuses.

"Whoa, no," Zang said, laughing. "Never sip liquor with a screw-top cap, girlie."

He shot back his own refill, by way of proof.

Carey clinked his mug against mine, and we downed

our drinks. It was exactly as bad as before, but at least it was over with quickly. I gestured for a refill, and Zang obliged, smiling the whole time like we were old friends.

"So," Carey said. "Zang, this is Kaitlyn. Kaitlyn, this is Zang."

"Charmed," Zang said, and shot me a practiced bad boy smile, all full of the promise of sexy mischief. I'd seen that same smile on every glam rock album in the '80s, but his eyes were still flat, like a lake on a windless day.

"Make him promise not to kill me, no matter what I say," I told Carey.

He looked back and forth between me and Zang.

"I don't think he can promise that," he said.

"I can," Zang answered, his voice atonal. "I can promise that I will not harm you, no matter what you say. The words you things bleat are largely irrelevant, anyway."

"Seriously?" Carey said. He eyed Zang with equal parts apprehension and appreciation.

"It has been a long time since you knew me," Zang said. "I have become more practiced."

Carey raised his eyebrows, a gesture of appreciation.

I looked to Zang, with his coma-patient face and black shark eyes, standing frozen at the table like he was waiting for input.

"What the hell are you thinking?" I screamed. I meant to consider the risks more carefully before speaking, but it just exploded out of me. "Bringing that thing here to my house? Are you working with them now? Did you turn on us?"

Carey tipped his mug back, swallowed once, hard, and blew out fumes I could smell from across the room. He shuddered.

"Zang is, well, he is and he isn't one of the Empty Ones. He's hollowed out like them, but maybe not quite as much. There's a bit more human left in him than there should be. Now, that doesn't make him safe. I wouldn't trust him alone with my puppy, for fear he'd eat it."

"I probably would not," Zang said, emotionlessly.

"Yeah." Carey shot him a skewed glare. "If you say so. Anyway, Zang's a monster, that's for sure. But he's good on his word. A long time ago, he told me if I ever needed him, I could find him at the Drunken Monkey Style every Sunday at closing time. When you said we needed to find another angel, I gave the place a call. Turns out the Monkey went out of business fifteen years ago. Terrible bar. Fully deserved it. But the whole neighborhood went yuppie, and the old Monkey is a yoga place now. Zang still showed up every Sunday night and waited until the doors shut."

"They tried to make me leave a few times, over the years," Zang mused. "It did not go well."

"This is the bad idea." Carey shrugged. "I told you it was stupid, and dangerous, and possibly insane. Now, you could say all those same things about Z himself—but whatever he is, he's not on the side of the angels."

"In all of the Empty Ones," Zang said, "there is a very small remainder of the person we used to be. That remainder is all that remains of our humanity. Much of my mine is rage. Even as I love the angels for what they are, and long for the nothingness they promise, I hate them. They are the things that did this to Jie and I. They must pay."

"You want to end this?" Carey asked. "Zang is all the way in, and he's our best chance at finding an angel."

"And so you invited the thing to my apartment? When I was all alone, and without so much as a warning?" I slammed my mug down on the end table beside the couch. Pale brown liquid sloshed over the lip. The little ceramic handle broke off in my hand. I whipped it at Carey. It bounced off of his chest.

"Well, he was early—" Carey said.

"I was not," Zang interrupted him. "I was exactly on time, as I am always."

"Well, fuck it, then. I guess I was late. Besides, I figured you could handle yourself."

"Against an Empty One?" I laughed, bitterly. I picked my mug back up, the ragged edges where the handle had been attached scraping against my palms. I bolted back the rest of the whiskey.

"Sweetheart," Carey said. "Not a week ago I saw you bleed out on a highway and come back to life, then step through time or whatever the hell you call it. I didn't figure you needed the protection of a crusty old homeless man."

"So it's true, then?" Zang said. "She can devour the angels?"

"Devour? No, I—" I wanted to protest, but I didn't have a better word for it. "Yeah, I guess that's what I do."

I felt sick. Maybe it was being confronted with the reality of what I'd been doing, or maybe it was just Carey's ten-dollar whiskey churning in my gut.

"And you believe that if you find another, you can kill them all?" Zang's voice and face were still devoid of humanity, but he'd taken an eager step forward while speaking.

"Yes," I said, figuring that this wasn't the time for hedging. "If you get me near one, I can end all of this."

"Well fuckin' excellent!" Zang exclaimed. "What are we waiting for?"

The abrupt shift back to humanity startled me. I dropped

my mug. It bounced off of the couch cushion and hit the ground, shattering. The piece nearest me was just the fat cat's face, removed from its body. Its expression was accusatory. "Why aren't you helping me?" it seemed to be saying. "Can't you see I'm in trouble here?"

TEN

Carey. 1982. Los Angeles, California. Chinatown.

The Empty One and I just stared at each other very, very awkwardly for the first few minutes. I guess he'd spoken his piece, and I just couldn't think of a damn thing to say. I felt like if I talked I might break whatever spell we had going here and he'd come after me. I wasn't in any shape to run yet. So I kept my big mouth shut. For about as long as I could manage that, anyway, which turned out not to be long.

"What?" I said. "You waiting for me to beg? You should do some stretches before you go fuck yourself. Make sure you don't pull something."

"Me?" The Empty One laughed. "Nah, I'm just not sure what to do in this situation. I've never saved a gweilo as ugly as you before. Do I throw you back, or keep you?"

Holy shit, what? An Empty One with a sense of humor?

"You're not gonna kill me?" I asked it.

"If I wanted you dead, I would've let those dudes back there do it." He smiled and it was almost halfway convincing.

"So, what, you're gonna hollow me out and make me

one of your groupies? I'd prefer the killing, if it's all the same to you."

He blinked a few times. His mouth twitched and the smile broke. His face went slack and his voice fell flat.

"You know what I am," he said.

I couldn't tell if it was a question or not.

"Yeah, are you . . . do you not know who I am?" I asked.

"I do not. Should I."

Okay, that was supposed to be a question.

"You're fuckin' A right, you should! I'm Carey. I've taken down more of you bastards than I can count. I'm like the Lex Luthor to your Superman. Wait, no—the other way around. You assholes are Luthor. *I'm* Superman."

"If you fight the other Empty Ones and their spawn, then you and I are on the same side," it said.

Is it fucking with me? What could its game possibly be? Maybe it's hoping that I'll lead it back to my base or something, so it can kill all my friends and allies in one fell swoop. If so, joke's on it. I don't have any.

"If you didn't know who I was, why did you save me?" I asked.

"I did not," it answered. "I just killed the spawn attacking you."

The spawn?

"Holy crap," I said, and slapped myself in the head. "Those guys were Unnoticeables."

"You did not know."

"Well, no. Normally I can spot the blurry-face shtick from a mile away. But I just figured those guys were Chinese. You all look alike to me, anyway."

"Wow, man," the Empty One said, adopting human mannerisms. "That's like, super duper *extra* racist."

I laughed.

"An Empty One that can get offended? I'm not buying it."

His human mask fell away again.

"That was the correct response to your provocation. Was it not."

"Yeah, it was. You got me there. So . . ." I looked around the square, still empty, still pissing fat streams of rain. "What now?"

"I just saved your ass," the Empty One said, back to feigning humanity. "I think you owe me a beer."

It held out its hand to me, and like a jackass, I took it. It pulled me to my feet and started to walk away. I followed. I was starting to get my wind back a little bit, but I decided to hang back some anyway. I played up a limp and hugged my chest, like I was still in bad shape. If this fucker turned on me, I'd need all the surprise I could get. It turned around and saw me hobbling slowly after it. It walked back toward me and grabbed my hand. I tensed up, ready to fight or flee or at least spit in the bastard's eye before he tore me apart. Instead it heaved my arm around its shoulders and took my weight off my "bad" leg.

It's fucking helping me.

Everything has gone insane.

The Empty One said its name was Zang. It took me to a dark little hole of a bar behind a Chinese restaurant a few blocks down. It said something to the bartender in their weird language, and they both laughed at me. The bartender ducked down and pulled out a few cans of Old Milwaukee from somewhere below the bar. He cracked them open— one with each hand—and spun them around to face us.

Then he retreated to a shaky metal stool and resumed watching his tiny TV set, hidden beneath the cash register.

The whole place seemed to be carved out of one solid block of wood—all the same deep brown color; over-varnished and heavily abused. A small rough-hewn bar made out of a single scratched slab. Wooden stools with faded and split red leather, secured by brass rivets. Wood paneling on every wall, holding up a couple of liquor posters, a Chinese calendar, and a dart board that in no way left enough standing room to actually play the game. The whole place smelled like fried pork and spices. Wafting through the speakers, so faint you almost couldn't hear it, wailing, twangy foreign music plinked away. Above that, the canned laugh track of whatever the bartender was watching, and angry ranting from behind a swinging door that led to the kitchen.

I took a deep swig from my can. However not my style this place might be, they had the only two things that mattered: cheap beer and a working refrigerator. Oh, god damn. Beer. The first tangy slap on the tongue, followed by the carbonated bite, then the soothing cold of the liquid running down your throat, coating your belly in its beautiful, healing beerness.

Being a bum has some disadvantages. Chief amongst them that you never have any money, so when you do, you gotta prioritize your drunk. Beer isn't actually that effective. You have to go for the fortified wine, or the rotgut, if you want to sustain an economically feasible blitz. That had been my life for a while. But beer was always my favorite. I hadn't had a cold one in weeks. Months maybe. I just couldn't justify paying the money.

Speaking of . . .

"There's no way I can pay for this," I told Zang.

"I figured," he said. "I've got a deal with the bartender."

"I don't even know where to start with you. Whatever the hell you are," I said.

He laughed. It was easy and natural, but he carried it on too long and cut it off too abruptly. None of the wind-down of a human laugh.

"What's to say?" He sipped from his own can. He savored it, eyes closed, head tilted back, even shivered a little at the end. He looked like he was really enjoying it, until I recognized something in the mannerisms.

They were mine. Exactly what I had done, just a few seconds ago.

"If you've got a free beer deal worked out in this place, you can start from the *very* beginning," I said.

"All right," he said, atonally. "I will tell you a story."

ELEVEN

Zang. 1871. Los Angeles, California. Chinatown.

There was a young man named Zang. Zang was not his birth name, but a name he took later. Zang does not speak his birth name, even in stories.

His parents were Liu and Fung, and they came from China to America because they had been told it was a magical place of riches. They believed these things because they were poor and uneducated, and did not recognize empty promises when they saw them.

They arrived in Los Angeles, California in 1860. There were no riches. But there was work. It was bad work. Hard, demeaning, and unceasing. There was no going back. Though to be honest, things were not much better back in China. People like Liu and Fung are not given chances. They can only take them.

Liu and Fung accepted their situation, because that is what broken people do: They accept.

They worked hard. They saved what little they could. Zang had been raised by Liu and Fung his entire life. He had been born poor, and uneducated. He should have become accustomed to it. He did not. He longed for things beyond his station. He lied. He swindled. He cheated. He did many things he should not have done. But he did not assault. He did not murder. He did not rape.

Zang wanted to avoid a life of pointless toil, like Liu and Fung. It was not a stupid goal. It was a worthy goal. But Zang become confused, and mistook status for security. He saw there were some Chinese people in Los Angeles, California, that were doing well. Or at least, better than Liu and Fung. Zang wanted to be like these people, who were called the Tong.

The Tong were called gangs, but that was not entirely correct. They were everything. They were protectors, exploiters, warriors, murderers, saviors, and salesmen. The Chinese in Los Angeles were not treated like people. They did not have the rights of people. All they had were the Tong. If they did not have the Tong, they had nothing. Zang wanted to have the Tong. He did not want to have nothing.

Zang worked very hard for a man named Sam Yuen, who ran a Tong. Life became better for Zang. He had to lie. He had to cheat. He had to swindle. But he did not assault. He did not murder. He did not rape. This was enough for Zang. Until one day he met a girl. She was very beautiful. She was very sweet. Zang was never much for poetry. If you asked him, he could only say he loved her, and that he did not know what that word meant before her, and that he would forget what it meant after her. The girl felt the same about Zang. This girl's name was Jie. Jie was not her birth name, but a name she took after. Zang does not speak her birth name, even in stories.

For a time Zang and Jie were very happy. They wanted for nothing more than they had. This is not often permitted to last.

A man from a rival Tong named Yo Hing also thought Jie was very beautiful. He did not lust after her for himself. He lusted after her for the price she would draw. Yo Hing took Jie, and sold her hand in marriage to a man who had the money to buy it.

Zang did not accept this. He was in love, and that is not what people in love do: They do not accept. Zang went to Sam Yuen and he demanded that they take action. Zang was in no position to make this demand. But Zang was a very good liar. He was a swindler. He was a cheat. He spoke to Sam Yuen about reputation and honor. He said that affronts like the abduction of Jie were bad for business. Sam Yuen agreed with this, though Zang did not. Zang loved Jie, and no longer cared about business.

The two Tong went to war. Many people died in this war. They were Chinese people in Los Angeles, California. Chinese people in Los Angeles, California, did not matter. And then one day, in a shootout between the Tong, a white person was killed. White people in Los Angeles, California, did matter.

On October 24th, 1871, five hundred of the white people of Los Angeles, California, gathered together and marched on a place called Negro Alley. Strangely enough, this was where many Chinese people were found. The five hundred white people of Los Angeles, California, (this is said to be one tenth of the city's population at the time) attacked Negro Alley. They assaulted. They murdered. They raped. They tortured and killed seventeen Chinese people. Seventeen Chinese people dead for one white person dead. Apparently this is the exchange rate.

On October 24th, 1871, Zang and Sam Yuen were informed that Jie was being held in a saloon in Negro Alley.

Sam Yuen gave Zang and four other men permission to raid the saloon in Negro Alley. They did so. There they found Jie. She was tied to a stained mattress, bleeding from every orifice. She had been assaulted. She had been raped. But she had not been murdered. Zang felt two things in conflicting measure, as humans sometimes do. He felt anger at what had been done to Jie, and he felt relief that Jie was still alive. What had been done to her did not diminish her in Zang's eyes. He untied her wrists and ankles. He wrapped his coat around her shoulders. He sat on the bed with her and held her in his arms.

From outside, many men began yelling, and there were gunshots. The four other men with Zang went downstairs to the saloon, and found five hundred white people descending on Negro Alley. Yo Hing, of the rival Tong, had made his fortune by being very kind to the white people of Los Angeles, California. He often sold out the Chinese for the benefit of the white people, and this made him money. This is what he did again, on the night of October 24th, 1871. Seventeen Chinese people would die, and many more would be wounded terribly, both in soul and body, so Yo Hing could send a message to Sam Yuen. That message was: I can do whatever I want. You cannot.

We are now done with Sam Yuen and Yo Hing. They are history, and are used only to bring Zang and Jie together at precisely the right place, at precisely the right time, for something miraculous to happen.

As they sat there crying and whispering promises to each other, an angel appeared in that dirty room with its bloodstained mattress.

This was not an angel in the way that Jie and Zang understood. This angel did not care for humanity. It viewed humanity as a series of problems. The code that dictated their personalities and existences was sloppy, repetitive, and poorly written. This angel could reach inside a human and solve those errors, and the human would cease to exist. The energy that human was using, had used, and would use, would then be freed up, and the angel could take it and use it for a better purpose. To this angel, humans were fuel. This angel needed fuel.

It looked inside Zang, and it looked inside Jie, and it saw something very unique: Their solutions were intertwined. Much of Zang's solution lay inside Jie, and much of Jie's solution lay inside Zang. Now that they were together again, it was a simple matter of shunting bits between them. Zang and Jie were solved.

Partially.

In some humans, there is no complete solution. There is always an answer. There is not always a neat answer. Sometimes, there is a remainder left over. Most of what made the person what it was has departed, leaving only a vacant shell. An Empty One. There was one thing the angel could not simplify about Zang and Jie: their love. Their affection did not come from a reasonable place. It could not be traced back to childhood experiences or subconscious fears or basic genetics. In this way, their love was like madness. And madness cannot be solved. Zang and Jie were left with their love.

It is here that many listeners pause in the story. Here, they issue wistful sighs. They profess opinions on romance. They do not stop to consider what a terrible thing love is, when taken on its own. The Empty Ones that had been Zang and Jie loved each other. But they had no compassion. They had no empathy. They had no loyalty. They loved one another, and nothing else.

For over a hundred years, Zang and Jie were together as Empty Ones. Over one hundred years that they spent torturing, murdering, and destroying anything that came between them, no matter how slight or accidental the trespass. They were worse than normal Empty Ones. They were paired. They exalted in each other, and that made their casual cruelty even worse.

One hundred and eight years after they had been solved, Zang and Jie met another angel.

It was here that the unit of Zang and Jie divided.

Jie was grateful to the angel. She worshiped it like it was a god. She was happy for what she was—simplified, pure, empty—and wanted only to help the angel.

Zang felt these stirrings, too. The thing that he was now enjoyed its new state. But the thing that he used to be, the man, remembered what had been taken from them. He remembered what Jie's love was before the angel. And he was furious.

Jie worshiped. Zang attacked.

Jie was heartbroken and furious. She was being asked to choose between her lover and her god. It was a choice she could not make. Zang was heartbroken and furious. He was being asked to choose between his lover and vengeance. It was a choice he could make.

He chose wrong. He chose revenge.

Zang thrust Jie aside and dove at the angel. He was taken inside of it, to a screaming white void of impossible angles. The world inside of the angel was painful and horrible, but it was not chaotic or mad. It was order itself. The Empty One that was Zang understood order. He looked into the churning intersections there and tracked their path. He found his way to something familiar. He found his way to himself.

This was the same angel that had simplified Zang and Jie, 108 years ago. It had used their energy. It had burned away their lives. But there were very small pieces of them left. Zang seized those pieces with everything he had. He took a small part of himself back. And he took a small part of Jie back, too.

When he awoke, all of the skin had burned off of his body. His eyeballs had cooked in their sockets. He could see nothing. He could barely hear. He heard Jie. She told him that she could not forgive what he had done, and that if she saw him again, she would hurt him. That is the true tragedy, she said: that neither of them could die, so she could never kill him, as he deserved.

Jie departed. Zang healed.

He sought her out, to explain what he had done and why. To try to give her back the pieces he had stolen from the angel. But she was true to her word.

She hacked him into pieces and scattered them around Los Angeles, California. It took weeks for his body to grow back from the neck-stump of his severed head. She buried him in concrete. It took months to dig himself out. She burned him, she shot him, she beat him, and she poisoned him. She never listened to him. But he never stopped trying.

Zang, through his divine theft, had become more human than the other Empty Ones. But he had not become human. Not even close. He was still a monster, just one with a conscience. He still did not understand people. He still harmed people. All that was different now was that he could regret it.

Zang had no place in this world, and had lost his only place in the world of monsters. He did the only measurably good thing he could think to do: He began killing his own kind. He found the weak and faceless spawn of his kin, the Unnoticeables, and he beat and broke them. He thwarted the plans of the Empty Ones. He knew their secrets. He knew of the ritual. He kept them from bringing about new angels, as best he could. And he sought out Jie, over and over again, hoping that this time, she would hear him.

That is the story of Zang, and there is nothing more to it.

TWELVE

Kaitlyn. 2013. Los Angeles, California. West L.A.

"What's the holdup?" Zang laughed. He was standing just outside my door, bouncing up and down like an excited child. "Let's go kill ourselves something beautiful!"

"Could you not do that?" I said.

"What?" He smiled. All innocence.

"It's creepy when you pretend to feel things," I said to him. "I mean, it's creepy when you're all blank, too. But it's a slightly more tolerable kind of creepy."

"I'm not pretending now!" He laughed. "This is the best day of my life!"

I looked to Carey for backup. He just shrugged.

"He's really not pretending," Carey said. "About the only thing that makes Zang genuinely happy is hurting the angels. We just told him he can kill one. This is his happy face."

I looked to Zang. He was smiling with his mouth open, the tops of his perfect white teeth just visible, glitter in his eyes.

I shuddered.

"Can we at least leave a note or something for Jackie?" I asked.

"Sure thing," Carey said from behind me, in the living room.

He grabbed a pen and paper from the little IKEA desk I keep tucked away in the corner, mostly covered in laundry that isn't dirty but doesn't quite qualify as clean. He scribbled something down, then followed me out the front door. He slid it shut behind him, the edge of the note tucked between the door and the jamb.

It read:

> *Jackie,*
> *Gone killin*
> *B back soon*
> *—the A team*

"That's not exactly helpful," I said.

Carey laughed.

"What do you want me to say?" He slipped into an impression of a prissy little British girl. "My dearest Jackie, with much reluctance we have gone to rid the world of the vilest angels and their ilk. Think of us always, your friends and confidants, the esteemed Mr. Carroll, the genteel Ms. Kaitlyn, and oh yeah, this fucking monstrous half-guy you haven't met yet. His name is Zang. He's cool."

"Thank you," Zang said, flatly.

"It's just the last time we talked," I said, "I promised her I wouldn't do any angel stuff. If she comes back here and sees this, she's going to freak."

"Where's she gone?" Zang asked.

"Back to see her parents," I answered.

"No worries then!" he said, all chipper. "She won't be coming back."

"What do you mean?" I said.

"Oh, she'll be dead or hollowed out or something. With Marco gone, that'll leave Jie in charge of the search. The first thing she'll do is convert any nearby family or friends, just in case you try hiding out with them. Don't worry about Jackie," he said, idly picking at his nails. "She's been lost for a while."

I wonder if anybody else has ever taken an Uber to a rescue mission.

Jackie used our only car when she took off to visit her folks in Brentwood. Zang had taken the bus to my place, and Carey sacrificed his beaten-up old motorcycle trying to rescue me from an unholy church, back when this all started. That left us with public transportation, taxi, or other. The cab company said it would be twenty minutes before they could pick us up. The bus would also take too long—there were three transfers to get to Jackie's place. Yes, we had to go back inside my apartment, turn on my laptop, and Google how to get there. Even as my best friend was probably being emptied out by freaks that used to be her own parents, we were on the L.A. Metro website selecting "quickest trip."

So we downloaded Uber. They had a car at our place within three minutes. It was a silver Prius with a bashed-in rear bumper. The driver was Nigerian, this was his very first fare as an Uber driver; he was trying to make some extra money to pay for singing lessons. That's why he'd come to Hollywood, you see—he was convinced musicals were going to be the next big thing, and he wanted to get in on the ground floor. In the meantime, he worked as a valet at a nightclub downtown—he can totally get us in if we came by on Friday, that was when Frederich worked the door, who was very cool and would let us in without even paying the—

I stopped listening somewhere around then.

I wanted to laugh at the absurdity of the situation, but I couldn't. I was full to bursting with a scrabbling panic. It occupied every inch of me. It clawed at the insides of my chest, closed my throat, made my scalp and forearms itch. My eyes kept welling up like I was going to cry, but I couldn't. Every word I spoke sounded distant in my own head, like somebody had recorded my voice on a cheap tape recorder and was playing it back from outside the car. I stared out the window and picked at the cracking vinyl on the back of the passenger seat.

Zang sat by the other window, happily chatting away with the cabbie.

The . . . Uberie? What the hell do you even call these people?

I guess he appreciated the chance to practice being human. His small talk was all off, but like most everybody in L.A., the Uberie didn't care: He was only listening long enough to find his turn to talk again. Carey sat between Zang and me. He was whispering stupid platitudes to me, about how it would be all right, and it would also be okay, and did he mention it would be all right?

I wanted to elbow him in the teeth.

All of this happened inside a bubble full of a dense gas that deadened both sound and emotion. I couldn't listen to them prattle on if I wanted to. Nor could I cry, or scream, or leap out of this car and sprint down Santa Monica Boulevard tearing out my own hair—which I very much *did* want to do. I was stuck inside a god damn Prius, killing time in the waiting room outside of fear and rage.

"Can we not take Santa Monica?" I leaned in between the seats and spoke to the cabbie, cutting off Zang in the middle of a charming little anecdote about the time he started a fire in the restroom of a bar that stopped serving him.

The Uberie tapped his cell phone, mounted on a little plastic thing plugged into his CD player.

"It says this is the best way," he insisted, pointing at the map on his screen. There was a solid line running straight down Santa Monica and all the way off screen.

"But it's not," I said. "Traffic's always rough through here, especially on a nice day, and the buses are constantly making stops, slowing everything down. If you take a right on—"

"They have this little map, you see," the Uberie interrupted. "It tells you the best way to go."

I fell silent, trying to suppress the urge to shove his precious app right down his throat.

"Speaking of fire," the Uberie resumed his conversation with Zang. "I know this lady, this very cool lady, she does a dance with fire down on the promenade. She says you can make—"

"If you don't take the next right and get off of Santa Monica," I said, reaching forward and gathering up a healthy portion of his arm fat between my thumb and forefinger. "I will pull the skin off of your testicles."

I pinched the fat and twisted as hard as I could. He screamed.

"You're crazy!" he yelled, and started cranking the wheel like he was gonna pull over. "I'm not driving you anywhere. You get out! You! Out!"

He slammed the brakes, leaving the car stopped diagonal to the curb: the front vaguely pulled in the direction of "over," while the rear blocked traffic for an entire lane. He flipped on his hazard lights though, so obviously it was fine.

The driver started to turn around to yell at us face-to-face, but Zang leaned forward and wrapped his hands around the man's throat from behind the driver's seat. The Uberie froze up like somebody had just flipped his off switch.

"I do not have the grip strength to pulverize your spine," Zang said, in his dead man's voice. "Not while it is fresh. I do have the grip strength to pulverize a dried spine. I know this from experience. But yours—no. It is still ripe. It is filled with fluid and therefore pliable. It will not crush. It will bend and squeeze. I can still sink my fingers through the flesh of your neck until I reach the spine, however. At that point I will wrap my right hand around the base of it, just above your collarbone. My left will remain higher on the spine, just below your jawline. By wrenching in two different directions at once, I will be able to break the spine and then twist your head until the tendons and veins rupture. I will then be able to pull your head off. It is a lot like taking the lid off of a very stuck jar."

We were all quiet.

"Please do not do that?" the Uberie finally ventured.

Zang considered the request for a moment.

"Okay," he said. "But only if you drive exactly how and where the girl says."

"Yes!" he sobbed.

Zang did not release him.

"And one more thing," he added, switching back to his faux human voice. "You gotta tell me about that fire dancer! Do you have her number?"

* * *

The Uberie drove quickly and precisely through Santa Monica and up into the Brentwood hills. Zang had his hands around the driver's throat the entire time, all while making the most terrifying small talk in history. The Uberie told him about the promenade performers he knew, what they made in a day, what they did for that money, what scams they pulled on the tourists when the day's take was light. Zang told him about the shows he'd seen lately, the chicks he'd banged at them, and one very detailed story about chasing down and mauling some sort of giant rodent on the concrete banks of the L.A. River. He swore it wasn't a rat. The Uberie told him it was probably a nutria—they had them everywhere, he said. He sobbed violently.

We came to a very gradual and careful stop in the roundabout of Jackie's parents' driveway. I'd been here a few times before, but I'd never driven it. At least, not in L.A. I couldn't afford a car. I mean, I came down here with one, but after sixteen tickets for not moving it on street cleaning days, I had to sell the thing. Now my internal geography of L.A. was based on bus lines and the views from the backseats of wealthier friends who could decipher the arbitrary code of the street sweeper schedules. We were somewhere in Brentwood, was all I knew. Somewhere very, very expensive, where people like me didn't belong. You had to have better teeth than me to live here. They had to be that unnatural shade of shining white, like a fresh sheet of blank paper.

The same color as Jackie's parental home, incidentally. I don't know a thing about architecture. I don't know what you call this style, but it reminded me of New England somehow. Just bigger and gaudier. Like a house on a movie set built to look like New England. No big floor-to-ceiling windows here. Just dozens of small ones that looked out onto an utterly weed-free lawn with short, soft grass the texture of velvet.

The Uberie made a strangled noise of confirmation. We were here.

"I will choke you now," Zang informed him, matter-of-factly.

The driver tried to protest, but only gurgled.

"No!" I said, "no killing!"

I leaned up between the seats and tried to pry Zang's fingers free. They were like iron. Like iron that had been welded to the driver's skin. I might as well have tried to break the grip of a statue. The Uberie looked at me with hope in his eyes.

"I know," Zang answered. "I will choke him into unconsciousness, and then put him in his own trunk. This way he will not alert the authorities. At least, not soon."

"Oh," I said. "Okay."

The hope in the Uberie's eyes turned to hate for a second, then it turned to nothing and he was out.

Zang released him, stepped out of the Prius, popped the trunk, and hauled the driver back there like an unwieldy grocery bag. Carey got out, too. He stretched his arms and yawned. I got out last. I made it all the way to the door and paused, my finger resting on the button for the bell.

"Should we—" I turned to Carey and Zang, then heard a latch click.

The door swung open. I had not yet rung the bell.

It was Glenn, Jackie's dad.

"Hi, Glenn," I said. "We're here for the trap."

He leapt out and caught me in a big bear hug that, shockingly, did not end with him strangling me. He let go and then held me out at arm's length, to survey.

"You look great!" he finally decided, with a firm nod. As though the matter had been up for debate, but was now settled. Forever.

"Who are your . . ." Glenn leaned to peer over my shoulder at Carey and Zang.

Carey had his hands in his pockets. His shoulders tucked low. He was intently staring at something off to his right, deliberately not making eye contact. Zang stood too erectly, like a soldier at attention. Then, after seeing he was being observed, dropped quickly into a slouch and shot Glenn a pair of thumbs-ups and a shit-eating grin. It was the least convincingly human thing he could've done at that moment.

". . . friends?" Glenn finally ventured, giving me a worried look.

"Oh, right," I said. "This is Carey, we uh . . ."

How the hell would two fairly normal girls like me and Jackie possibly know a scumbag like Carey?

"He's in Jackie's improv class," I said.

Glenn rolled his eyes, but in a controlled way, that signified he was used to this.

"And I don't know that other guy. He's just the Uber driver. He's going to stay out here and wait for us," I said, the last part while staring directly at Zang.

He shrugged and walked around the Prius to the driver's seat. He collapsed into it. The car rocked with his weight.

"Come in!" Glenn said. "Was Jackie expecting you? She didn't say anything, but then, she never does. . . ."

Glenn stepped aside and held an arm out to the foyer. There were crudely carved wooden benches to each side, rough and unfinished in a way that signified each probably cost more than a midsize sedan. Aged tile floors, wrought iron fixtures, an old brass coatrack with only two coats on it: Jackie's pale blue, puffy hooded vest thing, and some kind of thin purple duster.

Who else was here?

I stepped past Glenn, reasonably sure that an Unnoticeable wouldn't bother bear-hugging me before flaying me, and motioned for Carey to follow. He spat on the driveway first, and sulked after me with his head down.

What was his problem?

I guessed that if I felt out of place here, this must be like walking on the sun for Carey. Sometimes it's easier to live up to the preconceptions people have of you, rather than trying to fight them. I get that.

Still . . . maybe try not being such a dick?

"Can I take your uh . . . coat?" Glenn asked Carey.

Carey's ancient leather jacket was mostly held together with duct tape and patches for punk rock bands. It was a double-breasted motorcycle-style number, black, with spikes on the shoulder pads. I tried to picture it hanging on their antique brass coatrack. It was like picturing the Pope doing shots. It just wouldn't work. Carey shook his head.

"We won't be staying long," he said.

We wouldn't? Right. Of course we wouldn't. We were just here to check on Jackie, make sure she was alive and okay, maybe give her a warning, then we were off to . . .

What, exactly?

I never did catch Zang's plan. I heard that Jackie might be in trouble and we dropped everything to rush out here. Whatever it was, I suppose it was still on the table, supposing things turned out okay here.

Glenn smiled and motioned for us to head on through to the living room. Carey was closer to the doorway than me, but he still waited for me to go first. A tour guide in hostile territory. I stepped through into an immense space dominated by a huge brick fireplace. More wrought iron all around it—pokers, grates, strange devices with hinges and bellows that clearly hadn't been employed since the 1800s. The room was divided into tasteful little subsections: a reading nook with leather armchairs and oak bookshelves, each laden with tasteful-looking tomes that I'm sure had never been opened; a few old-world rocking chairs in front of the fireplace; a small couch and lounge combo centered around the main window, looking out onto the front lawn.

Jackie's mom, Brin, sat there. Prim to the point of being on edge. Her posture ramrod straight, knees together, hands folded in her lap. She jumped to her feet when she saw me, and went through a strange variety of expressions. Like each feature of her face felt a different emotion at the same time, and it took her a minute to gather them all together under the same banner. Finally, she smiled at me. We were an awkward length away from each other. The hug was expected of us, so we both had to walk like twenty feet with our arms outstretched.

"Katey!" she said, and I wrapped my arms around her.

She had the lightweight frailty of the elderly. Somehow felt less solid than younger people, like she was just made of less durable materials. Her sweater smelled like roses.

"We weren't expecting you," she said. Her eyes were full—like she hadn't been crying, but maybe she meant to.

"Brin," I whispered. "Is everything okay? Is Jackie okay?"

"Just fine, honey," she said, and took my arm. She walked us toward the dining room. The loose soles of Carey's Chucks slapped and shuffled behind us. Even his walk felt the need to clarify exactly how unhappy he was to be here.

"So, uh, Carey, was it?" Glenn asked.

Carey grunted affirmation.

"You know my daughter from her improv classes? You must be quite the comedian yourself, then."

"I'm a fucking laugh riot," Carey said.

Glenn laughed nervously.

Brin and I rounded the corner into the dining room. It, the kitchen, and the TV room occupied one very long, relatively narrow end of the house, no walls separating them. At the far end of the stretch, the television was on, blaring something I couldn't quite make out, but could tell, just by the bitchy tone and inappropriate soundtrack, was some kind of reality show. I remembered they had a big fluffy white sectional back there, ultra sleek and low profile. The shitty television programming said Jackie was watching, but I couldn't see the couch from here. The kitchen was blocking the way. It was a series of tasteful islands; all the appliances were brushed steel and probably made by some company in Italy that had only made toaster ovens for the last six hundred years.

The dining room, closest to us, was dominated by yet another slab of rough hewn wood. This one was maybe twenty feet long, with a dozen archaic and severe-looking wooden chairs lining the sides. At the head of it sat a Chinese girl with silver hair. She was gorgeous, but in a cold way. Like a statue. Like she'd been carved out of a single block of smooth marble, and never meant to move. She looked up at Brin and I when we walked in, but showed no expression. Not even a nod of acknowledgment. Glenn followed next. He put his hand on the small of Brin's back. Carey shuffled in last, still gazing at the floor and the walls with disdain and disinterest.

"Katey," Brin said. "This is another friend of Jackie's, she's staying with us for the weekend. Her name is—"

"Oh, fuck!" Carey said, from behind me.

The Chinese girl saw him and smiled. It was the only thing not pretty about her.

"Run!" Carey screamed.

THIRTEEN

Carey. 1982. Los Angeles, California. Chinatown.

I didn't know what the hell to say when Zang finished his story. It sucks, for sure. And I felt bad for the guy in it, but that guy was long dead. And like fuck am I going to console an Empty One, even if he was buying me beer. Hey, speaking of . . .

I pointed my beer can at the old Chinese bartender and made a shotgun noise. He looked at me. I shook it, to show him that it was empty. He didn't move, just looked at Zang. Zang nodded, and the old guy got up to fetch us two more cans.

"So, what?" I said to Zang. "Now you're a good guy? You're like the punk rock Batman, righting wrongs and defending justice and shit?"

"Nah." He laughed. "I just want to kill as many of those fuckers as I can."

I briefly spun through some monologues about doing the right thing for the wrong reasons and all that garbage, but that would just be me playing devil's advocate. Lecturing the guy not because I disagreed with him, but because I wished I did. That seemed like it would take a lot of energy that I just didn't have, so instead I said:

"Huh."

And I raised my beer can. He clacked his against it, and we drank.

"I gotta piss off soon," Zang said, fully back into his asshole punk persona. "Places to be, people to kill."

"Yeah?" I said. "Who and where and do you want a hand?"

"Seriously?" he asked.

"Seriously," I said.

"I might take you up on that. A little birdy told me about a gathering of mystical shitheads going on tomorrow night. A little birdy who doesn't have much of a face left anymore. Meet me at the entrance to the old zoo in Griffith Park at midnight if you're looking to kill some time and some ass-holes. But not tonight. This business is personal, and besides"—Zang spun his finger at the bartender, in a wrap-it-up gesture—"you've got dishes to wash."

"What?" I asked. "I think you've got your slang crossed, man. You need more practice talking like a human."

Zang laughed as he shoved open the door and stepped out in the rain. It swung back inward after him, carrying a watery breeze scented with ozone and exhaust.

I looked at the bartender. He had one hand on the bar, sweeping away our empties into a bin. The other hand came up with a monstrous cleaver; a few big notches in the blade said it wasn't for decoration. He motioned toward the gray door to the kitchen, behind which it sounded like some sort of Chinese civil war was starting.

"Motherfucker," I said.

I stood up, pulled my jacket off, set it on the far end of the bar, and clocked into my new temp job.

*You stupid bastard. If you know one thing by now, it's this:
There's no such thing as a free beer.*

That god damn Chinaman had me scrubbing pots until
two in the morning. I don't know what fucking payscale
the Chinese work on, but three cheap beers does not equal
four hours of hard labor. Unless . . .

Son of a bitch, Zang had me paying for his beers, too!

I wanted to hate him for it, but damned if I wouldn't have
done the same in his situation. He was actually pretty good
at passing for a real punk.

After my shift, the Chinese at least gave me some fried
rice and a cup of greenish tea. I ate it sitting on a milk crate
out back. It had stopped raining, and the air felt lighter.
Like the water had grabbed onto some of the particles of
bullshit that accumulated in the L.A. air and washed them
down the gutter. The bars were closed, and the shows had
let out hours ago. The only people left in Chinatown now
were the workers, just closing up shop, and the junkies and
drunks looking for a dry place to sleep it off. I plucked
through my bowl of rice as best I could.

The rotten sons of bitches had given me chopsticks.

Chopsticks. For rice.

How the hell was a man supposed to eat like that? It was
like using tweezers to shave your head. One of the chefs came
out to eat with me. He squatted down on a milk crate of his
own, picked up his set of chopsticks, and plowed through his
bowl in a little over a minute. That must be some Zen kung
fu shit they all learn at a special monastery or something,
because I gave up after about five minutes and resorted to
shoveling rice and bits of pork into my face with my fingers.

I drank most of my tea, dipped my sticky fingers into last warm inch of water to rinse them off, then dumped the rest down the drain. I set my bowl and cup next to the door—my dining partner had locked up behind him—and ventured out into a shut-down Chinatown.

The place was like a theme park modeled after what a racist assumes China looks like: lots of pagodas and unnecessary archways, neon signs, and cheesy dragons. All dark now, of course, and abandoned. I sidestepped the puddles as best I could, but the holes in my ratty Chucks had my socks swamped in a matter of minutes. It took a good three hours of walking with soggy feet and an uninsulated jacket just to make it back to my crash spot. But the Los Angeles streets were as empty as they ever got, the buildings had been washed as clean as they ever got, and I was about as fed as I ever got, so all told, I'd had worse nights.

FOURTEEN

Carey. 1982. Los Angeles, California. Griffith Park.

I liked Griffith Park at night. You could forget you were in L.A. No people, no cars, no freeway noises—just insulated wilderness. If you turned away from the sprawling metropolis spread out below you like a blanket of light, you could almost convince yourself you were off lost in the wild, untamed woods somewhere. And then you tripped over a broken toaster oven or got a used condom stuck to your shoe and it all came flooding back.

I found Zang standing utterly motionless at the entrance to the old Griffith Park Zoo. They'd closed the place back in the '60s when the Los Angeles Zoo opened, and the movers had emptied the place of anything valuable. The hobos disagreed, and ripped it apart even more, until there wasn't anything left worth trashing. The punks and the teenagers disagreed yet again, and started using the old concrete cages, enclosures, and auditoriums as a combination of party spots, bedrooms, and mass bathrooms. Then the taggers came and covered every visible surface in crudely drawn cocks and obscenities. Now you had to wade through a small ocean of discarded beer cans and used hypodermics to get anywhere. Despite being a mandatory stop on the L.A. homeless tour, I'd only been here once before. This is probably the first, last, and only time you will ever hear me say this: I was just too good for this place.

Zang was standing ramrod straight, still as a statue, his gaze locked on something deep in the darkened interior of the zoo. I'm sure with his creepy Empty One senses he heard me coming a mile away, but if he did, he didn't show it. He didn't move until I physically touched his arm, at which point the spell was broken and he abruptly transitioned to the half-staggering drunken punk persona he spent so much time practicing.

"Hey, man," he said. "Good to see you!"

He reached over to hug me, and I jumped backward so quickly I lost my footing and went sprawling.

"What the fuck was that?" I said, bracing myself to run.

"A hug?" He momentarily dropped the human façade. "I read the social cues wrong. It happens often. I will note your distress."

"Fucking underline that note, too," I said, standing up and brushing myself off.

Just playing the odds, I'm sure I caught a dirty needle to the ass when I fell and had now contracted eight forms of hepatitis.

"You ready to do this shit or what?" Zang said, feigning normality again.

"Do what shit, exactly?" I asked.

"You lucked out, man," he said. "This is angel night. We've got about a dozen Unnoticeables in there, two Empty Ones, and one poor dumb fucking human about to get himself angel-fied."

"Holy shit," I said. Memories came flooding back to me.

An underground train station. A crude plywood stage in an English marsh. Screaming light. Death. "What do you expect us to do about it?"

"I don't know." Zang shrugged casually, like I'd just asked him how he felt about the Packers. "Fuck it up?"

"Listen, man," I said. "This isn't my first shitshow. I've seen this kind of thing happen twice before and it's gone south both times. Quickly and dramatically. I know you can't die and all, but I can die *real* easy."

"And what?" Zang laughed. "You got so much to live for? Last night I told you what I'm all about: hurting them however I can. I don't care what that costs me. I thought you felt the same way."

I wanted to argue, if only by reflex, but nothing came to mind. A few years ago, I could count all of my friends on one hand. Now I could count them on one finger, and I was including beer as a friend. I slept in a filthy bag on the sidewalk between a Korean butcher and some sort of pornographic comic shop. And every night I thought about the time I had to leave my best friend for dead. Watch him get torn apart, from the other side of a chain-link fence that I was too weak to climb.

There were parts of me still striving for some kind of life, some kind of happiness. But that was just instinct. Some stupid lizard part of my brain that thinks I deserve those things, despite all I've done. Survival is a hell of an urge, but it's got nothing on revenge.

"Fuck it," I said. "What's your plan?"

"I think you'll like this," Zang said. "Step one: We go in there and hit everybody as hard as we can. Step two: We grab the human candidate. Step three: We run away."

"I like it," I said. "Easy to remember."

There were no lights in the old zoo, and a hell of a lot of empty beer cans to step on in the dark, giving away our position. Zang, being an inhuman asshole, didn't bring a flashlight. He didn't need one. Me, being a broke dipshit, couldn't afford one. Zang made much quicker progress than me. My process basically consisted of putting my foot down really slowly, and if I felt a crunch, trying again. It was like walking through a minefield made of eggshells. I lost Zang's silhouette a few times, but he at least seemed to get that, and would do his creepy vacant robot thing while waiting for me to catch up.

Finally we rounded a corner and saw lights up ahead. A handful of tiki torches—the cheap, disposable kind that suburban housewives buy to decorate their tacky barbecue parties—were laid out around what used to be an amphitheater. The main stage was backed by a concrete slab cut to look vaguely like one of those Mayan pyramid things—two sets of blocky stairs meeting each other at the highest point in the middle. Dead center in the stage area, a chubby kid a few years my junior wept in wide-eyed terror. He was kneeling, his hands bound in front, looking to all the leering non-faces of the Unnoticeables surrounding him for help that would never come.

A few feet behind the chubby kid stood a god damn mammoth of a man. He was eight feet tall if he was an inch, stocky in a way that tempted you to call him fat, but with so much muscle beneath you'd never survive actually doing it. He had a scraggly, filthy beard that hung down to his waist, his long hair pulled back in an equally long ponytail. He wore a pair of filthy, blood-stained denim overalls, black combat boots, and nothing else. He was holding an honest-to-god fucking battle-axe.

Like something out of a fantasy movie.

Where would you even get one of those things? Is there a murderous giant psychopath store down at the mall?

Zang hissed quietly beside me. I turned to follow his gaze. At the very top of the pyramidal slab, sitting primly on its apex, was a petite Chinese girl. Late teens, early twenties at the latest. Short denim jacket, bright yellow tank top, torn blue jeans, and white ankle boots. Legs crossed at the knee. Her head tilted curiously at the sobbing kid below, taking in the scene like a raptor watching prey. The guttering light from the torches reflecting off her bright, silvery hair.

The god damn evil bitch that killed Randall.

"Jie," Zang said. Somewhere between a curse and an exclamation of awe.

"That's Jie?" I whispered. "That's your fucking star-crossed lover? Your girlfriend killed my best and only friend in the world."

I grabbed his arm and dug my fingers in as hard as I could. Zang didn't even blink. He slowly rotated his head to face me. I'd say he looked me straight in the eyes, but even when they were staring right at you, those eyes never seemed to actually see anything. They looked through you, to a place a thousand miles gone.

"That is Jie," Zang said flatly. "And the only human thing left of me is the love I have for her. I have tried to kill her dozens of times. I would crush her skull in an instant if I had the means. If you have any ideas on how to accomplish that, I am listening."

Guess everybody's got a crazy ex. Can't hold that against the guy, can I?

"Shit," I said.

Probably best to let the subject drop for now.

"I was more down with this plan before I saw the monster in the overalls," I said. "What the hell is that bastard? Where do you even buy a battle-axe?"

"That's Alvar," Zang said, adopting his human affectation. "The Empty Ones are immortal, but most of us are pretty recent converts. Just since we picked up the ritual, and started summoning angels more frequently. Back in the day, Empty Ones were rare, but they did exist. That big son of a bitch is the oldest one I know of. He's had the axe since the Middle Ages, at least. I don't know anything else about him. I don't think anybody does. The only time he speaks is right after a kill, to recite a number: the new tally of how many victims his axe has taken. I'm not sure what number he's on. He says it in German."

I felt my bladder spasm, and it was only thanks to years of training with massive quantities of beer that I managed to not piss myself right there and then.

"Isn't he wonderful?" Zang said, smiling at me in the dark.

"That's not the word I was thinking of."

"You can take him," Zang said. "I'll take Jie."

"Like fuck am I fighting the axe-wielding grizzly bear. I'll take the skinny Chinese girl, thanks."

"Wow," Zang said, gently clapping me on the shoulder. "That's really brave. Thanks, man."

Oh. Shit.

"Wait, why is Alvar easier than—" I started to ask, but Zang cut me off.

"Well," Zang said, eagerness in his voice. "Nobody lives forever."

He hopped atop the rock we'd been hiding behind and

yelled: "Curfew call, assholes! Time to go home to mommy."

The crowd of faceless kids turned to look at us as one. Surveying their shifting, featureless faces, I immediately felt the telltale migraine building behind my eyes. I focused instead on my target, Jie, who had responded to the surprise with only the slightest inclination of her head in our direction.

"Butcher them," she said.

The Unnoticeables whooped and hollered as they ran for us, like an Indian war party out of an old Western. Alvar, the mountain of beef and terror, said nothing. He quietly hefted his gargantuan double-headed axe over one shoulder, and began moseying toward us.

Zang leapt from his perch atop the small boulder and clotheslined the closest Unnoticeable—a skinny kid in black jeans and a Kiss T-shirt, the rest of his features lost to the supernatural blur. Zang was up in an instant, moving nearly faster than my eyes could track. He grabbed the downed buttrocker by the ankles and whipped him around in a huge circle, leaning backward to use his own body as a counterweight. At the peak of his arc, he let the kid go, sending him flying into two more Unnoticeables. They caught him right across their necks. All three went down like a *Three Stooges* routine.

The other Unnoticeables witnessed Zang's inhuman speed and strength and stalled out. They looked to each other, then back up at Jie.

I don't know much about the Unnoticeables. They're like cleaner fish to the sharks that are the Empty Ones. Just there to provide a brief service and occasional snack. But I know that the Unnoticeables worship the Empty Ones like gods. They set out toward us thinking they were attacking humans, and now found one of the things they revered the most turning on them. It must be like Jesus Christ descending from his cross to throat-punch a bunch of devout Christians.

Jie made an irritated hand motion, shooing them back to the fight, but the Unnoticeables were still torn. How do you choose sides in a war between gods?

That question, like all philosophy, was irrelevant bullshit.

Zang took advantage of the distraction and was among the Unnoticeables like a fox in a chicken coop. He snapped, tore, gouged, and maimed without hesitation. He pulled one of the Unnoticeables' jawbone off and used it to wail on the one next to her. He headbutted another so hard its nose exploded, blood rocketing out in every direction like a firework. The last he just brutally and ceaselessly crotch-stomped until it stopped moving. In the span of a few breaths, all of the Unnoticeables had been not just beaten, but fucking dismantled.

Alvar didn't seem to be impressed by the display. He didn't even speed his stride, just kept loping toward Zang at an unhurried saunter.

Zang looked back at me.

"Eyes on Jie," he said, then turned and broke into a dead run at Alvar.

I couldn't have registered less with Jie. She only had eyes for Zang. Not that she looked at him with anything resembling affection. When Zang first saw her sitting above the abandoned auditorium, there was plain and unmistakable hatred on his face. But as Jie watched Zang slide between Alvar's legs and jump up onto his back—snatching and clawing like a furious housecat thrown atop a passive bear—there was nothing on her face. Not hate, or love, or even faint irritation. Just little bird-like twitches of the head as she observed the struggle. I took advantage of being in her blind spot, grabbed the nearest solid object, and chucked it right at her head.

Too late, I realized "hurl stuff at the invincible monster's head and hope it works out" was a shitty plan.

Even worse: As soon as it left my hand, I realized that the object I'd thrown was an inexplicably full beer can. I mean, it was a Coors, and it was probably old, certainly room temperature, and undoubtedly peed on at some point—but still, an abandoned soldier on this battlefield was a damn miracle.

At least my aim was true, and the can nailed Jie straight in the forehead. It wasn't enough to hurt her, but it was enough to throw her off balance. She windmilled her arms, trying to stay atop the concrete slab, but it was too little, too late. She went tumbling backward into the dark. To either side of the auditorium, the concrete walls stretched out, high and unbroken. Whatever it was she'd fallen into, it would take her a bit to get back around to me.

The Unnoticeables were in pieces around me, Jie was indisposed, and Alvar was currently occupied—if not the least bit bothered—by Zang's attack. Nobody was watching the chubby kid, who had once been the center of this fucked-up stage show. I ran to him, hauled him to his feet, and started him running. I had no point of reference for the nearest exit, aside from back the way we came. So that's where we went, blindly crunching empty beer cans and stumbling over broken appliances.

The kid didn't say a word as we ran. Whatever had happened tonight had broken something in him, and I sure as shit didn't have time to fix it. He moved his feet in the general direction that I dragged him, and that was good enough for now. We crouched beside the entryway, our breath coming in stuttering gasps.

I strained my eyes, peering into the darkened interior of the zoo, but caught no sign of Zang.

How long is considered a polite length of time to wait for a sociopathic hollow monster before leaving him for dead?

About five seconds, I decided.

"We can't stop here," I told the kid. "Keep running."

The kid was on the heavy side. He was afflicted with one of those bowl cuts that looks like Mom just upturned a mixing bowl on his head and went to town with the clippers. He was wearing a bright blue windbreaker and cargo shorts. Socks with sandals. Not exactly a champion for the ages, but god damn if he uttered a single word of complaint, despite clearly being in worse shape than even I was.

He just nodded once, resolutely.

Tears streamed down the kid's face. He breathed only between hiccups. But he was ready.

I slapped him on the arm by way of encouragement, and we both set out at a fast jog, back down the path toward civilization. We'd barely made it to the first bend when a shadow stepped out from between the bushes to our left. I grabbed a fistful of the kid's windbreaker and we skidded to a halt. The shadow was short and skinny and it moved with a lethal grace.

I had an awful feeling I knew who it was, and she wasn't going to be too happy to see me.

But Zang stepped into the half-light from the distant streetlamps instead, his face cleaved nearly in two by a massive, gaping axe wound. Still, he smiled at us when he said: "You got the candidate out! Good job, man. How the hell did you take out Jie?"

"I threw a can of Coors straight into her face," I said.

"Haha," Zang said. "Holy shit. She's going to eat your fucking eyeballs for that."

"Thanks, man," I answered. "That's really comforting."

The fat kid's eyes had gone wide at the sight of Zang. His breathing, already labored, only quickened. He couldn't yet speak, but I got the gist.

"Hey," I said to him. "Don't worry. I know it's weird, but this one's on our side. You're safe now."

The kid looked at me like I was trying to sell him a time-share, but finally he nodded again and smiled at me.

"We'll take care of you," I said to him.

"We sure will," Zang added.

He moved in the space between blinks. His fist crashed into the fat kid's face so hard it got stuck inside what was left of his skull. Blood and brain matter splattered across my shoes. The kid's shattered facehole made a noise like when you try to shake cranberry sauce out of the can. Zang wriggled his fist, trying to free it from the ruins of the kid's skull. Finally, it came free with a moist pop, and the kid's twitching carcass hit the ground. His sandaled feet tapping out a dead man's soft-shoe on the asphalt path.

"What the fuck did you do?" I screamed. "What the fuck did you just do?!"

"What?" Zang looked at me, innocent confusion on his face.

"You killed him!"

"Yes."

He still didn't see the problem. I had forgotten, for just one second, the kind of creature I was dealing with. I fell for the goofy mannerisms and the human shell, like everybody else. Like an asshole.

"But why?" I dropped my volume, remembering that we literally weren't out of the woods yet.

"He was a candidate," Zang said, his voice gone flat. "What we interrupted back there was the ritual to create a new angel. Sooner or later, the other players would have arrived, he would make the choice required of him, and a new angel would be born."

"But we got him out of there," I said, my tone like I was trying to explain shoplifting to a toddler. "He was safe."

"Yes," Zang said. "But for how long? He was fat, and running was difficult for him."

"Holy shit," I said, putting my arms behind my head. "You killed him because he was kinda chubby?"

"Yes," Zang answered. "He may have slowed us down. He may have gotten himself caught again, at which point Jie would have resumed the ritual. The only safe way to deal with that candidate was to eliminate him. That ensured that no new angels could ever be made from him. That harms the angels. I want to harm the angels."

"But I was a candi—" I caught myself, too late.

Zang's posture grew stiff. He turned his blank eyes on me.

"I did not know that," he said. "Did they complete the ritual?"

Oh, shit. What was the right answer here? The one that doesn't get my skull punched inside out?

"Yes?" I said, opting for honesty—mostly 'cause I couldn't think of any decent lies right then.

Zang relaxed, lapsing back into the façade of humanity.

"Well, all right!" he said. "Damage done! They can't use you again for a long time, and we'll cross that bridge when we come to it."

"And uh . . ." I gestured toward the kid's corpse, now still. "Is this what you mean by 'crossing that bridge'?"

Zang winked.

It was fucking hideous.

"Now we gotta go, man," Zang said. "Unless you wanna wait around for a hot date with Alvar and his axe."

"I do not," I said.

My heart was hammering and my guts were clenched so tight I was probably turning yesterday's tacos into diamonds, but I feigned a smile. Probably the worst acting in history, but the guy didn't know a genuine human reaction from his own asshole, so he bought it. I would have to play it cool for a while, until I could spot an opening and get away from him without getting my own face pulverized.

Zang turned and jogged down the darkened path, cutting through the squat pines with their skeletal arms and needles like dried straw. I followed a few steps behind, trying not to puke.

I figured Zang would take off again once we got back in town. When it became apparent that he wasn't, I tried a few awkward good-byes, but he didn't get the hint. He walked with me all the way to my crash spot in Koreatown.

Well, shit. Now I have to find a new crash spot, unless I want to wake up to a skinny Asian guy stomping me to death for kicks some night.

We ducked into the short alley I called home. I leaned back against the exposed brick of the butcher shop wall. It was cool against my back, even through my leather jacket. The strength went out of my legs. I'd been running or walking all night, fueled on nothing but fear, adrenaline, and some stale bread I'd snagged from the Vietnamese bakery down the street. I slid down onto my butt. Zang squatted against the wall opposite me. He didn't say anything. His face was slack and his arms dangled by his sides, like somebody had pulled the plug on a human being.

"I've got a question," I said.

"Shoot," he said.

"Back at the zoo, when I said I'd take Jie and you should take the giant with the axe, you said I was brave. . . ."

"Yes."

"Why was Jie the brave option there? That guy was like a Buick with a beard."

"The Empty Ones' strength doesn't come from size. When the angels gift us with the void, we cease to be disgusting meat machines. We do not eat, drink, or breathe, unless we choose to. We are not human. Alvar was just a shell, as I am a shell. The size of the shell does not matter; the power within is the same."

Zang tilted his head a little, considering something.

"Or very nearly the same. Perhaps Alvar is a bit stronger than I am," he continued. "But not in a way that is meaningful. The thing you have to fear most in an Empty One is not their strength, but their viciousness. Alvar is a simple thing. He lives for battle. He likes to kill. He does not like to torture. One swing from that axe, and Alvar would be done with you.

"Not so with Jie. Jie likes to take her time. Jie is very creative. Fifty years ago in Santa Barbara, a woman spilled her drink on Jie and did not apologize profusely enough. Jie took her to our home at the time, whose occupants we had butchered and replaced. She slit the woman's belly open and hooked her intestines up to a very large antique music box the previous owners had acquired. Jie forced the woman to crank the mechanism of the music box herself. Jie sat and listened to the song of a woman disemboweling herself for three hours until the woman, at last, collapsed into death."

Holy. Shit.

"And I just hit her in the face with a beer can," I said.

"You did indeed," Zang said. "Very brave. Or very stupid. I do not fully understand the difference between the two, so I gave you the benefit of the doubt."

"It was probably the second one," I conceded.

"Yes," he said. "That seems right."

We stared at each in other silence for what felt like hours, until the exhaustion finally caught up with me and I passed out in my clothes, sitting atop my own sleeping bag. I had terrible dreams. Pretty Chinese girls clawing into my stomach, grabbing the ends of my intestines in their mouths and slurping them out like spaghetti. Giants with bloody, multi-edged axes—each head the face of somebody I'd gotten killed—swinging them into me, splitting me in two. Dead, black dolls' eyes inches from my own. Just staring, wide, unblinking, unseeing. . . .

"Gah!" I yelped, and reflexively slapped Zang away.

That last one wasn't a dream, I guess. When I awoke, Zang was laying down beside me, his own face inches from my own, silently staring into my eyes.

"What!" I exclaimed, not asked. Then asked: "What?!"

"You were sleeping," Zang said.

"Yeah, what the fuck were you doing?"

"Pretending to sleep, so as not to arouse suspicion in passersby." He gestured out at the sidewalk beyond the short alley, already bustling with the early risers of

Koreatown. Shop owners, mostly, just opening up their doors.

"Why the hell were you doing it right next to me?" I asked.

"People sleep on beds," Zang said. "You only have the one blanket. It would be strange if I did not appear to be sleeping on a bed."

"It is way stranger that you snuggle right up to me on a single sleeping bag and fucking stare at me all night," I said.

"To you, it is," he answered. "Not to them. You know what I am; they do not."

"Okay, fine! Fuck!" I shoved him back and sat upright, rubbing the sleep off my face. "Just shut up for a minute while I wake up."

So, what? Now I have an evil sidekick? How the hell am I going to get out of this?

"Don't you have any plans today?" I asked, when I'd finally scraped the last of a shitty night's rest away.

"We do," he said.

"We?" I asked. "What are we, a couple now?"

"Yes."

Just . . . yes?

"I, uh, I was joking," I said. "Look, man, it was great working with you and all, but I've got my own life."

"No, you don't," Zang said. I blinked, and he was standing. I didn't even see him move. "You have no life. You are useless. You are trash. At least as far as society is concerned. You are doing nothing. You have no purpose. But you have skills and knowledge which are useful to me. You will help me."

My first instinct was to defend myself, but I looked around at my stained bedroll and my stolen JanSport full of hobo treasures, and I couldn't muster a good counterargument. Instead I simply said:

"Do what?"

Zang smiled. A big, goofy grin.

"Fuck shit up, of course!"

FIFTEEN

Carey. 1982. Los Angeles, California. Westlake.

I'd been with Zang a week, and so far his mission consisted of a lot of standing quietly outside people's houses, watching them through the windows.

It was pretty creepy, even by my standards.

He explained that he was watching other potential candidates, trying to tell which one the Empty Ones would pull next, since we'd cost them one angel already. The procreation cycle was thirty-six years, he said, but that was per angel. The one we'd cock-blocked, for lack of a better term, wouldn't be able to try again for a few decades, but there were plenty of other angels, and the Empty Ones don't take days off.

The first night we watched a hot teenage girl try on outfits for like an hour, which was all right, then we watched a chubby guy repeatedly and obsessively measure his own dick for twenty minutes—starting from different points, hard, soft, using a ruler, using a measuring tape—and that was less than all right. But mostly we watched people watch TV.

I'd had a few opportunities to slip away from Zang in the past seven days, and I took every single one. But I never made it more than a block or two before he stepped out of some darkened alleyway, or up from between two cars, and just stared at me blankly until I turned around. But to be honest, I wasn't even sure I wanted to leave anymore.

All that quiet time I'd spent crouched in strangers' bushes with nothing but an evil mannequin for company, Zang's words kept echoing around in my head.

You don't have a life.

You don't have a purpose.

You're trash.

He wasn't wrong. I failed out of high school. The closest thing to a job I'd ever had was busking on the subway, and I was god damn terrible at it. Any friends I once had, I'd insulted, turned away, or gotten killed. What was I going to do with my miserable excuse for a life, go back to college and fix air conditioners?

The only remotely useful thing I could do was fight these psychopaths and their faceless pet dickheads. Maybe cost them an angel or two in the process. And the more I thought about it, the more I realized that was all I really, truly wanted. The drinking wasn't "to have a good time" these days; it was so I could sleep without hating myself so actively it kept me awake at night. The punk shows, what few I still bothered with, were just a distraction—me going through the old motions, trying and failing to recapture the feelings they used to bring about. The cigarettes were only killing time, and myself. Why was I holding out on Zang?

We weren't any different. Something took away his humanity. I pissed mine down the gutter. Might as well do something useful with the pitiful shells we had left.

"I won't take off again," I said to Zang one night, squatting on the roof of a low parking garage across from a Section 8 apartment complex.

We were watching a Mexican girl with a vivid red dye-job dance with herself, all alone in her shitty studio off Wilshire. Zang was squatting at the very edge of the roof like a punk rock gargoyle.

"Cool, man," he said, without so much as glancing away from the girl's windows.

Here's a fun fact I'd learned: Zang only blinked to pass as human. On these long stakeouts, he didn't bother. Yes, that's exactly as fucking unsettling as it sounds.

"I'm serious," I said. "I've been thinking about it, and you're right. The only worthwhile thing I can do is fight these things with you, and it's not like anybody gives a shit if I live or die. Why am I holding back? I won't take off again, at least not without returning. So you can quit watching me like a hawk and popping up outta Dumpsters and shit every time I go for a walk."

"Nah," he said. "I'll probably just keep doing that for a while."

"No, really," I said, standing to stretch my cramped legs. "I'm in. I'm with you. But I have some conditions."

"Such as?" he asked.

"No more murdering people," I said.

"That's a deal breaker," he said, and laughed.

But I knew he was serious.

"Okay," I said. "Well, no more murdering people unless we talk about it first."

He was silent for so long I thought he was ignoring me. When he finally spoke, it startled me so badly I damn near jumped out of my skin.

"All right, then," he said. "Then I get counter-conditions. One for one."

"Okay," I said, already mentally flipping through the various atrocities he'd probably ask me to commit.

"You can't leave for good without talking to me first," he said.

Shit, and here I thought he was going to demand virgin's bloody hand delivered nightly. Can't pass up a deal like that.

"Done," I said. "Second condition: No more keeping me in the dark about the Empty Ones and what we're doing. I ask a question, I get a straight answer."

"Fine," he said, immediately.

Wow. I really expected pushback on that one.

"But you have to practice conversing with me for one hour every night," he added. "And you gotta be honest about whether or not I'm passing for human."

I laughed, but he didn't so much as smile.

"Yeah, sure, man," I said. "Last condition: You gotta allow me time to do human shit. I need to piss and crap; I need to eat; I need to sit down for a while sometimes; I need to grind for beer money; I need to masturbate in relative privacy. I need *me time*."

"That's cool," he said, still staring, unblinking, at the girl, now hand drying an infinity of plates. "My last condition: If we see an opportunity to harm or destroy Jie, we take it, without argument."

Theeeere it is. That's the one that's going to get me killed.

Ah well, has to happen sooner or later. I basically made peace with my own impending doom the second I opened my mouth to tell this monster I'd be his new partner.

"Deal," I said.

We lapsed into uneasy silence for a moment. Well, uneasy

for me—I don't think there was such a thing for Zang.

"I'm glad we made this system," he finally said. "It was just in time."

"Yeah?" I said.

"Yeah," he said. "We need to talk about murdering this girl now."

SIXTEEN

Jackie. 2013. Los Angeles, California. Brentwood.

Normal!

Damn, I don't even remember what that is. It makes me think of white people in khakis and button-downs, laughing on a picnic bench somewhere. And you know what? That's not too far off from life at my parents' house. My mom likes long skirts, and my dad's worn jeans every day since he became his own boss, but otherwise they fit the picture to a T. And they did have a picnic table in the backyard. . . .

It was weird, being back at their place. I can't call it "home," because I had never lived here. My parents moved out to L.A. to be closer to me, which was so codependent it was creepy, but whatever. It meant I got to skip out of my sad bachelorette's apartment once in a while and eat artisanal cheeses up in Brentwood. The only price I had to pay was the regular lecture about how I could stay at their place permanently if I wanted—I could even take the guest quarters out back if I needed my privacy.

Yeah: me all sneaking boys past my parents at age

twenty-five. I don't need help feeling pathetic, thanks. I can manage that one just fine on my own.

Now, I'm not gonna front here: I wasn't out to prove I could get by without Daddy's money. I love me some money, Daddy's or otherwise. I wasn't slumming in L.A. for the fun of it.

Hey, don't scoff—that happens! I know some rich white girls that live as close as they dare to Compton just for the thrill of it. (Spoiler alert: It's not very close.)

My parents would buy me whatever stupid frivolity I needed. They'd buy purses and fund vacations without a second thought. But they'd never help me pay my bills. I think their longterm plan was to live close enough so that I could get a taste of the good life whenever I wanted it, but never pay my rent or anything, so that I didn't get too comfortable to move back in with them. Seriously. That's how devious they are.

They're pretty awesome.

But as brilliant as the plan was, it wasn't working. They mistakenly thought I was more spoiled than I actually turned out to be. I know! I was surprised to learn that, too.

It turns out that as long as I could afford food and the occasional night out binge drinking, I could live with the occasional fridge-roach. Mommy and Daddy's little slice of temptation was just a nice vacation spot for me. I wouldn't let it become the real world.

But damn, could I ever use the vacation right about now. I had become so accustomed to life on the road that I'd forgotten just how shitty, well, *everything* was: shitty beds impressed with the sad, chaotic grooves of thousands of strangers. Shitty coffee left too long on the burner. Shitty hotel chairs that were never broken in because they got shoved away into the corners while the bed pointed toward the TV. Shitty drive-thru food eaten joylessly in parking lots—hastily hiding your shame every time some passerby looked in the car just as you took a huge bite of fried mystery meat. Shitty showers with shitty water pressure and shitty towels that felt like somebody had masturbated into burlap. And then . . .

My parents' house.

Even as a kid, I never felt fully at ease in my mom and dad's home. They weren't monsters; they never yelled at me for touching anything. But it still felt like I'd been accidentally locked inside a museum after hours. Their belongings were always put together just so, arranged by some abstract sense of appropriateness rather than by purpose. If you used a blanket and left it crumpled up in a pile, you'd come back to find it neatly folded up and draped over the chair at a jaunty angle. The exact same jaunty angle it had before you so ostentatiously disturbed it, in fact. The entire house was guest soap. Technically functional, but frowned upon to use.

But if you put that unease in the back of your mind, and let yourself just run rampant over their distinguished collection—socked feet up on the flawless varnished redwood coffee table; slumped deep into the enormous couch so white and flat it looked like a salt plain, no hairs marring the surface, no unsightly balls of lint clinging to the throw pillows, no butt grooves on the cushion—it was a damn sight more comfortable than life on the road.

I was nestled deep in an angora blanket, doubtlessly hand woven by an indigenous artisan whose story my mother would know by heart, and crumpled into the alabaster couch, eating chocolate ice cream straight out of the container like some sort of maniac. The gargantuan flat-screen TV blared the whiny protestations of an obnoxious, overly hip MTV reality show. I had lost track which one. This teenager could be pregnant, or she could be headed to rehab. Maybe she needed scaring straight. Whatever, her point was that her parents didn't understand her. That's every teenager's point.

I was acutely aware that I was cancer to this house: an ugly, low-rent tumor squatting in the den, not even having the decency to realize that one *does not use the den*—it is there as more of a conversation piece; an idea to entertain, distantly, before opting to retire to the study instead. And I was the happiest malignant lump you'd ever see.

Mom and Dad had been weirdly accommodating since I showed up, unannounced, at the front door. They loved seeing me, of course. I was their one and only baby girl. But they had some unspoken rule-set for visits that I never fully grasped. I guess I was supposed to call first, even though, at the end of every visit, they were firmly adamant that I could stop by anytime. One time I specifically remember my dad shouting "no need to call first!" as we waved good-bye. And yet every time I took them up on that offer, their faces told a different story. Their expressions were invariably both amused and disdainful, like a maître d' at a fancy restaurant forced to address a rapper by their hip-hop name.

Monsieur 2 Chainz, the wine list, if you please, their arched eyebrows and puzzled smiles seemed to say.

But that wasn't how it went down this time. I showed up at the door after an extended and unexplained absence, and they threw their arms around me like I was a soldier returning from war. When I crashed out on the couch and immediately flipped on the television, they didn't politely invite me to sit with them in the garden instead—they just stood in the kitchen and smiled at me.

When the weird Asian girl showed up, I was six deep into a binge-watch of *Catfish*. This fat kid in an anime hoodie was fucking irate that the girl he fell in love with online was also fat, because she'd used an outdated profile picture from when she was skinny. His own avatar was a hunky male character from a CW show about demons and stuff, but he didn't seem to appreciate the irony.

The Asian girl didn't say anything to announce her presence. She just stood there, silently watching me watch offended internet trolls for God knows how long.

"Jesus!" I said, when I finally noticed her.

I jumped, and melted drops of chocolate ice cream danced precariously across the bottom of my spoon, both eager and afraid to ruin something as valuable as the angora throw.

"Not quite," she said, and smiled.

"That's uh . . . a pretty creepy thing to say. Who are you? Are you supposed to be here?"

This chick looked like she was nineteen, tops. She had platinum silver hair cut into a jaggy punk bob, and black lipstick. She was wearing red short-shorts over torn fishnets, and a skin-tight Descendents T-shirt. She didn't exactly fall into my parents' usual "elderly rich white person who looks like they stepped out of a commercial for insurance" social circle. She could have been somebody's rebellious daughter, I guess, but seeing her standing there with those flat eyes and that uneasy grin, it seemed more likely she'd broken in to vandalize the place.

"Oh, honey," my dad said, stepping out from the kitchen like he'd been waiting for his cue. "This is a friend of ours, uh . . . Jie. Jie, this is our daughter, Jackie."

The uncomfortable way my dad said "Jie" told me he barely knew her name. His clumsy Anglo tongue hadn't had time to get used to the exotic syllable yet.

Like hell this was a family friend.

Alarms went off inside my head. My stomach seized up like a menstrual cramp. I started salivating excessively . . .

That's a weird fear response; good to know, body.

"Mom, Dad," I said as calmly as I could. "Can I please talk to you in the other room?"

Jie's smile collapsed. She looked through me with her blank eyes, the same expression a shark has, just before those white eyelids roll up.

"You're a quick one," she said, her voice now absent of all its former tone and melody. "Restrain her."

My parents looked at each other askance.

"What are you, mental?" I laughed.

It was forced, obviously—putting on a brave front I absolutely did not feel. In fact, at the time, I was genuinely wondering whether I was peeing myself, or if I could just add "legs get oddly warm" along with "extra spit" to the big list of Things Jackie's Stupid Body Does When She's Fucking Terrified.

"Who's going to restrain me?" I said. "You're the only one here."

Jie swiveled her head around like an owl to stare at my mother.

"Sorry, sweetie," my mom said, and took a step toward me.

"What? What the hell are you . . ." I backed away from her, but I knew there was nowhere to go. The only exit from the den was through the kitchen, which would leave me trying to fight my way past Jie and now, I guess, *my own dad*?

"Why, Mom? Did they . . . get to you? Did they turn you?"

I squinted at her face, trying to see if it had gone strangely indistinct like those of the Unnoticeables. But no, it was still my mom. With her crow's feet and worry lines and matronly braid.

"No, honey," she said. She was advancing on me slow, with her hands out, like I was a strange dog she didn't want to spook. "But they promised they wouldn't hurt you. They don't want you, they just want your friends."

"My friends? You mean K? Mom, please—" My butt bumped against the low bookshelf marking the end of the room. "You can't. You've known Kaitlyn like, all of her life. You can't just . . ."

"We don't have a choice," my dad chimed in, with his sitcom-father-wrapping-up-today's-moral voice. The disingenuous tone he used when he thought I was being unreasonable. "These things, they aren't human. This one put your mother's garden shears through her own eye just to prove a point. Last week I snuck away when they weren't watching and called the police. They showed up within minutes . . . to hand me back over to her. There are dozens of them all around us, right now. They're in the garage and the guest rooms. In the neighbors' houses. Just watching. They don't sleep. Sweetie, some of them don't even blink."

"No, Dad." I was watching him while he spoke, and my mom took the opportunity to inch closer to me. Almost within arm's reach now. "K, she knows all about them. She's got these powers now, she can fight them!"

"What's the point in fighting them?" my mother said. She had tears in her eyes. "You heard what your father said. We've seen it. They don't die."

She reached out, hands shaking, to grab my wrists.

What am I gonna do, punch my mother?

I let her guide me toward the couch, and sit me back down. My dad came over with a roll of duct tape and bound my hands and feet together. They were both crying now.

"This will all be over soon, darling," he said.

My mother kissed me on the forehead, and then drew the angora throw back up over my shoulders, tucking me in.

SEVENTEEN

Kaitlyn. 2013. Los Angeles, California. Brentwood.

My first instinct was stupid, because it wasn't to run, like Carey was screaming at me to do.

My first instinct was to tell him to calm down, explain what he meant, work this thing out. By the time I realized how irrational that was, the Chinese girl was already moving. She wasn't quite as fast as Marco had been, with his short bursts and spastic gestures, like a spider lunging at prey. You could see Jie moving, fluid, like mercury on glass. By the time your brain had fired its feeble instructions to your clumsy limbs, begging them to react, she was already somewhere else. She didn't even look hurried as she darted across the room, like she knew my limitations; knew my useless body could never respond in time, so she only put forth the barest effort to come out ahead. She loped across the kitchen in a few quick bounds and raised her hand. I tried to put up my own to block my face, but I was already staring at the ceiling, flat on my back, the pain of the blow still dancing up my nervous system.

Shouts, a yelp of pain, a meaty snap—like somebody had

slapped down a big fat steak, flat on the floor. Footsteps, glass crashing. More shouting.

I blinked rapidly. Shook my head. I rolled up onto one elbow and the world flowed sideways, like somebody curiously tilting a snow globe. There were sharp and brutal movements happening in my peripheral vision. Dark shapes snapping at each other, like fighting fish. Brin and Glenn were huddled together just a few feet away. They were kneeling, their arms around one another, biting their lips and sobbing. Carey was on the floor just outside of the kitchen, blindly scooting backward across the hardwood planks.

The dark shapes caught one another and paused for a moment: a slender man in a black leather jacket with his hand around a young Asian girl's throat; her fingers sunk deep into his cheeks, blood welling around the wounds. Then his other hand descended into a blur. It impacted her stomach and the shapes were a smear of madness again.

I dragged myself over to Jackie's parents, and tugged on Glenn's sleeve.

"Where is she?" I said. "We've got to get out of here."

"Please," Brin said, without looking at me. "Just go with them. Just leave us alone."

Me? What the hell did I do?

"Brin, where's Jackie? We have to leave! Now!"

Glenn looked at me with steel and fire in his eyes, where usually there was only goose down and Burberry.

"No," he said. He released his grip on Brin. "You're not going anywhere."

He grabbed both of my wrists and pinned them to the ground, above my head. He straddled my chest, using his knees and weight to lock me in place.

"Glenn, what are you—" My head was still swimming. I

was trying to focus on a central point—the light fixture on the kitchen ceiling right above me—but it kept slipping down and to the left.

"They only want you," Glenn said. "Just you, and they'll leave us alone."

"You don't understand," I said.

My tongue was made of cotton, too big for my mouth. My vision ebbed, a tide of blackness momentarily creeping in.

"I understand," he said, "that this is the only way to keep my daughter safe. You love her, too, Katey. Wouldn't *you* do this for her?"

Something snarled in the study. Partway between a trapped fox and a train whistle. It was not a human sound. A moist tear and a thump, like a wet paper bag full of meat had lost its bottom. Droplets of blood arced through the air above Glenn and I, a parabolic spray of crimson painting the pristine white kitchen.

"Jesus!" I said. "Glenn, we all have to get out of here! We don't have time!"

"I can't, Katey," he said. The resolve on his face wavered, but only for a moment. He set his jaw, and tightened his grip on my wrists. "There's nowhere to go. They're everywhere."

I kicked my legs, but couldn't find good purchase at this awkward angle. I bucked my hips and twisted. I was stronger than Glenn, I knew—he spent his whole life carefully nurturing the doughy physique of the comfortably rich—but there were dampers on my muscles. The blow to the head sucked the energy right out of my limbs, like waking up and immediately trying to make a fist.

This isn't going to work.

I stopped struggling. I closed my eyes. I heard Glenn sigh with relief. I pictured my breath entering my nostrils and flowing down my throat, like a diagram in a commercial for allergy medicine. Blue arrows moving through the airways of a generic human being, in cross-section. Hold. The resistance building in my chest was a red circle, enlarging. I exhaled, and orange arrows flowed outward. I got rid of the imaginary cross-section of a person. I pictured colorful arrows traveling through me, a circle enlarging. I got rid of the arrows, now just colors streaming in and out: blue, red, orange. Now no colors, just flow—shapeless, smooth, and even. Stillness.

I opened my eyes and the air was full of silver—glittering metallic particles drifting lazily on unseen currents. All color had been washed out of the world, leaving it overexposed and wan; the ghostly afterimages your eyes assemble after staring directly into a flash. A jagged black outline surrounded Glenn. It danced and surged about the perimeter of his body, though Glenn himself appeared to be frozen. I was still pinned by his weight. More so, actually—his fingers were statues that had been carved around my wrists. I couldn't have moved them an inch, even at full strength. I turned my head and saw Brin, similarly chased by a spiky black aura, and also immobile. I bucked and heaved under Glenn, but his body didn't budge in the slightest. He wasn't heavy; it just felt like he'd been glued in place. It felt like everything around me had been fused permanently to its spot, in fact. I was the only mobile thing around.

Think, Kaitlyn. What did you do the last time this happened?

Dammit, I didn't do anything. Not consciously, I just found myself in this nothing place—this world between worlds—and I stepped out of it.

No, that's not right. Remember.

I saw something first. I saw options. I saw pathways.

I looked again at Glenn, and noticed that his outline was not spiking and dipping at total random. It more or less followed his form, as it rapidly moved in thousands of different directions, simultaneously. I focused on one of those directions, and a ghostly outline of Glenn split off from his body. It shunted to one side a little bit, its weight thrown slightly off balance, then recovered. I followed a different outline, and saw a similar result. Again and again I concentrated on discerning distinct outlines from that ragged black aura, and again and again Glenn shifted only slightly before returning to his original position.

I kicked my heels in frustration.

Maybe you're thinking about this wrong.

I glanced over at Brin, instead. Her aura was substantially more active than Glenn's: it flung itself wide, all the way across the room, or retracted until it was nonexistent. I picked out one of those possibilities, and a faded image of Brin rolled on her heels, scrabbled backward across the kitchen, and hid in the den. I tried another option, and this one crawled over to assist Glenn in holding me down. Another potential pathway found Brin just squatting there and sobbing until some unseen force lifted her up by her hair, then bashed her face into the floor so hard that her skull splattered like overripe fruit.

God. What the hell? Is that what happens if an Empty One gets to her?

I isolated another outline from the ragged, squirming mess, and this one crawled toward me again. I was about to let my focus fade and release the potential Brin to return to her point of origin, but then she reached out and grabbed Glenn's wrist instead of mine. Her aura merged with

Glenn's—their potential actions tied together now, and they struggled. She pried at his fingers. He turned his head and shouted something I could not hear. Brin reached up and slapped him across the cheek. It stunned him enough to loosen his grip.

There.

I focused on those low-opacity images, and mentally filled in their details. They brightened and solidified, just a touch. I squinted at them harder, picturing Brin's kindly crow's feet, her intricately braided hair. I drew out the stubble on Glenn's face and the weave on his shirt. The faded figures grew more and more vivid, until they were too painfully bright to look at. I blinked. The world unpaused. Brin was squatting beside me now, waiting on bated breath for Glenn to respond. He lifted a hand from my wrist and felt at his face. I swung hard with my free hand and connected, right where the hinge of his jaw met his cheekbone. His head snapped around and connected with Brin's, and the both of them tumbled into a loose heap on the floor beside me. I squirmed out from under Glenn's legs and crawled toward the den. I knew it dead-ended, no exits but back the way you came, but it was in the general direction of "away" from whatever the hell was going on in the study. That was all that mattered.

Something grabbed my ankle.

God, no. I'll turn around and see those blank eyes, fingertips like claws tearing into my skin, rejoicing in the arterial spray—

It was Glenn, looking dazed and lost. The blow had momentarily sapped his strength, and he pawed at my legs weakly. I felt a moment of pity for him. I really *would* do the same in his situation, if I thought it would help. But I knew it wouldn't. I knew a deal with an Empty One meant less than nothing. They might let you go, because you're nothing to them. Or they might tear you limb from limb, again, because you're nothing to them. It's too risky to gamble a life on, even one as messed up and crazy as mine had become. I tried to tell Glenn all of this with my eyes, as I reared my other foot back and kicked him in the face.

I don't think he got the message.

His head rocked back sharply, then lolled forward and smacked the kitchen floor. Brin let out a mousy "eep," and covered her face with her hands. She tucked her feet up under her and rolled to her side, becoming the tiniest, most unobtrusive ball of human that she could be.

In the room just beyond the kitchen, Zang and Jie were fighting like trapped tigers. I only caught brief glimpses of them: a pretty young girl pulling a long strip of flesh from a man's neck with her teeth. A man's hand wrapped around a delicate throat, the flesh bulging out between his fingers. A wrist snapping backward. A fistful of silver hair. But for the most part, they were just a bloody, screaming blur.

I took advantage of the distraction and ran from the kitchen. In the den, a TV half the size of my apartment blared some offensively hip folk-rock as a sixteen-year-old girl stared dramatically at the ocean. Behind her, a teenage boy in a backward ball cap and a white T-shirt that came down to his knees was freestyle rapping to nobody in particular.

God, who watches this crap?

A stifled moan from behind me. I whirled and put my fists up, ready for some shifting-face monstrosity to come hurtling toward me. I saw the source of the noise: a pale girl with a dark brown pixie cut, laid out on a pristine white couch, her hands and feet bound with duct tape, a bundle of cloth stuffed in her mouth, her green eyes wide and pleading.

Jackie.

I dove at the couch and tore at her hands. I pulled at the tape, but only succeeded in making it tighter. Jackie made another muffled plea. I looked up and she shook her head furiously, working her jaw. She wanted the gag out. I caught the edge of the fabric protruding from her lips. It was white and lacy, like a doily. I pulled, and a pair of expensive panties unraveled from her mouth. When it was out, she gagged and spat.

"What the hell?" I asked, holding the damp underwear between thumb and forefinger.

"They're my mom's," Jackie said, with intense bitterness. "That Asian bitch put them there."

"Oh my god." I hurled them across the room and shook my soiled hands. "That's so fucked up."

"Tell me about it," she snapped. "But do it while you're untying me."

I went back to work on the tape, this time suppressing my own adrenaline enough to actually peel it apart. I freed her hands, then she sat up and we both worked on her feet. The instant they were loose, she leapt up from the couch and ran to the kitchen. I tried to catch her, but I was too slow. She made it around the dividing island and saw something that froze her in place. I was only a few steps behind her, and saw it seconds after.

Jie was a network of bloody lacerations. Half of her ear had been ripped off, and her silver hair was matted with gore. She stood in the center of the kitchen, holding Brin and Glenn by the backs of their necks like disobedient puppies. Their faces were a bloody mash, their bodies utterly limp, remaining upright only because Jie held them that way.

"This is what happens when you fuck with me," Jie said, matter-of-factly, and she bashed Brin's and Glenn's heads together so hard that their skulls gave way, melding them into one.

My first instinct was to cover Jackie's eyes. I blocked her view with one hand and pulled at her with the other. She moved like she was sleepwalking. I steered her easily back into the den, and we retreated to the far wall. The bulk of it was taken up by massive, nearly floor-to-ceiling windows. I grabbed a triangular metal end table, and whipped it into the glass as hard as I could. It rebounded and clipped me in the head. Blood streamed down my forehead and into my eye. I blinked and swore. The glass wobbled slightly from the impact. Barely a scratch from where the table hit.

"It's shatterproof," Jackie said, her voice flat and distant. "My parents are afraid of L.A. riots. *Were* afraid."

She laughed, bitter and hollow.

"Riots in Brentwood," she said, looking at me with unfocused eyes. "Can you imagine?"

"Oh little pigs," a lilting voice sang behind us. "Where do you run to?"

Jie leaned casually against the island dividing kitchen and den. She twirled something red and meaty in one hand. It looked to be a human jawbone.

"I'm going to pull your parents apart and stuff them inside of you," she said, looking to Jackie. "If you're nice, I'll let you pick which orifice."

Jackie hummed tonelessly.

"Let us go," I commanded, with all the authority I could muster.

Good job, Kaitlyn. What a super compelling argument.

"No," Jie said. Though strangely, she did seem to give it

some consideration before answering. "I don't see a very good reason for doing that."

She paused, waiting for me to provide one.

"B-because it's the right thing to do?" I tried.

Jie laughed, high and trilling. It was clearly practiced: a socialite expression, a thing to unfurl at old-fashioned cocktail parties in response to ribald anecdotes. It didn't fit this situation at all, much less her current "punk girl that gives head for beer" image. I wondered, for the first time, how old the Empty Ones really were. I wondered how many public personas they had adopted over the years. How many people they had pretended to be.

"No," Jie said. "I think I'll just torture you both to death."

I tried to find that still place inside of me again, tried to go stepping between moments, but I felt too loose and shaky. Like there were still ripples on the pond from the last time I'd thrown something in. Back in Mexico, I could see everything that Marco had ever been. It was so easy to just . . . pick him apart. Like pulling a thread on an old sweater. But now I felt like I'd taken a blow to the head—well, I mean, I *had* just taken several, but that's not supposed to affect me anymore—and now I just couldn't focus. I guess the between-space takes a different kind of toll.

I pushed Jackie behind me, putting my body between her and Jie. It might buy her a few seconds, I guess.

Jie quirked her head, listening to something. I didn't hear it at first, but whatever it was, it was increasing in volume. An industrial whine, like a giant drill spinning up. Through the windows behind Jie, I saw a Prius take the corner into the driveway too fast, briefly and madly tilt up onto two wheels, come down with an out-of-control shudder, veer around the median and then barrel, unbraking, straight through the wall of the study. Jie barely had time to turn her head before the car was on her. She folded under the front bumper and disappeared. The Prius sat at a severe angle, its right front tire parked atop her. The passenger door kicked open, and Carey spilled out.

"What is with you chicks?" he yelled. "I told you to run!"

He led the way, limping back across the wreckage he'd just generated and onto the driveway. I grabbed Jackie's wrist and pulled her toward the ruined kitchen. I pushed her up on the half-destroyed island, then crawled over myself. I heard a ragged breath being drawn from somewhere beneath the car. The shocks jounced and settled. Fingernails scratching on broken tile.

Jackie obeyed every prompt I gave her, but the second I stopped guiding she just shut down. She ground to a halt and stared straight ahead. I dragged her through the study, stumbling and tripping over shattered furniture, to the top of the driveway. We paused on the street. People were just coming out of their homes, drawn by the noise of the crash. I surveyed their gawking faces, and more than a few of them slipped right out of my mind. Their expressions were unreadable. Their features were a blur. Unnoticeables.

A horn honked.

Twenty feet away, a black SUV idled. The horn sounded again, longer this time, then the passenger door opened and Carey leaned out. He gave us an exasperated look.

"Do I need to send you a formal fucking invitation?" he asked.

I bolted for the car, hauling Jackie along with me. The second we moved, roughly half of the gathered crowd moved with us. I yanked open the rear door and shoved Jackie inside, then jumped in myself and slammed the door just as something hit the truck. Balled fists battered angrily on the rear windshield. I was thrown back as the SUV accelerated, then forward as it braked briefly, lurched to one side, and sped up again. I sat up and watched the street disappear behind us. A dozen indistinguishable figures still chased after the truck, though it was clear they'd never catch it. Only a handful of the neighbors were looking around in genuine confusion.

God, they really had taken most of the neighborhood. How many people were lost, just for the off chance at getting to us? To me?

A good half of the skin on Zang's neck was missing. His pink muscles twitched and jumped as he jerked the steering wheel. I could see part of his face in the rearview mirror. Enough to know one eye was also gone—just a dark red, wet hole that pulsed bloodily.

That reminds me . . .

"Are you okay?" I asked Jackie.

She blinked at me.

"Am I what?" she said.

"Are you okay?" I repeated. It was going to take a while for her to get through the shock. She'd probably be dazed and unresponsive for—

"That's what I thought you said," Jackie snapped. "But I wanted to give you a chance to think about how fucking stupid it was before you repeated it. But no! You doubled down! You're a gambler, K. You're like Kenny Rogers without the mustache. Well, without *as good* of a mustache."

She laughed, high and cruel.

"Hey," I said, keeping my voice gentle. "I know, okay? I know what it's like to lose somebody like that. I know what you're going through right now, but I need you to stay with me, okay?"

"You have no idea what I'm going through," Jackie said. She fiddled with the button for the window.

"I do. When Stacy died in the fire, I—"

"Fuck your dead sister," Jackie said. She looked me straight in the eye when she said it.

I made a bunch of disbelieving sounds, but no actual words.

"That is not the same thing," Jackie continued, poking at the little toggles set into the armrest. "Your sister died what, fifteen years ago? You told me yourself that you barely remember it."

"That doesn't mean I—"

"What did her skin look like, when she burned?" Jackie asked.

Holy shit.

"No answer for that? What did it smell like? Did she scream? For how long?" With each question, Jackie stabbed at the controls. They didn't respond. "My parents died like five minutes ago, K. And I am a god damn adult. I saw every second of it. Every detail. I watched my mom's face disintegrate *into my dad's*. I heard how it sounded. Look!"

She showed me her bare wrist, the soapy white skin spotted with red.

"That's their blood! That's their fucking face blood, Kaitlyn! Your distantly remembered, romantic little childhood trauma isn't like this! It isn't the same! And oh my god, why doesn't this window roll down?!"

She yanked the switches as hard as she could, and punched the armrest when they didn't break. Her barks of fury quickly devolved into hyperventilating sobs. I tried to put a hand on her shoulder, but she slapped it away.

"Oh hey," Zang said, entirely too chipper for the

situation. "Got the child lock right here. There you go."

Jackie's window rolled down of its own accord.

"Who the hell is this guy?" she said. "No, *what* the hell is this guy? Is he like you, K? I saw him moving in the house. He's crazy fast. And I'm pretty sure—yep, I'm definitely staring through his empty eye socket into his brain right now, yet he's still driving a car. Somebody wanna fill me in on this?"

"That's Zang," I said, then faltered.

How do I tell her that he's an Empty One, one of the things that just butchered her entire family right before her eyes? And that he's on our side? Especially when I'm not even sure of that last part. . . .

"He's an Empty One," Carey said. "He's on our side."

"He's . . . a what now?" Jackie said. "He's one of those things? Like the Asian girl?"

"Yeah," Carey answered. "Actually, she's kind of his girlfriend."

"Ex," Zang added.

Carey laughed.

"Ex-girlfriend," he corrected.

Jackie was silent for a long, stunned moment.

"Would you pull the car over?" she finally asked, dangerously polite.

"Nope," Zang said. "We detoured to save you, but we have somewhere important to be right now."

"Save me?" Jackie said, carefully. "That's what you call this? Saving me?"

Nobody knew what to say.

"Kaitlyn . . ." She turned to me, slowly, like any sudden movements would see her head fall off and bounce away. "I was gone for, like, a day, and in that time you not only met, but teamed up with one of these monsters? Then you brought them all to my home, and watched as they massacred my parents right in front of me? And now you have one chauffeuring us around?"

Jackie laughed that insane giggle again.

"We didn't bring them to you," I said. "Jie was there first, she had you tied up and your house surrounded, if we didn't—"

"There's no 'we'!" she shouted. "There's you. There's you and the monsters, and I'm starting to think you're one and the same. This all started with you—you and your creamed jeans over Marco."

"What? You set me up with him! You insisted!"

"Oh sure, and there was soooo much protest. You couldn't wait to climb that flagpole. And you know why? I think you knew. I think you sensed what he was. One freak to another."

Fuck. You.

I didn't say it—I knew Jackie was just messed up and lashing out at me—but I sure thought it as hard as I could.

"You did this," she said, quietly.

"Jackie, come on, I didn't—"

"You did. This shit has been floating around you ever since you were a kid. You and your mutant little finger."

I froze inside. We'd fought before, sometimes even viciously, but Jackie never brought up my extra pinky. Not even as children. It had always been out of bounds for her.

"You've been a god damn weirdo forever, and I keep trying to drag you into normality. In school back in Barstow. Moving out here to L.A. Taking you to those parties. It was charity work: me, just trying to show you what real people are like. But it was all a waste. Because you're not one. You're one of the monsters."

I kept my mouth shut. But I couldn't keep the glare out of my eyes.

"Oh, you don't like that?" Her laugh again, like icicles crashing on frozen ground. "Little Katey still thinks she's human? When's the last time you slept, K? Weeks?"

It's been months.

"When's the last time you ate?"

What?

"You don't even realize it. You haven't eaten in days. Maybe longer. Do you even need to? I wonder, how long can you hold your breath now? *Are you sure you still have to breathe?* Or is it just going through the motions for you? You're not my friend. You're not even the weird little girl I once took pity on. You're already gone, Kaitlyn. This is a car full of monsters. And I want out. Now. Please."

She folded her arms and waited.

"I'm still mostly human," Carey piped up, breaking the sullen silence. "I mean, some say I've got a python for a dick, but that's just metaphor."

Nobody laughed.

"Should I pull over?" Zang asked, his voice flat and empty.

This situation was clearly beyond the scope of his limited humanity.

"Yeah," Carey said. "What the hell. Why not? If she's not gonna laugh at my jokes anymore, it's not like we need her."

I should say something. Stick up for Jackie. She doesn't mean what she says. She's just hurt.

I should say something.

I can't help but notice that I'm not saying anything.

When was the last time I ate?

"If we do not need the girl to kill the angels, then she should go," Zang agreed.

"What?" Jackie said.

"You should go," he repeated.

"You know how to kill them?" Jackie said. "As in, all of them?"

"We think so, yeah," Carey answered.

"Then keep driving," Jackie said. "I'm in."

"You don't have to—" I started, but Jackie cut me off.

"I'm not helping you," she spat. "I'm hurting them."

"I like her," Zang said.

He delivered it like a punch line in a sitcom. The more I saw of the dead-eyed, emotionless vacuum of The Empty Ones in their natural state, the more intolerable their human façades became.

"If that thing touches me," Jackie replied, pointing at Zang, "I'll castrate it with my teeth."

"I *really* like her." Zang laughed.

We fell into an awkward silence. I thought of a thousand things to say to Jackie—the most heartfelt condolences, the perfect explanation for what had happened, the best anecdote to remind her of our friendship (when we were thirteen, and she got her braces caught in my hair, clearly)— but I didn't voice any of them. There was a hollow anger in my stomach over the hurtful things she'd said, followed by a dull and aching emptiness whenever I thought about how true they were.

When was the last time you slept?

When was the last time you ate?

Just going through the motions.

You're already gone, Kaitlyn.

I knew that if I didn't get out of my own head, I would do some serious and lasting damage.

"Fine, then," I said, answering a question nobody asked.

I locked eyes with Zang through the rearview mirror. "You said you could find an angel. . . ."

"Costa Soberbia," Zang said.

"I don't know what that is."

"It is a place where we will go and kill things."

Carey sighed and slapped Zang in the arm—the flesh there was already gluing itself back together, like watching somebody tear up a wad of Play-Doh, but in reverse.

"Tell them the whole thing," Carey said.

"It is a very long story," Zang said.

"It's an hour-and-a-half drive, and apparently nobody in this car is going to be any fucking fun. We've got time for long stories."

EIGHTEEN

This story is told by Zang. This was a very long time ago. The exact year is lost. The location is the city of Eridu in Sumeria.

In ancient Eridu, there was a man. This man's name is not important, because names are not important. They are road signs in the desert, indicating nothing. Man itself is not important, and so believes that by giving itself names it can stave off—

"Jesus, fuck, Zang," Carey snapped. "Leave off with the loony speeches, all right?"

"Yes, fine," Zang said.

This story involves angels. This story involves Empty Ones. This is not the story of the first angel. The angels have been and will always be. This is not the story of the first Empty One. As long as humans have been, there have been Empty Ones. This is the story of how the Empty Ones learned to best serve the angels.

When society first began, the angels came. Man thought that society was a blessing, but society is an abomination. The universe is a lifeless, unthinking, beautiful machine. It is void of doubt, and fear, and hate. It simply is. The angels understand this. When man first inflicted thought upon himself, he embedded within him the most dangerous of things: a language. A language is a code. A code can be manipulated. And so the angels used mankind's own curse to save it. They found man, and they reduced his code, until he was once again nothing. All of the energy that man had been wasting on frivolous complexity was then used to feed the angels, and to further serve the universe. This was good. This was right. But this was not enough.

The code of humanity was sloppy. Sometimes, it did not reduce cleanly, and there were remainders left over. These remainders you know as the tar men and the Empty Ones. The tar men were lucky. They are the animalistic part of man. They are not burdened with thought or desire. The Empty Ones were not lucky. They are the thinking part of man. They were cursed to know the perfection of nonexistence, while also doomed to exist forever. But the Empty Ones did not live in hate. Hate was man's house. The Empty Ones instead dedicated themselves to helping mankind, by assisting the angels in their quest to reduce the needless complexity of life. They sought to return humanity to the universe.

So they watched. And they waited. For a very long time.

They discovered that the angels were patient creatures. They appeared rarely and seemingly at random. They blessed only a few humans a year with oblivion. This is fine for the angels. They are beyond time. This is bad for humanity, who are mired in time. Man would have to wait millennia—more, perhaps—to be fully returned to the universe. The Empty Ones could not stand to let humanity endure such torture. They sought a way to force the angels to not only appear, but to procreate. More angels would speed the job.

One day, in man's oldest city, the Empty Ones found their way.

The Empty Ones knew they must work within the world of man to save him. So they lived in his city, and attained positions of power. They took nothing men and nothing women from the city streets, and they experimented. The people they took sometimes suffered greatly before expiring, but their pain was trivial when weighed against the pain of the species. The man in this story did not agree. One such experiment involved the man's youngest daughter. A deformed young thing with one extra finger on her left hand. The man loved her despite this inferiority. He mistakenly believed that blood ties create a relevant bond, and lapsed into a state of insanity that caused him to act irrationally. He sought justice for his daughter.

This man had two other children. They were much older than the daughter. They were males. They were strong and willful. All three fought the Empty Ones. They struggled against the systems that the Empty Ones had put into place. They killed human soldiers employed by the Empty Ones. They kidnapped bureaucrats enforcing the will of the Empty Ones. They burned a structure used by the Empty Ones for their experiments. In this, they made a mistake.

The man was hurt badly while escaping the fire, and his sons, suffering from similar familial insanities, refused to abandon him. They helped him to flee, but he slowed them down. The chase was short lived. Their pursuers were mostly human, but among them were two Empty Ones. No matter how hard the three fought, they could not prevail. One son was wounded, badly. At last it was clear to the remaining son that he must flee. But he could not escape with both his father, and his brother. He looked to his father, who was old, and hurt. He looked to his brother, who was young, and may have healed. The son chose to save his brother and abandon his father. At that moment an angel honored them with its presence.

By virtue of the son's actions, something within the father's code had become ready. The angel used the complicated series of tragedies that the man called a life to create something meaningful. It created another angel.

When it was done, the Empty Ones rejoiced at the miracle. They sought to replicate these events. It took years of practice, but at last they managed. They re-created the chase, just as the father and sons had fled. They re-created the pain, the panic, and the emotional distress those original three endured. They re-created the choice they made, and the abandonment that followed—the young choosing the young over the old, as all life must do. And angels appeared.

The process was not perfect. Not just any human could serve in the roles. There were certain personality archetypes that had to be present: A personal tragedy in the distant past, which left psychic wounds that could not heal. A reactionary disdain for authority. An absence of clear want and direction. These aspects made up major chunks of the original man's code, and so for the ritual to work, future candidates must share those attributes. As the ritual was refined, more angels were brought to Earth. More humans were solved, some of them incompletely, and so more Empty Ones were made, who, in turn, performed more rituals, to bring more angels. The ultimate solution of humanity sped ever forward, and at last its return to the universe was imminent. The cycle of creation will peak soon, and there will be nothing left but angels and Empty

Ones. The Empty Ones know they cannot be solved. They are forever cursed. They realize this. Yet still, they try to save humanity from suffering existence. It is their sacrifice.

NINETEEN

"Okay," Jackie said. "That's a bunch of crazy bullshit. Thank you for sharing."

"It may be," Zang said. "I was not present to account for it. This is what the Empty Ones believe. This is what they strive for. But the ritual is real. Everyone in this vehicle can account for that."

A small, stone church in a walled compound at the base of dark mountains. A burning light, jarring static, white space . . .

"So what does that have to do with now?" I asked.

"They're doing another ritual tonight," Carey said. "Poor son of a bitch is probably already going through the ringer."

"The chase would be on right now, yes," Zang said.

"Once he's all done up to their liking," Carey said, "an angel will turn up to put its celestial dick in his ear—"

"The angels do not have genitals," Zang corrected.

"Figure of speech," Carey said.

"Those are difficult." Zang nodded.

"And that's when you do your angel-murder thing. If

your uh . . . *vision* . . . is real, then that's the end of all this stuff. But hey, even if you're wrong . . ."

"You will still kill an angel, and all of the Empty Ones around it," Zang finished. "Jie will be running tonight's ritual. I will see her dead."

"But why are *you* doing this?" Jackie asked. "Nobody finds that weird? This fucking thing starts ranting about how perfect and beautiful the angels are, and how disgusting people are, and nobody thinks 'oh shit, this guy is probably leading us into a trap'? *Seriously?*"

"If I wanted you dead I could steer this car into oncoming traffic. It would not matter to me," Zang said, his voice as barren as a desert. "But I do not want that. Jie and I are connected. The angels created us together. They made a mistake. The thing I am cannot help but worship them. The thing I used to be remembers what they took away, and cannot forgive it. And Jie . . ."

There was genuine longing in that pause. A dusty, nostalgic kind of regret, like an old man looking at a picture of his wife, back when she was young. . . .

"Jie should not continue like she is," Zang said. "She wouldn't want that. She doesn't deserve it."

We all allowed him a moment of silence.

"And what's Costa Suburbia?" I asked, when I thought enough time had passed.

"So-*ber*-bia," Carey corrected. "It's a subdivision they built back in the seventies. Supposed to be real high class shit. Where the families of studio heads could live safely, without ever being in danger of seeing a Mexican that wasn't mowing their lawn. Built it right on the beach on top of these gigantic cliffs. Then a big one hit in seventy-one, and the whole thing collapsed. Didn't even get to finish

KILL ALL ANGELS 181

construction. The earthquake broke the cliffs clean off, and sent the whole neighborhood a couple hundred feet down into the ocean."

"So we're going scuba diving?" I said.

"No, most of it still sticks up above the water at low tide."

"Jesus, these guys sure do love their dramatic set pieces." Jackie laughed.

I smiled at her. She returned to staring out the window.

"It is not for dramatic effect," Zang said. "The place is abandoned. The ritual draws much attention. There is often screaming. Bloodshed. Then the angel comes . . ."

"Lights up the joint like a million-watt spotlight," Carey finished.

Every hour is rush hour for *about* an hour in every direction of Los Angeles. That sucks at the best of times, but try sitting in a stolen SUV with an old, smelly, homeless punk, a girl who blames you for the death of her parents, and a psychotic immortal who's mostly preoccupied with driving and growing back his face. The silence was beyond awkward.

Carey spun the radio dial back and forth, scoffing and swearing at every single radio station before settling on NPR. They had some old punk guy from back in the day talking about how he's doing this spoken word stuff now. Carey kept making wanking hand gestures and giving the radio the bird, but he didn't change the station. In the pauses between segments, I could hear the soft *squick* of Zang's flesh melding back together. It was a relief when he finally jerked the truck to a stop in an empty, cracked, and weed-strewn cul-de-sac overlooking the sea. Jackie yelled at him for the teeth-rattling stop, but he started droning on about "ceasing momentum in the most efficient way," so she just stepped out of the car and slammed the door. I followed.

The sky and the ocean were the same color, separated by a thin shimmering band where the ghost of the sun still lingered. I could hear waves far below, their echoes confused by the furrowed stone of the cliffs. There was a hidden architecture down there somewhere—half-glimpsed hard angles, flashes of white tile—but I couldn't make out details. The sun had barely set, but it was midnight in the cove below. It must be shadows from the cliffs, I told myself.

I wasn't terribly convincing.

Carey and Zang took turns spitting off the cliff, then argued about who managed the greater distance. I stood upwind of them, for obvious reasons. Jackie was alone, huddled on the farthest outcrop she could find. She hugged her bare shoulders and shivered, her short brown hair whipping in the wind.

You should go talk to her.

She's gotta calm down eventually. You'll both put this behind you, and it'll all be like it was.

You just have to take the first step.

Be the bigger person.

Say something.

"We should go," I said. "If we're going."

I turned away from Jackie and started picking my way down the path. That was a generous description: It was a slippery, sandy animal trail, tracing the line of least resistance across unstable boulders and shimmying along crumbling cliffsides without much consideration to such paltry human concerns as "safety" and "terror."

"Stop," Zang said.

He grabbed me by the wrist and yanked me straight off my feet. I flew backward and landed on my tailbone in the dirt.

"What the hell?" I yelped.

"My bad," he said, and gave me a goofy teenage smirk. Then it dropped away, and he continued tonelessly. "Working these bodies is difficult. I meant you no harm. I should go first on the path. I can see better at night, and sudden falls will not harm me. You are valuable tonight. You cannot be risked."

He turned and started off without another word. Carey shrugged at me before disappearing over the precipice himself. Jackie went next. I got up and brushed the dust from my butt. Picked a few pieces of gravel from my elbows. Then I followed them down. I tried not to dwell on the implications of that word: "tonight."

The trail started out dangerous and then graduated into a slow-motion suicide attempt. You could actually see where each type of hiker realized this was an idiotic venture, and turned back: The path was most worn right up to the edge of the cliff, where everybody with a functioning brain took one look at the crumbling goat trail and its several-hundred-foot drop onto jagged rocks and crashing waves, and decided that the mall sounded like a better weekend outing, after all. The more confident hikers ventured over the lip and onto the thin, deceptively slippery sand before turning back. The daredevils made it all the way down to the first switchback, where they likely took a few danger selfies so they'd have something to post on Facebook besides their lunch orders and cute pets. The tracks all but faded after the turn, dissipating into a scant few dares from drunken teenagers and a handful of reconsidered suicides.

We had past that point an hour ago.

But we weren't even afforded the weak comfort of

isolation. After a particularly difficult section—Zang had to straddle a gap where the trail either crumbled away, or else never existed in the first place, and then serve as a kind of human bridge for us—I fell to my knees and gripped the reedy, windswept grass like safety handles built into the earth. Beneath my clenched fists full of straw, I saw fresh footprints. Not enough to trample us a clear and usable path. Just enough to remind us that we weren't fording this ridiculously dangerous trail to reach some untouched nature reserve, where we would take dumpy vacation photos and then laugh about our near-death experiences with the other insufferable expats back at the hostel; we were descending into a den full of monsters. Falling to our deaths on the way there would be our best-case scenario.

I couldn't see the sunken city from the path. I could barely see the ground beneath my feet, during those few times I could pull my fear-paralyzed eyes away from them. The city was somewhere below or behind us, looming in my mind like a haunted house in a horror flick. I envisioned us rounding the cliff side into a dramatic fog break, the mist parting to unfold an ornate tapestry of broken towers and mossy brick.

In actuality, we hopped down a series of descending boulders, placed just too far apart to take them like stairs, and when I looked up, we were there. Standing in a sandy inlet tucked behind an outcropping of rock. The waves broke against the far side, leaving us with a small, but relatively peaceful little beach. A trail of gravel chased the cliff-base back into the darkened bay. The waves boomed back there, too, echoing across the rocks like terrestrial thunder. Zang allowed us a paltry few minutes to catch our breath, but you could tell he wasn't happy about it.

Carey leaned upright against the rocks, trying to play off his exhaustion with an apathetic James Dean slouch, but his legs were shaking and his face was drenched in sour sweat. Jackie sat cross-legged at the edge of the shore, slumped, shivering, and silent. I was mentally exhausted— my adrenal glands having been burnt out hours ago by the rapid-fire near-death experiences—but I looked for tiredness in my muscles and found none. I flexed my fingers. They didn't ache, like they should. They weren't scraped and bleeding, barely able to close into a fist. They felt strong. Even my extra pinky, which up until recently I hadn't been able to move much at all, now clenched and unclenched easily.

I'm no stranger to physicality. I made a living pretending to be action heroines. And I've even done some climbing— nothing serious, just for fun—so it makes sense that, after that trek, I would be in better shape than an elderly hobo who drinks Pabst for dinner, and a girl who thinks eating ice counts as exercise because it takes more calories to chew than it's got. But I shouldn't be this well off. I shouldn't be at the top of my game. I shouldn't be spoiling for a fight.

But Christ, I am.

"Do you need rest?" Zang asked, his voice flat. He stared into the dark.

I made a noncommittal noise.

"You should be tired," he said. "They are tired."

"I'm fine," I said.

"I know," he said. "I said you *should* be tired."

I squinted at him in the half-light. He gazed unblinking at the black curtain that hung across the bay like smog. Like there was some poisonous factory in there churning out shadow as pollutant.

"How many have you taken?" he asked, still not sparing me a glance.

"How many what?" I started, by reflex, but I thought better of it. I knew what he meant.

Why play coy with the monster? The monster knows its own.

"Two," I said. "I've killed two angels. This will be the third."

"Good," he said. "That means you'll be strong and slow to injure, but will not yet turn on us."

"Turn on you?"

Zang blinked and slowly adopted his human mask. It looked painful, watching that smile carve itself into his flesh.

"I'm just fuckin' with you!" he finally said, and laughed. He nodded to Carey. "You guys ready to roll?"

"As I'm going to be," Carey said.

He seemed to have trouble pushing himself upright. His knees crackled when they took his weight. Jackie said nothing. She just stood and faced us, quietly awaiting the next order.

"Follow behind me closely," Zang said. "When I pause it means the footing has become dangerous. Grab my hand and I will guide you. Make little noise. They are not vigilant, but they are not entirely oblivious."

"They?" I said.

"The Unnoticeables that live here," he said.

"How many?" Jackie said. Her voice was like steel.

"Only ten that I can see," Zang said. "But they are not the ones to worry about. Jie takes too much from her followers. She does not leave them enough to function like normal humans, and we should be able to avoid their attention."

"So what should we worry about?" I said.

"The tar men," Zang said. "I cannot see any now, but

even my vision is not keen enough to pick them out in the dark. They will be here. And they will be quiet. And they will be nearly invisible until they are upon us."

"What do we do then?" Jackie asked.

"You will probably die," Zang answered. "That is why you should make very little noise. Let's go."

He took a step and disappeared into the dark. We followed.

TWENTY

Carey. 1982. Los Angeles, California. Westlake.

"But I don't want to murder the girl," I said for the third time. Slowly now, like I was talking to a little kid or a moron.

"But it is necessary," Zang said, with the exact same inflection I used on him.

Is he fucking mocking me? Or is he just parroting back what I say to—how did he put it—practice at humanity?

"She hasn't done anything," I said. I gestured up at her window. A bright square of yellow cut out of the blue denim night.

I wasn't kidding. Zang and I had been squatting on the roof of a garage just below her apartment building for a few hours, and all we'd seen her do so far was a little dancing, a lot of dishes, and iron half a shirt. I've never seen somebody do so much nothing, and I've been unemployed for . . . ever, I guess.

"This is not about what she has done," Zang answered. He alternated between patronizing, frustrated, and totally empty—varying tactics to see which was the magic button that would make me understand.

"We don't even know if she's going to do anything," I said.

"This isn't about what she's going to do."

"Then what the hell is this about?" I snapped.

"This is about what she could do, if we do nothing."

Butting up against the far side of the little parking garage was a run-down three-story adobe building. One window opened right out onto the upper level of the complex, which must've really killed the ambience when people lived there—throw open the shades and take in all that lovely fresh exhaust, why don't you? The building was empty now, but somebody had obviously been ducking out that window to use the roof of the garage as their smoke spot. Not too long ago: It hadn't even rained since they vacated, leaving their old butts nice and dry. None of that precious nicotine leaching out through the paper, staining it the color of tea. Plus whoever lived there must have been a millionaire; they left a half inch of untouched cigarette on nearly every butt. I gathered up a handful of them, twisted the stems between my fingers to loosen the tobacco, poured it all together, and rolled it back up in one of my own papers.

What? Oh, this is what you're gonna judge me for? Not for running away and letting my friends die, or the rampant alcoholism, or being a general no-good parasitic drain on society—secondhand smokes is where you draw the line. Fuck you. Nicotine doesn't care if it gets in your system via used butts or blown gently up your ass by a Swedish supermodel. Drugs are drugs.

I took a drag.

Come, partake of our beautiful Lucky Strike garage tobacco, aged on the ground, next to a broken bottle and an old burrito wrapper, gently toasted over a period of weeks by the warm California sun. . . .

I blew smoke in Zang's general direction. He didn't flinch. He didn't even blink.

"Blink," I told him.

He did.

"You have to remember to blink if you're gonna pass as human."

He started blinking mechanically, once every five seconds.

"Okay." I laughed. "Stop, that's way worse."

He stared at me blankly, awaiting further input.

"You want to kill the girl," I said.

"Yes," he answered.

"It's like the fat kid in the park all over again," I sighed.

"Yes," Zang answered, with something like relief. "She is a candidate. If we don't kill her now, the angels could use her to procreate. The angel she would birth could kill others, and it, in turn, could use another like her to procreate again. That angel could kill more people, spawn more angels, and so on down the line. To not murder that girl now may be like murdering thousands in the future."

"Jesus Christ," I said. "I knew you guys were messed up in the head, but to hear you actually walk through your fucked-up thought process—I don't even know where to start with what's wrong with everything you just said. You're acting like all of this has already happened, just because it could happen."

"Yes," Zang answered.

"That's . . . that's dumb, man," I said.

"That is how the angels think," he said.

"The angels are dipshits, then."

He considered this. You could actually see him mull the statement over like it might contain valuable information.

I used the quiet moment to stare up at the girl. She was cute, in that "I'm so hard up, I'd screw a hole in the ground" kind of way. Which is the only way I know, to be honest. Shoulder-length bright red hair brushed flat, not all teased up into a fire hazard like the chicks go for these days. Wide eyes, big lips, not exactly skinny—at least by L.A. standards—but I liked that. These L.A. girls, they look normal on TV, but once you actually get here and see them in person, there's something off about them. Those little stick bodies make their heads look bigger than they should be. Like walking caricatures drawn by hacks busking on the promenade. At least this redhead looked like she wouldn't break in half if you—

"I don't think the angels are dipshits," Zang finally replied.

It snapped me out of what was obviously turning into a jerk-off fantasy. Probably for the best, considering that I was staring up at some strange chick's window in the middle of the night, perched atop an empty garage with a soulless psychopath. Any way you cut it, those are suspect conditions for a hard-on.

"Look," I said, gesturing at the girl with my garbage cigarette. "You're never going to beat them by thinking like them. You're just going to make the same moves they'd make. That makes you easy to predict. That's why I'm still alive: They can't predict my moves, because even I don't know what they are."

"That does not sound like good strategy," Zang said.

"Well, it works. If you wanna beat these bastards, you gotta think like a human. What is the humane thing to do here?"

Zang considered this for a minute.

"Wait until she falls asleep before breaking her neck?" he ventured. "That way she suffers no fear or pain."

"You're making progress, I guess. But no: A human would go up there and talk to her. Tell her what's coming, and give her a chance to run or something."

"Again, that does not seem like a sound strategy."

The redhead heaved a sigh so exaggerated I could practically hear it across the street. She held up the shirt she'd been ironing: a white blouse with a triangular black mark the exact size and shape of an iron.

I laughed.

Then I saw it.

"You're right," I said. "She's not going to run."

"What is she going to do?" Zang asked.

"She's going to fight," I answered.

The girl spun and flung her ruined shirt away. She ran her hands through her hair and pulled at it in frustration. She stomped and paced, jumped and swore, finally returning to the window just to flip the bird to her iron. It was a weird-looking gesture, being performed with six fingers and all.

"Hey," I said, when the redhead opened the door. She wasn't stupid: She left the chain on and had one hand tucked awkwardly behind her, probably holding a weapon. "My name is Carey and I promise I'm not a rapist."

Not your best opener.

"O . . . kay," she said, slowly closing the door.

"No, wait! I just need to talk to you about—"

"Sorry!" she said, in that chipper tone you only use when

you're trying to defuse dangerous psychopaths. "I gotta go. My boyfriend needs something. More steroids, probably."

She shut the door carefully, like any sudden motion would set me off. Then a series of solid and final thunks as she clicked every lock she had into place.

I knocked again. She didn't answer. Probably already dialing the cops.

"Can I come out?" Zang asked.

I told him to hide in the bushes while I knocked.

You know you're in trouble when I'm the most presentable face of your organization.

"Yeah," I said. "I think I screwed up the nice approach."

Zang stepped out from his hiding spot inside a pair of brittle acacia. An errant thorn dragged across his cheek while he moved. It drew blood. He didn't notice.

"There is no time for courtesy," Zang said. "We are not the only ones watching."

"We're not?"

"No, the Empty Ones will have Unnoticeables watching over all potential candidates."

"Christ," I said. "How do you guys even know who to watch?"

"It is complicated."

"No," I poked him in the chest. "That's part of our deal. You answer all of my questions right away or this whole thing is off."

"You are right," he said. "I simply did not think there was time. It all begins in the year thirty-six hundred B.C.E.—"

"Oh holy shit." I threw up my hands. "Fine. We'll do answers later. Get the door."

He shrugged his patchwork leather jacket into place with a practiced motion he probably learned from watching

Happy Days, gave me a cheesy double thumbs-up, then jump-kicked the girl's door into splinters.

Never forget what he is.

You spend enough time alone with something—doesn't matter what; a dog, a plant, a car, a friendly looking garbage can in the alley beside a butcher shop in Koreatown that has a couple of dents that almost look like eyes—and you start to treat it like a person. Like a friend. If I'm ever in danger of falling into that trap with Zang, he only has to move to snap me right out of it. When they drop the mask and stop pretending like the shell they hide in is remotely human, the Empty Ones move like apex predators. Not in a poetic sense, either. No "great beasts dancing in the night" or whatever. It's like watching a grizzly bear bumbling about in the woods.

"It's so big," your stupid brain thinks. "Big means slow."

And the bear seems to know you make that assumption. Seems to play off of it. It moseys around like an adorable dope. Like some great big snuggly, sun-addled cow. Then you step wrong and snap a branch, and you've got its attention. Suddenly it's moving at you like a freight train. There's no transition period between slow, lovable fuzzball and hurtling mountain of teeth and claws. It is death; it always *was* death. The cute stuff before was the act, and the thing that's killing you before you can blink is the reality. You get that same feeling when you watch an Empty One move—really move, without the handicap of pretend humanity. There's a little shiver in the back of your soul that recognizes the murderous trick you've been falling for.

Zang was up the walkway and through the shattering door in a heartbeat. Straight through it like a cannonball and inside, chasing down the girl without so much as a faltered step. She didn't even have time to scream.

I stepped through the wreckage of the entryway and found them in the kitchen. Sure enough, she'd been calling the cops—or at least thinking about it. She still held the receiver. Zang stood behind her, his whole body pressed against her back. One hand across her mouth, one around her left wrist, isolating the butcher knife she also held. His fingers dug into her face, pooling the baby fat in her cheeks up around her nose and eyes, which had gone wide with terror and confusion. There was no way she could have reacted to the threat in time, so her nervous system just misfired. She froze in place like a statue, not struggling in the least, now just hoping not to make the situation worse by accidentally twitching.

"Hey again," I said. I gave her a friendly wave.

She didn't seem to appreciate it.

Okay, well, so much for first impressions. I guess it's the hard way.

"You didn't let me finish earlier," I said. I plucked the phone from her hand, noted the dial tone with relief, and hung it back on the receiver. "*I'm* not a rapist, but oh man— my friend here sure is."

Her eyes slowly slid to the side, trying to see who held her.

Zang gave me a disapproving glance.

"I mean . . . aren't you?" I asked.

"Yes," he said, "among other things. But it is not a flattering introduction."

"That's Zang," I told the girl. "I'd say he's the worst person you'll ever meet, but that would be calling him a person."

I yanked open the door to her faded pink '50s refrigerator. There was an untouched six-pack of Coors squatting on the lower shelf, shining like the Holy Grail. I snagged it and raised it toward her.

"Cheers," I said. "Now, if you come with us peacefully we're not going to hurt you. Hell, I wouldn't hurt you even if you made a fuss. But Zang, he's not good at restraint. He might just mean to brush your hair out of your eyes, and instead he accidentally puts a fist inside your skull."

Zang sighed.

"Is that wrong?" I asked.

"No," he said. "It has happened before. But I am practicing and getting better. It happens less often now. Some credit would be appreciated."

A tremor ran through the redhead, but she tamped it down.

"So blink twice if you're gonna play nice," I said.

She blinked. Then again.

"Good girl," I said.

I nodded to Zang. He twisted her wrist a little bit at the wrong angle, and she dropped the knife. One by one, his fingers pried themselves loose from her face. A bright red handprint there, already fading. As soon as his pinky left her cheek, the redhead heaved an elbow into Zang's chest and barreled toward me. I hopped out of the way, holding the precious beer above my head and out of the danger zone. She wasn't expecting that. She had her shoulder down and all her weight forward, figuring I'd grab for her and she'd have to plow her way through me. Instead she went headfirst into the wall opposite the kitchen door. She left a skull-sized hole in the drywall, but she didn't let it faze her long. She was up and crawling as soon as she hit the floor. She only made it a few feet.

She looked up to find Zang blocking the front entrance.

He was leaning against the jamb and idly picking at his nails in another of his human affectations.

"How did you . . . ?" She leaned back on her haunches to peer past me, into the kitchen where Zang had been just seconds before. It wasn't humanly possible for him to get there so fast.

"Not humanly possible" still surprises some people.

"See, you thought I was exaggerating earlier," I said, peeling a can from the six-pack in my right hand and offering one to her. She didn't take it.

It's weird how none of these people want a drink when you need one most. Ah well, more for me.

I held the beer up and bit the tab, levering it back with my teeth. Probably a bad habit, since it left both of my incisors chipped, but on the other hand, it left all of my beers open without me having to set the rest down and risk them being stolen by parasites. It's all about priorities.

"All that stuff I said about him being a monster, accidentally putting a fist through your skull and whatnot—you thought I was trying to be scary. I'm not scary," I said, and gestured at Zang with the five-pack. "He's scary. I'm just accurate."

"Please don't rape me," the redhead said, almost too quiet to hear.

Ah, shit. Overplayed the hand.

I just wanted her scared enough to listen—not broken. I forget just how fucked up it is being a girl, when shit like this is a real possibility instead of an overblown threat.

"We don't have much time," I said. "There are bad people coming."

She blinked at me.

"Worse than us, even," I said, laughing.

She didn't join in.

"Look, we're not going to rape you, hurt you, or even rob you—I mean, aside from this beer here—you just need to come with us right now, and without making a lot of fuss. That sounds bad, I know. But I swear we only want to talk to you for a few minutes, and then you can walk away."

"I don't believe you," she said.

"No shit," I answered. "Why would you? But you've seen how fast my friend here is—you can't run away from him, and he'll be on you the second you scream. You don't really have a choice."

"For what it's worth," Zang said, all smiles. "I've never raped anybody *to death*."

The girl shuddered.

"Thanks, man," I said. "Real big help."

Neither Zang or me had a car. I'm a worthless, homeless drunk, so I can't afford one, and he's an inhuman maniac with no social skills, so he feels right at home on the bus. We had to walk our captive away. Zang and the redhead strolled hand in hand, and I almost felt jealous—been a while since I touched a woman without being asked to leave the premises afterward. I consoled myself by remembering that it wasn't a romantic gesture; it was so he could pull her arm off if she tried to run.

She didn't.

When the Empty Ones touch you, you feel it right away—how wrong they are. There's none of the minute human communication that naturally comes through our skin. No sweating, no little twitches of the palm, no flush of the skin. It's like being grabbed by a statue. Like they put your tiny baby arm in a hand carved from stone, and then held you there until you grew into it. Those immutable fingers aren't just holding you; they may as well be a part of you. You know instantly that you cannot get away without gnawing something off.

A Chinese punk in a stained and torn leather jacket holding hands with a pretty Mexican girl in her pajamas in the middle of the night draws a few looks, even in Koreatown, but something in Zang's manufactured smile told folks they didn't want to look too long.

A few blocks from the girl's apartment there was an empty lot that still held the skeleton of an old liquor store. The front façade had been burned out and the roof caved in, but most of the back of the building still stood. Enough to at least hide us from the street. Intermittent blue and red lights from the neon sign of the hotel across the street lit the place like a disco morgue. The building felt like it was specifically constructed to be a crime scene. You could just feel all the previous murders staining the shattered concrete floor. Whatever promises of safety I'd made to the girl, she sure as hell wasn't buying them now. Zang released his grip on her wrist and took three huge, awkward steps backward. He looked around the room, took another half-step to the left, then froze.

We both stared at him. He didn't offer any kind of explanation.

"So," I said, "what's a pretty girl like you doing in a place like this?"

Not even a smile. Huh. Must be uptight.

I offered her a beer again. Still, she refused.

Definitely uptight.

"Here's how it is," I said. "From the top down: There are

these balls of light—we've been calling them angels, but that's just a name—and they do something to people. Kind of take them away—"

"They are solved," Zang interrupted. He was still utterly frozen in his strange straddling stance. "All of life can be reduced to an infinitely complex series of interactions. These interactions can be assigned something like numbers, and—"

"Look, she just needs the CliffsNotes version for now," I cut him off. "The balls of light take people away, only sometimes that doesn't work entirely and you're left with a fucked-up shell of a human. That's what my buddy Zang here is—oh and hey, that's his name, by the way. I'm Carey."

I waved.

She didn't wave back.

Offer the beer again.

. . .

Nah, better to just power through.

"Anyway yeah, my friend here was emptied out of everything human and now he's like some sort of immortal psychopath, only he's trying to be better."

"I am better," Zang said. "I have killed far fewer people this year than any other since I was turned. That is an objective improvement."

"Right." I nodded. "So he's *getting* better. Uh, what am I forgetting?"

Zang quirked his head at me, awaiting permission.

I nodded.

"The animus and the shadow," he said.

"What?" I said.

"You call them 'tar men' and 'unnoticeables.' I should add that the latter is not actually a word and—"

"Right, right." I turned back to the girl. "So the ball of

light solves a human and you get Zang here plus a thing that looks like a walking grease stain and melts you if it touches you. The Empty Ones also do something to people that makes them, like, less than people."

"The animus—the tar men—they are destruction. It is all they do, and all they know. We are the anima. We are creation. It is all we are, and all we know—we seek to give birth to ourselves, but the great tragedy is that we cannot procreate, no matter how badly we are driven to. When we try, we only succeed in draining some of a human being, not emptying them out as our own creators do. Together, the anima and the animus are the essence of the dual nature of humanity, split apart by—"

"Hey," I said. I held up a finger. Zang dutifully fell silent. "So for the cheap seats, you got evil balls of light that sometimes disappear people, and other times turn them into tar men and Empty Ones. The Empty Ones further feed off of folks, turning them into these kinda faceless people who are hard to remember, even when you're looking at them. That's more or less it."

"Not quite. She does not yet know where she fits into this," Zang added.

"Holy shit, I forgot how complicated this gets," I said. "Okay, so you're a candidate. You're like, uh . . . you're like an angel egg. And they need to fertilize you so you can— look, I failed biology. Or I would have, if I had ever gone. The angels need people like you to make more angels, but I think you're special. You've got an extra finger on your left hand. I knew a girl like that once. She was also a candidate, but she could do amazing things. She could fight the angels, and we think you could fight them, too."

Nobody spoke. I cleared my throat.

It was about as quiet as L.A. can get, which means there was distant traffic noise, some faint screaming, what sounded like a cat dying nearby, and a trickle of falling water that was probably a hobo peeing on the outside wall.

"You are so, so nuts," the girl finally said. "I didn't even know you *could* be this nuts. I thought that only happened in movies. I thought real nutty people just hit themselves, or thought the devil talked to them. I never thought nuts could be *this* complicated and weird. Anyway, I'm really sorry you're so nuts, but it's not my fault. I didn't do it. Can I please go?"

I sighed. Zang did nothing. Didn't even blink. Thought I talked to him about that.

You're an idiot. You should have started with proof in the first place, and then explained.

"Hey, Zang," I said. "Do something fucking crazy. Rip off your arm or something."

Zang instantly shrugged out of his ragged leather jacket and sunk his fingernails into his own flesh, just below the elbow. He worked quickly and efficiently, tucking his fingertips under the loose flaps of skin and prying them up from the muscle below. It was like watching an old fisherman fillet a catch. Clearly wasn't his first rodeo. Within seconds he had skinned his entire forearm down to the wrist. He pulled it over his hand like an old sock, and wriggled his fingers free. He shook the flesh glove out, spraying fine droplets of blood all across the floor, then inverted it so the skin was on the outside again. He stepped forward and handed his own arm to the girl. Then he took those three huge, awkward steps backward again and settled into the exact same position and stance he'd left.

The redhead was trying to scream, but she couldn't catch

her breath. It sounded like a deflating balloon.

"Now watch as it grows back," I told her. "How long is that going to take?"

"Skin takes the longest," Zang said. "Perhaps hours."

"What? Shit, that's no good. It's the growing back part that'll convince her. Now she just thinks you're extra *super* crazy. Why didn't you say something?"

"You asked me to pull my arm off. I did that."

Fucking literal monsters, man. They're the worst.

"Okay, well, do something else that'll convince her you're immortal like I said."

Zang thought for a moment, then placed one hand on each side of his skull and twisted. His neck snapped. The girl yipped like a frightened squirrel. Zang's head lolled backward, settling loosely between his own shoulder blades. He had to turn around to face us again. He stared at me questioningly, a faint smile on his inverted lips.

"Will this do it?"

The girl was still making that breathless shriek, her eyes gone the size of dinner plates. I gestured toward Zang with the now-three-pack in my right hand, as if to say "what do you think?"

She nodded.

Good start.

TWENTY-ONE

Kaitlyn. 2013. Los Angeles, California. Costa Soberbia.

I could taste the salt in the air, and feel the crashing of the distant waves reverberating through the ground, but I still couldn't see anything. I moved forward by tentatively feeling ahead with the toes of my shoes first, then slowly settling my weight onto them and just hoping I didn't slip on the slick rocks.

I hoped wrong.

Often.

Judging by the scuffs and soft swears issuing from somewhere behind me, Jackie and Carey weren't faring much better. I bumped into Zang's butt more than a few times, when he'd pause to listen for something in the air and neglect to tell us. The sounds of the ocean grew less thunderous, eventually fading into a distant lull. I heard that same sound every night, except mine was emanating from the 405 when I left the windows in my apartment open.

Traffic and the ocean.

Breaking waves and the highway.

It all faded into white noise as we traced the ragged path

deeper along the darkened bay. The rocks beneath my feet became more angular, and I realized we'd left the path behind at some point and were now crawling over shattered asphalt, the sharper corners smoothed by a few decades in the water. Damp denim pressed against my face.

Zang's butt.

I sighed and held my own hand out behind me, not willing to give Carey yet another excuse to "accidentally" press his face into my ass. A few seconds later I felt his stubble abrade my palm as he brushed into me. Hopefully he was extending Jackie the same courtesy.

I wouldn't count on it.

Zang had paused for far longer than usual, but I guess he didn't feel the need to offer us any explanation. I reached out in the dark and felt around until I contacted his thigh. I tugged on his pants like a lost child trying to get the attention of an adult. He slapped my hand away.

More silent minutes crouched painfully between sea-slick slabs of broken pavement, listening to the static of distant waves.

I reached out and tugged again, this time more urgently. Instantly Zang's lips were brushing my ear. I shuddered, just to have him so close.

"Do not do this thing you are doing," he whispered.

"Why are we stopped?" I whispered back, unsure if he was still close enough to hear me . . . or if volume even mattered to a thing like him.

A pause, and then his cool breath in my ear again.

"You said you have taken two of the angels?"

I nodded. Then felt stupid for it. I was about to speak instead, but apparently Zang saw the gesture.

"You should be better than you are," he said. "You are

too attached to your humanity. You do not accept that you can do things beyond them now. The others that came before you embraced this. This is why they were better, and you are worse."

This conversation is turning strangely critical for a "save the world" mission.

"Listen harder," he continued, before I could protest.

I did, and heard nothing. Just the terrestrial rumble of the waves beneath my feet.

"For what?" I asked, barely able to hear my own voice.

"You need to stop thinking you are human," he said. "You assume limitations you no longer have."

I felt a twist of anger in my belly.

"I *am* human, and I don't know what the hell I'm supposed to be listening for."

I felt a hand land on my ankle. It pawed around, confirming that this was, indeed, an ankle, then it proceeded carefully up my thigh until it rested on my ass. It tapped.

I turned around and whispered in Carey's general direction.

"Knock it off, pervert."

"Why are we stopped?" he whispered back.

"I don't know," I said. "Zang's being a jerk."

"I will need capable allies to help me get through here," Zang replied. "I am trying to turn you into one."

"Real funny," I said.

"Who are you talking to?" Carey asked.

"He can't hear me," Zang said. There was something off with his voice. It was so soft I could barely hear it, but so harsh it was like screaming in my ear. "You shouldn't be able to hear me, either. I'm standing ten feet away from you now."

Goosebumps tracked down my forearms.

"Now, listen for what's below the sounds you hear."

I held my breath for a moment, then exhaled slowly. I tried to find that same mental space I'd occupied when I stopped time—or whatever it was I actually did—back in Jackie's parents' kitchen. I modulated my air, letting it out slowly, bringing it in even slower, trying to erase the transitional period between inhale and exhale. I felt the broken pavement: The irregular grooves became mountains, the slight dimples became valleys. I could feel the difference in textures where they'd once painted the traffic lines, though those had surely faded years ago. I felt every tiny droplet of water in the air as it landed on my skin, though I'd been continually soaked from the moment we set foot on the beach. I listened to the grating of metal on . . .

Metal?

It was like Zang said: a sound somehow below what I could hear. It was almost a tactile sensation; I could sense it in the tiniest bones of my ear. There was something metallic out there in the dark, whirring softly. Like a weathervane spinning in the wind, though there was no wind back here. Whatever it was, its joints were old and rusted—they labored and caught, paused, and reluctantly resumed. The noise was coming from somewhere far ahead and off to the left of us, where the broken asphalt opened up. I could hear the peninsula ahead.

That's weird. That's a weird thing to be able to hear.

The remnants of those great waves that crashed against the breakwater shushed along the perimeter of a landmass extending out into the water a few hundred meters in front of us, their soft lapping showing me the shape of the place. The bay wasn't covered overhead—we weren't in a cave, but at the bottom of a gargantuan sinkhole. You could see the night sky if you looked up, but none of the light made it down this far. I got the feeling the sun didn't shine here during the day, either—it had the atmosphere of a place that lived entirely in the dark. The mustiness of a forgotten closet. The stillness of an attic you didn't know you had.

"What is that?" I said, little more than mouthing the words.

Zang still heard me.

"Look," he said.

In my head, I began to sarcastically explain what dark means to humans, but he was right: If I looked *beyond* the dark, I could actually see. Not very well—it was like the city at night, those few darkest hours before dawn still barely navigable by the secondhand light of distant streetlamps.

I could see that the four of us were squatting in a shallow ditch made of broken pavement slabs. Just beyond us, the street opened up a bit into something like a cul-de-sac. Deep cracks ran all throughout the pavement, but it was largely intact. You could see how it all happened, when the earthquake first struck and the neighborhood sank. It didn't fall straight away, as I'd initially and probably naïvely assumed. There was a landslide, and the whole place slid down a steep grade that had since eroded away. The jagged path we'd been walking was the main fault line where Costa Soberbia had broken away from the land above.

Beyond us, forming the bulk of the peninsula was a nearly intact suburban neighborhood. A few dozen houses were peppered here and there, mostly high-end ranches, new builds back in the '70s when the neighborhood had stood whole. They were now in rampant disrepair—what few rooms hadn't collapsed in the slide slowly gave way to the ocean air and neglect. Not enough sunlight down here for weeds or any other plant life, just the occasional skeleton of a tree or carefully planted shrub lining what had once been a pristine lawn. At the far end of the peninsula, where the pavement jutted farthest into the water, one building stood out from the others. It must have been a few stories tall before the fall, but only the ground floor and a few crumbling remnants of the second remained. Still, the first story seemed mostly intact—even the door remained.

There were people scattered all throughout the broken streets, wandering pointlessly like background characters in a poorly coded video game. A chubby lady in a tattered sundress stood before a rusty mailbox, opening and closing it incessantly. Three pale children in sea-worn rags huddled together in the center of the cul-de-sac, idly kicking nothing back to one another, as though they once had a ball but had long since lost it. Just beyond them, a skinny man in filthy denim shorts pushed a manual lawnmower back and forth over a dirt lot.

The whirring sound.

There were other faces, I saw now—most of them half-glimpsed through holes torn in the crumbling houses. Each was going about some forgotten task, or else just standing there blankly, waiting for input. When I tried to focus on their details, I came back with only a blurry impression and the start of a headache. If I'd been anybody else, I would have chalked that up as a trick of the dark.

"What are they?" I asked Zang.

"Unnoticeables," he said. "You've seen them before."

"Not like this," I said. "The ones we saw were almost like people. They talked to us and did things. They blended in."

"We create the Unnoticeables," Zang said. "Because it was what was done to us by the angels. We try to empty them out of their painful human complications."

The first night I met Marco. Struggling with the door in his Mercedes. His lips against mine. Something mercurial sliding past them, into my stomach, draining me . . .

I fought back sudden nausea.

"It is a pathetic attempt at re-creation," Zang continued. "What we birth is nowhere near as beautifully austere as the things the angels create. But still, the Unnoticeables are useful. We leave them enough humanity to function, to fit in, to be our eyes in your world. Most of us do, anyway. Jie does not. Jie takes as much as she can from them, and leaves them like this. Shells that only barely remember what it was to be alive."

"What are you muttering up there?" Carey whispered from behind me. The abrupt change in volume made me jump.

"Hush," Zang said.

"What?" Carey whispered.

"Hush!" I said, right in his ear.

He flinched and fell back onto his butt. His eyes went wide and he pawed around in the dark, feeling out for me.

Right. He can't see . . . because he's still human.

"So what," I said to Zang. I could see him now, perched atop an outcropping of natural rock amidst the asphalt debris. "I have super senses now?"

"No," he said. "You are not hearing or seeing anything. You are just aware of things as they are, without being limited by the crude meat machines that are your eyes and ears. If you continue consuming angels, your awareness will extend. You will see things that happened in the past, that will happen in the future—distant places, potential events. You will become unstuck from the hindrances of time and distance, as the angels are."

The outlines I had seen in Jackie's kitchen—potential paths laid out before me. The visions in the desert—the cube in cross-section, the thing beyond the edges of the universe, waiting . . .

"But for now," Zang continued, "it is enough that you are not entirely useless. Come. Do not let them see you."

"Or what? They'll mow their lawns at me?" I asked.

"They do not like new input. They do not deal well with change. They will scream. And if they scream, the tar men will come."

Oh, right. It's kinda weird that you can just forget all about the flesh-melting monsters in the shadows.

I turned back and saw Carey and Jackie, both frozen in awkward squats, straining to hear or see something through the darkness. Pity lurched about in my stomach— at first for them and how sad and limited they seemed, and then for myself and what I was becoming.

There are better places to mope than a sunken city populated by monsters, Kaitlyn.

I moved toward Carey, making just slightly more noise than I had to, to let him know I was coming this time.

"We're here," I whispered in his ear. He still flinched. "There are Unnoticeables everywhere, but these don't really have brains. We just have to avoid upsetting them and we'll be all right."

"What happens if we upset them?" Carey sneered. "They gonna call their shrinks?"

"Just shut up for now," I answered. Then added, "and also in general."

Jackie was leaning against the far side of the ditch, her head tilted back to rest against one of the pavement slabs. Her eyes looked up at nothing, unfocused. Her hands were clenched into small, white fists, pressed into the thighs of her jeans. Her jaw muscles were locked, her breathing too fast.

I should tell her, too. The only way we're getting through this is just to talk, about anything . . .

"Tell Jackie," I said to Carey instead. "We're moving."

He did, and the three of us formed a crouching, single-file line. We held hands, so as not to get separated in the dark. I motioned for Zang to come over and join us, but he just stared at me blankly until I realized it on my own. He didn't have to guide us now—I was doing his job.

Should I tell Carey and Jackie I'm the one leading them? That's a bit of a complicated conversation to conduct entirely in terrified whispers. . . .

No, let them go on thinking I was just as blind as they were. What did it matter? They already thought they were being led through the dark by something inhuman. Technically, nothing had changed.

Zang went first, strolling casually toward the end of the cul-de-sac, then skirting around its edges, moving from shadow to shadow whenever the Unnoticeables looked away. I watched him for a while before following, to get a sense of just how much the Unnoticeables could see down here. They didn't seem to be doing much better than Carey or Jackie—they navigated more by memory than sight, like walking to the bathroom at night. They stuck to small, repeating routes, if they moved at all. As long as we stayed quiet and didn't stray to within a few feet of them, they'd never know we were here.

I squeezed Carey's hand twice, letting him know we were about to move, and then gave him a second to do the same for Jackie. I went up over the lip of the ditch first, then waited for them to follow. That's how we proceeded: me taking a couple of steps ahead, until our arms were fully stretched out, then waiting for them to close the gaps. We were infinitely slower than Zang, with our awkward little group crab shuffle, but we followed his trail just fine. We edged around the three children playing their long forgotten game in the center of the round. I gave them plenty of space, just because I could. I didn't need to look into those tiny, pale faces—even if I could have seen through the haze of the Unnoticeable effect, I didn't want to register those dull and sightless little eyes.

We approached the first home on the block, little more than the framework of a garage and some crumbling walls. Two more Unnoticeables sat inside what used to be the living room: rusty springs from a rotted-away couch, the framework of a collapsed table, a burned wooden box that used to be a massive TV set. The pair sat cross-legged on the floor, facing one another, each repeatedly reaching up to touch the other's mouth. They giggled softly when they found each other, went quietly blank for a moment, then started the game again. I don't know what memory they were trying and failing to relive, and I didn't want to guess. We moved on. Past the trampled white picket fence, now gone seawater gray, and into the next yard. A rusted metal swing set there, the seats rotted away, just rusty chains hanging from a steel bar, the whole thing looking like some ancient implement of torture.

At the next house, we lost Zang.

Well, I lost Zang.

Carey and Jackie didn't even notice. They were staring straight ahead, saucer-eyed, into and at nothing, their faces slack. The way we look when we know nobody is looking. I brought them to a halt while I peered into the darkened corners, trying to find something like a human body moving with purpose.

I thought of what Zang had told me earlier, about this not being sight in the sense that I know it. It was more like an objective awareness of my surroundings that came from a different place. I focused on that concept and felt the world shudder for a second, a single frame of my surroundings flashing before me—starkly lit, washed out, everything looking oddly naked and exposed. It was like the split second after a lightning strike. But the scene was gone as fast as it came, far before I could actually process what I had seen.

I guess my mind is still mired in this pesky humanity for a bit longer, anyway.

Something moved inside the house. The three of us were squatting in a damp dirt pit that had once been somebody's immaculately groomed backyard. Between us and the home it belonged to, there was a wide stone patio littered with the shattered framework of a few lawn chairs. They formed a semicircle, surrounding a twisted metal husk that used to be an old barbecue grill. The chairs had surrendered their fabric a long time ago, now just skinny aluminum bars reaching in toward the grill as though in worship. Beyond them, an empty space where a sliding glass door had once stood. Beyond that, nothing. Parts of this house still supported a roof, and I couldn't see into the darkness beneath it.

Come on, your stupid brain is just inventing that limitation. See through it. Look harder, you weak little hum—

There it was again. Something definitely moved in there. My stubborn eyes refused to pick out details from the wall of blackness inside the house, but they did register movement. It was quick and purposeful, not at all like the languid, dreamy fugue of the Unnoticeables down here.

"Wait here," I whispered to Carey, and before he could argue, I released his hand and crept toward the doorway.

I stalled at the threshold and gave it a few seconds, hoping maybe my eyes would adjust. When that didn't happen, I dropped to all fours and crawled blindly into the dark.

The carpet had the texture of cold, week-old oatmeal. It squirmed beneath my fingers like something living, trying to escape being crushed under my weight.

Oh Christ, I hope that's carpet.

Just guessing at the layout of the house, I supposed I was crawling through the master bedroom. It was the kind of obscenely immense space nobody could possibly use, meant mostly as a status symbol for rich housewives who'd fill it with superfluous couches and end tables—like they were all just dying to host cocktail parties in their god damn bedrooms. I thought of my own cramped but cozy little cave, barely big enough for the mattress, my soft, enveloping pillows and my fluffy comf—

Stop. No use pining for things you'll never see again. Besides, dummy, you don't even sleep anymore.

At the far end of the gargantuan bedroom, a collapsed wall let more light into a long and narrow hallway, at the end of which stood a larger room, its corners lost to shadow, though most of its ceiling was open to the elements. Something skirted my vision down there—a sudden and precise movement out of the light and into the shadow.

It has to be Zang. Please, God, let it be Zang.

I pawed further into the darkness, keeping my eyes on the single unwavering square of light that was the door into the hall. I was mere inches from it, speeding my crawl just to hurry out of this awful black space, when something cold seized my wrist with a grip like iron.

God damn it all, I screamed.

Like some knock-kneed ditz in a horror film.

Screw you, Kaitlyn.

A hand covered my mouth instantly, cutting off the sound almost the second it left me. A voice whispered in my ear:

"Quiet! What are you doing?"

Zang.

But if he's here, then what . . .

Shuffling footsteps coming from outside. Heading toward us.

"The Unnoticeables—they heard you," he said. "Back to the yard, quickly. If they don't see us—"

A sound like a zipper catching fabric and Zang was gone.

His hands were violently yanked from my wrist and mouth, but not before they brought me with him—hauling me off my feet and sending me sprawling on my side in the dark bedroom.

I could hear a violent scuffle somewhere very close to me, though neither combatant made a sound: just the muffled slap of fist on flesh, clothes tearing, bodies bumping into walls.

I spun, trying to orient myself in a sea of black. My face brushed into something smooth. It smelled like wet death and gave with sickening ease under pressure. I felt around it. The bed. I pressed my back against the waterlogged mattress, grateful for some semblance of solidity. Before me, the dark was absolute and unbroken. I must be on the far side of the bed, between it and the wall. The fight continued somewhere behind me, growing in intensity.

The blows came faster now, the thumps more violent. Still no sounds from the combatants themselves, though: no groans, swears, or even exhalations of effort.

I turned and peered up over the edge of the bed. Backlit against the empty frame of the sliding glass door, a snarl of silhouetted limbs twisted and clawed at each other. I slid around to the foot of the bed, as far away from the writhing black mass as I could get, pointed myself toward the door—the dim light of the open backyard shining like a beacon—and broke into a blind, dead sprint.

You never appreciate just how little faith you have in the world until you start running as fast as you can in utter darkness. I knew, objectively, that I had just crawled through this space moments before. That this whole section of street seemed to be relatively solid, and that the odds of some bottomless pit yawning open directly in my path right now were infinitely low. But still, I didn't trust a single footfall. Every stride I took was off the edge of a cliff into an eternal black void. They were hardest eleven steps of my life.

But I made it!

Out through the doorway—oh shit, can't stop—clipping my shin on a partially collapsed deck chair, sprawling into the grill—hands up, break the fall—catching a rusty spear through the soft flesh of my underarm—spinning, watch the head—hitting hard on the stone patio, feeling teeth break, tasting blood.

I stared at nothing for a few seconds, gasping like a landed fish and clutching at the ground, my brain still trying to catch up with all the damage that my body had just incurred. A broken shape slammed into the dirt directly in front of me. It rolled end over end, sickeningly slack, before finally settling into a limp and formless heap. It was so misshapen, it took me a minute to register Zang's scrappy leather jacket in there. Then his arms. Then his head, resting right next to his skinny, bare ankles. He'd been torn nearly in half.

I turned and looked for what did it. Looming in the doorway was a bearded mountain of flesh in filthy overalls. He had to be eight, ten feet tall, and you'd have to describe his weight in small cars. A Geo Metro, at least. With one hand, he heaved a monstrous axe onto his shoulders. I don't know anything about axes. I don't know what type of axe it was, but at a glance I'd say "the kind the bad guy uses in a fantasy movie." The thing probably outweighed me.

From behind me, Zang giggled softly, though his exhalations were thick and liquid. From somewhere far ahead, a high and breathless scream. It was immediately joined by another, and another, until they formed a choir of shrieking voices.

TWENTY-TWO

Jackie. 2013. Los Angeles, California. Costa Soberbia.

At first, it really was for revenge. I'd gone full Inigo Montoya for a few hours, the anger urging me on, filling me up, making me feel full and strong. Like a badass on a mission, instead of a skinny white girl in waaaaay over her head. But then . . .

Oh god, this is so stupid. I don't even want to admit it to myself.

I stewed in fury the whole car ride from Brentwood to here, scowling like a pixie-cut Charles Bronson. I even kept it up for the first few feet down that terrifying cliffside trail. But as soon as we came to that broken section, where the ground gave out and it was just broken rocks and crashing waves like a hundred feet down? All the anger left and I was just cold and I just wanted to go home.

So why didn't you, Jackie? Huh? Why, exactly, did you do the stupidest thing in the universe and crawl down into the Village of the Damned without so much as a flashlight?

Well I'm super glad you asked, Jackie. I didn't turn back because I didn't want to look like a pussy in front of the people that just got my parents killed.

No seriously, that was it. That was the whole reason. I'd made such a big show of coming with them, that I just couldn't bear to turn to Kaitlyn and Carey and Zang—all of whom totally dealt with and pretty much deserved this life—and tell them that I'd lost my nerve. So, instead, I was just going to lose my life.

I wonder when I got this stupid, exactly? Like, when was the precise moment it happened? When I hit my head in that skateboard crash in seventh grade? When I huffed spray-paint behind the 7-Eleven to impress Tommy Zucker? Or is it just a slow degradation of brains that continues even now? Maybe I'll just get stupider and stupider until one day I eventually wind up eating out of a bucket. God, I should be so lucky to live long enough for a feed bag.

I'm definitely going to die down here. No question.

Carey's hand in mine was actually pretty comforting. I always pictured touching him to be slimy somehow, like his personality could ooze out of his pores, coating him in a thin film of beer-sweat and sexism. Like actual, liquid sexism. But no, it was relatively dry, warm, and firm without being crushing. If I didn't know better, I'd swear he was either scared himself, or else trying to comfort me.

But I do know better.

All of these people are insane and selfish. Carey might not be technically inhuman, like that Asian guy and Kaitlyn, but there's still something wrong with him inside.

Kaitlyn, Jesus—it's weird to even call her that, now. I should come up with a new name for her. If only so I don't disparage the memory of my friend by pretending I recognize this awful thing that took her place.

Crazy K?

Killer K?

Kryptonite K?

These sound like B-list professional wrestlers.

Wait, am I really going to die with these as my last thoughts?

I guess I always figured when the end came you'd be thinking about something deep, but nope—my inner monologue is just as inane as ever. That's almost comforting to know.

But hey, gotta think about something down here in the dark. I couldn't even remember what it was like to see. I'd been staring so long into solid, unrelenting black that I'd be genuinely surprised if I ever saw something again. What actually was the last thing I saw?

Carey's exposed buttcrack as he crouch-walked in front of me, into the dark.

Great. That's actually perfect. Totally fitting with the rest of my life.

They say your other senses become heightened when you take one away, but so far that was bullshit. Instead of becoming Daredevil and echolocating my way through the blackness, all I could hear was the distant rumble of crashing waves and the occasional grumble from Carey. We'd been stuck here, squatting uselessly for what were probably minutes, but felt like decades. I'd asked him what was going on when we first stopped, but he just grunted at me and squeezed my hand. Now I was too busy pretending I was still a vessel of righteous anger—and not about to pee my jorts in terror—to pursue the point.

I stared deep into the hypnotic black for so long that I honestly forgot whether I was awake or asleep. Sleeping would make so much more sense: This was just a crazy nightmare brought on by smoking too much weed while

binge-watching *Home Room* on cable. This being reality—
me squatting here blind in an underwater monster suburb?
That was the absurd option. I could almost feel the plush
fabric of my parents' couch, hear the TV's canned laugh
track after J.C. Sable called Spaz a "real nerd's nerd." Smell
my dad grilling fish in the backya—

A short, sharp scream.

A scream was bad enough: That it cut off so quick was
gut-wrenching.

Was that . . . was that Kaitlyn?

*Oh, no, Jackie, there are tons of other girls just wandering
these pitch-black ruins—this is the new hip spot to be seen, meta-
phorically speaking. Pitch-black fucking monster ruins are the
new Silver Lake, don't you know? Of course it was Kaitlyn. And
she's in big, big trouble.*

The dull twist of fear in my belly actually surprised me:
Sometimes, no matter how hard you mentally write
somebody off, your gut still calls them a friend. A surge of
panic, up from the soles of my feet, creeping across the back
of my neck, tingling in the back of my skull.

Something tugged at my hand.

Oh, right: Carey.

What is he doing?

He's holding me back.

Why is he holding me back?

Wait, back from where?

Holy shit, where am I going?

The second Kaitlyn screamed, I began automatically
crawling toward the source of the sound. Like a totally and
completely insane idiot. And like a much more insane and
far completer idiot, I was still doing it.

"Stay put!" Carey hissed.

"We have to help," I pleaded, as much to the enveloping blackness as to Carey.

Let us see. Let us go. Let us help.

"We can't," he said.

His responses were uncharacteristically short and to the point. No elaborate swears or jokes about my tits. Either he was trying to stay tactically quiet, or the bastard was scared. And if he was scared . . .

"So we're just going to cower here?" I asked. "Like a bunch of frightened little girls?"

Wait for it. Please. Please be this stupidly macho. Please . . .

"Hell no," came the response, after an aching eternity. "You were just going the wrong direction."

He jumped ahead of me and pulled on my hand— apparently hoping I wouldn't notice we were still going in the exact same direction—and I followed. Between the two of us, we probably spent more time falling than moving. Turning our ankles on unseen dips, snaring our wrists in invisible tangles, each of us loping awkwardly on three limbs, unwilling to let the other's hand go and risk them being swept away in that sea of black.

The texture of the ground changed from loose dirt to smooth pavement. I took it as a sign we were heading in the right direction, though there was absolutely no good reason to believe so. Carey had started ever so slightly veering off to the left, but I knew which way was straight. I yanked his hand. He yanked back. I yanked harder and felt him stumble. I won that argument.

He fell in line behind me then, and I trekked through the void on my knees, outstretched fingers groping in front of me—hoping against hope they'd brush up against Kaitlyn's long hair or thick shoulders instead of sinking into some unseen monstrosity. I hit something hard and splintery, felt around until I recognized it—the siding of a house—and let out a thin, quiet sigh of relief that lasted so long I felt light-headed after. We scooted along the exterior wall of the house, arms out, feeling for a door, a window, a broken section, anything. Then my fingers brushed against something strange in the darkness ahead—it was cool, slick, and rubbery. It gave a bit beneath my touch, but not completely. I moved my hands around it: some kind of skinny, warped pillar. No, scratch that, there were two of them, leading up to a point in the middle where they met and grew thicker.

My stupid brain put it together seconds too late. Seconds after I realized it was skin that I'd been touching. The cool, damp skin of something that had lived down here in the dark for years. Seconds after I dumbly pawed my way up its legs and patted it right on the belly. Seconds after it started screaming its high-pitched, painful wail.

From all around us, the others answered.

TWENTY-THREE

"Heads up!" Rosa laughed, and tossed me the severed head.

I laughed with her, but it was pretty forced. Both because it was kind of a corny joke, and also because the head was still snapping at me. I juggled it like a hot potato, trying to keep the snatching jaws away from my fingers. When I finally got the head settled, she glared at me with piercing blue eyes. She was trying to say something, probably about my mother, going by the hateful expression, but seeing as she was at least temporarily parted from her lungs, the words came out as barely a whisper. I sure as hell couldn't make out what she was trying to say over all the screaming.

Rosa had one Unnoticeable in a headlock and another beneath her knee, pinning him to the concrete. There really didn't seem to be much fight left in them, not since we'd killed the angel. A few seconds after the ball of light first blinked into existence, Rosa kicked opened the flimsy steel doors of the tool cabinet we'd been hiding in, jogged over and hopped right into the shrieking spotlight like she was cannonballing into a kiddie pool. She made it look so easy. Well, hell, in all fairness it was pretty easy these days. Had been ever since we'd taken her first angel in the ballroom of that boarded-up hotel.

Damn, but you wouldn't recognize this chick as the same one me and Zang scared half to death in her apartment. It's hilarious now, to think of her all meek on her kitchen floor, like "please don't rape me." Now she held sparring sessions with Zang and dismantled him like your little sister's Barbie doll. If I so much as thought of mouthing off to her, I only had to rub the scar on my back where she dislocated my shoulder to give it another think. She took to the life like a lonely dog to a leg, but it took forever for her to believe us.

See, I'm of the opinion that once you see one impossible thing, you gotta consider that everything else *could* be possible. After I saw my first angel, looking like a cigarette burn in the film print of reality, shimmering with planes and angles that bent your mind, making a sound like an ocean of screams—well, ever since that night I pretty much accepted anything as a possibility. If you ran up to me on the street tomorrow and told me a gang of leprechauns was chasing you, the first thing I'd do is laugh. Then I'd start lacing up my boots in preparation for some magical-midget-stomping.

Not Rosa, though. We showed her Zang with his neck broken in half and still dancing around like a goober, and she believed that he was something supernatural, sure. But that was it. She had to be shown every little thing—the people whose faces fade away the closer you look at them, the other Empty Ones walking among us—we practically had to feed her to a tar man before she believed in those. Shoulda seen her face when her first angel popped in about three feet above the soggy, rotting floorboards of The Senator Hotel.

Me and Zang, we had to throw her into the angel when the time came. No shit: I held her legs. We did the ol' heave-ho. We were supposed to let go on three, but I was late. She disappeared into the shrieking white void ass-first.

Took her days to recover from angel number one, but ever since she opened her eyes, she's been the fucking Tasmanian Devil. I thought Meryll was strong, but Rosa could pick up a damn car. A small one. Well, at least the back half, anyway. Look, she ripped this chick's head straight off with her bare hands, and that's enough for me. Oh, speaking of—one second.

I dropped the head to the cement and kicked it away. No idea if that was the right thing—did Rosa toss it at me just to fuck with me, or was I supposed to do something? But at least it wasn't looking at me with those accusing eyes anymore.

We thought we'd find Jie here, in this run-down fur storage warehouse just outside Koreatown. There were plenty of Empty Ones inside—all Chinese except this one with the blue eyes—but that telltale silver bob was nowhere to be seen. This was the fourth angel we'd taken together, and still no sign of her. Four in eight months. Zang said it was remarkable that so many were in the area at all, much less that we'd taken every one—but like I said: Rosa made it easy.

After that first angel went down, Rosa just sorta knew where the rest would be. Not just angels either: She knew exactly where to find Unnoticeables, tar men, even Empty Ones. Not specific ones, or else me and Zang would've gone straight for Jie, but it was like she had some interior monster radar. That made it so easy it almost wasn't fun anymore—the third angel we took by just disengaging the parking brake on a nearby garbage truck, watching it bulldoze through a disused mansion in Carlsbad, then picking our way through the debris until we found a ball of light that—I swear to god—just hovered there looking confused. They don't have faces, I know, but there's no way the sucker was expecting that.

It's been like that every outing. No surprises. We're finally the ones doing the ambushing. I think that's why we let it go on so long: Zang had been riding me to "talk about the girl" since the second angel, but even he'd gone quiet after the garbage truck coup. We had a good thing going, and when you get hold of a good thing, you ride it until it goes bad.

Everybody knows that, right?

"You holding up a wall or what?" Rosa said. "Little help?"

I blinked.

I walked over and gave her my hand, easing her out from under a small pile of bodies. Guess I'd spaced out for the slaughter. It's not like I'd been standing here lost in thought for hours—it had been maybe a minute since she chucked the severed head at me, and you'd think she'd give a guy a tick after that, but no. The more angels she took, the faster she got. The faster she got, the more impatient she got. Every conversation you had with her lately, she'd be checking out the windows, looking at her nails, hurrying you on like you were telling a joke she'd heard before. You could see it in her, those little bits of humanity wearing away at the edges.

But then she smiled at you, like she was smiling at me right now—and face covered in blood and gore aside, she was glorious. There were a million prettier girls, a million better sets of teeth, and a million pairs of fuller lips. But none of them knew how to work it like Rosa. They say a smile lights up a room, well, Rosa was a damn disco ball. Her light left you all giddy and disoriented, staring and smiling like a nitwit just 'cause she flashed you some teeth.

"Take a picture buddy," she said, laughing and punching me in the shoulder.

It was a friendly gesture, but she still put too much into it. Sent me back on my heels.

"Sorry," she said, and rubbed the wound. She left her hand there a little too long, and the both of us got all dumb and bashful.

"Any time you're through," Zang said.

We looked up to where the other Empty Ones had hung him, before Rosa pulled them apart: He was impaled on a metal hook meant to carry fur coats along a conveyor belt. They'd sunk the hook straight into his spine, right between the shoulder blades, making for an awkward placement— he couldn't reach back to pull it out, and he couldn't get his hands on anything to lever himself off. He needed our help to get down.

"One second," Rosa said, stepping over the twitching torso of the blue-eyed Empty One, useless without its head and limbs.

She skirted the blackened asterisk left behind on the floor when the angel exploded—taking most of the Empty Ones and more than a few tar men with it—and stopped at the conveyor controls mounted beside the big rolling door.

"I think it's this one?" she said, slapping a faded red button.

The conveyor belt clanked into action, taking Zang with it. He glided slowly around the room, arms and legs drifting out as he took the corners, his body limply swinging about the ceiling, a look of blank unhappiness on his face.

Me and Rosa, Christ, we about had a hernia laughing.

TWENTY-FOUR

Kaitlyn. 2013. Los Angeles, California. Costa Soberbia.

The axe bit into the pavers right beside my head. Stone chips stung my face like angry insects, leaving bright tracers of pain across my forehead and cheek. The behemoth in the bloodstained overalls was standing over me, one foot planted on each side of my prone body. In the several stunned, disbelieving seconds I used to stare blankly at him—cut me some slack, I was *really* not expecting to find a giant with a battle-axe lurking in the ruins of that '70s split-level—he could have strangled me, crushed my head, killed me in a dozen ways.

But no, he really, really wanted to use that axe. He took his sweet time lining himself up for the blow—maybe he didn't expect me to be able to move yet—but he didn't seem upset when I rolled away at the last second. No frustration or surprise on what little I could see of his weathered face beneath the three feet of tangled beard. Just the blank, dispassionate stare of an Empty One.

I don't know why I was surprised.

Why else would he be down here? A maniac convention?

I just didn't know they could be so . . . overt. All the Empty Ones I'd met so far had one thing in common: They wanted to be able to pass for human. At least some of the time. No way this beast could walk down the street without somebody calling the SWAT team. Or Godzilla. Whoever it is that deals with psychopaths of this magnitude.

I army-crawled out from between his legs, scrambling up and over Zang's body, which was folded nearly in half along a wide gash in his stomach. There was still some spine and meat holding him together, but not much.

"Hey Alvar," he said, still that shadow of a giggle in his voice. "Long time, no see. What've you been up to?"

Alvar didn't answer. He just patiently worked his blade back and forth until it pulled free of the stones. He repositioned himself, above Zang this time, and heaved the massive axe up over his head. I grabbed Zang's wrist and pulled. The blade came down, sinking deep into the dirt where Zang's head had just been.

"Swing and a miss!" Zang cackled.

"Would you shut up?!" I snapped. "This isn't funny, he's going to kill us."

"Well, you say 'us' . . ." Zang laughed again.

"Well, he's going to kill me for sure and probably at least mess up your day," I said. "Help me!"

I tried to drag Zang further away, but hauling a normal body is hard enough. Dragging one that's been nearly bisected is basically impossible.

Jesus Christ, I should not know these things.

The giant's axe pulled free of the dirt easily, but he didn't come after us. He just stood there staring at me. Or at a spot a thousand feet behind me—it was impossible to tell with the Empty Ones.

Quiet.

Relatively.

The reverberating grumble of waves. The distant, high-pitched, panicked screams of dozens of Unnoticeables. My own ragged breathing.

"What's he doing?" I said.

"He's thinking," Zang said. "It's not his strong suit."

"What the hell is there to think about?"

"He likes to chop people apart with his axe," Zang said, lapsing back into his dead monotone. "It is not so much about the kill as it is the actual act of dismemberment. That was all that remained of him, when the angels simplified his code: his simple enjoyment of axe in flesh. That is not working right now. He is thinking about how to make it work."

While Zang was droning on, I was butt-scooting us even further away from the behemoth. I only made it maybe twenty or thirty feet. There was muscle now in the gap between Zang's halves—wet red fibers twining about each other on either side of the spinal column.

"How long until you can walk?" I asked.

"A minute. Maybe two."

"Do we have that long?"

"That depends on how long it takes him to think of a new strategy."

On cue, Alvar turned and lumbered back toward the ruined house. He paused on the patio, amidst the druidic circle of ruined lawn furniture. He laid his axe down gently, like you'd set a baby in its crib, then hefted the mangled barbecue in both hands and hurled it at us. I ducked most of it, but an errant scrap of metal clipped me in the temple. My vision swam. I felt a warm rush flood down my neck. Blood. A moment of fierce and blinding panic.

I'm going to die. I'm going to die.

And then I remembered what I was. Or at least, what I was becoming.

Stop thinking like a victim. Stop relying on others. You're turning into a monster? Fine. Use it.

I kicked loose of Zang's body and hopped away just as a chunk of flying deck chair caught him in the face. Alvar turned around to find another projectile, so I took the opportunity to close the distance.

Okay. Okay okay okay. This is dumb. This is really dumb. But you can do it: He's big, but he's slow. If you can get up on his—

It felt like somebody had strapped a bunch of ham to a wrecking ball and then hit me with it. Just a little give at first, then behind it, the immutable solidity of iron. Alvar backhanded me away like a bothersome fly the second I was in range. He moved like the other Empty Ones. That insectile, unnatural speed was even more disconcerting on Alvar. Seeing it set off ancient, disused alarms in the primal parts of my brain. Alarms left over from when we actually had to worry about charging mammoths and pouncing tigers. Gargantuan beasts closing in on us.

I couldn't tell whether or not it was just my head spinning, or if I really was still tumbling head over heels. It seemed like I'd been going forever. I pictured myself just comically rolling all the way out of the sunken suburb, back up the trail, into the car, little stars swimming around my head.

Did anybody get the number of that bus? Cue audience laughter.

"Pfffthahahaha." Zang laughed like he just watched me fall into a pool. "What was that?!"

"Humnurb," I said. Then, trying again: "Urmble?"

There was a particularly spinny blob in the upward-sideways direction that was doing something worrisome.

Alvar, probably gathering his axe and coming over to finish me off. Nice and slow. No hurry.

"Oh." Zang's voice went flat. "I see. You thought because he was big, that he was slow. You still believe in some association between physicality and ability. As though our strength comes from muscles; our speed dictated by mass. It is the same as with your eyesight. Why will you not listen? It is because we are partially unbound from this dimension that we are able to exceed its limits. We move quickly because there is a part of us not tethered to time. We strike hard because our power can be gathered and spent instantly—that power is, has been, and always will be there. The very notion of gathering is a petty and human—"

"Shurt ump!" I yelled.

I couldn't keep my balance, even on all fours. I felt seasick. Like it was the world that bucking, and not just me.

"Okay," Zang said. "I will. Just one more thing: move."

I was so addled that I just did what he said without question, my body two steps ahead of my conscious mind. I flung myself forward, felt Alvar's axe impact just behind me. I kept going, scrabbling madly in the dirt, falling on my face, scooting on my side, trying to stand, to run, tipping over and landing hard, trying again. It felt like running in a dream. So much effort to go such a short distance. I knew Alvar was still there, right behind me, that great blade looming above my head, just about to drop.

Everything in me switched over to survival mode. No thoughts, no worries, no strategy. Just pure and selfish fear.

Run. Run. Live. I have to live. Just run, never stop, survive, survive just you against the world just you—

She screamed.

Jackie.

It stood out from the choral shrieking of the Unnoticeables by virtue of its urgency. They screamed like a matter of fact. There was fear and anger and confusion in there, but mostly it was like they didn't know what else to do. Jackie's scream was deep, purposeful, and human. It was pure fear, and it was close. Just the other side of the ruined house.

How did she—

A burning slash raced across my back and then I was airborne. I heard the sound before I even felt the blow. A fleshy thunk with all the finality of a cleaver sinking into a carving board. Then my synapses caught up and started relaying the pain. Every one of my bones echoed the blow of the axe, right down to my toes. It felt like an earthquake localized entirely within my skeleton. Then the hot, wet, flowing pain of an open wound. I hit the ground, tasted dust and mold, and then nothing.

A sleepy, welcoming void.

A scream.

Black like velvet, draping gently over me, settling—

That scream.

Sinking into a warm ocean, no pain here just—

Who keeps screaming? It's very distracting. I'm trying to die here.

Oh, right.

My best and only friend. The only constant in my life. The one who pushed me to do more. To be more. To treat settling like a small death.

And now here's the big one. And it's so nice. I miss my bed.

But she needs me.

It felt like dragging an anchor up through a mile of mud, but I managed to open my eyes. Just blurry dirt.

That's helpful.

Move your head. Now your hands. On your feet. There's work to be done.

Alvar had turned away from me to focus on Zang, who was actively knitting himself together: both hands sunk wrist-deep in his own guts, shoving things into places, yanking on his pelvic bone, trying to get it to line back up with his spine. All the while Alvar thunking toward him with weary inevitability. It was like something out of a safari special on the Discovery Channel—you know that long shot they love so much, of a lone elephant trundling through a wasteland with no destination in sight? That's what it felt like, watching him walk. But I knew Alvar could move like a frightened spider if he wanted.

Why doesn't he? Is it just scarier this way?

Jackie screamed again. She was trying to make words: "No" or "stop" or "help"—but they kept getting cut off. Muffled by something. Like she was drowning and I could only hear the screams in the brief span between waves.

Up now. Up. Now.

But no matter how much willpower I put into it, one of my legs just plain refused to work. I managed to push myself upright despite feeling like a bloody Jenga tower in mid-collapse, and ran to Jackie's rescue.

Well, I guess it was more of a hobble.

The nerves in my spine lit up like Sunset Boulevard, but I made it all the way through the dirt yard, skirted the side of the house, and came out onto the cul-de-sac. It looked like somebody was holding a small rave for tuberculosis patients. A dense mass of emaciated and pasty bodies, all knees and ribs and skulls, jostling for space around some central, unseen point. It was from there—the vortex at the center of this maelstrom of angry, screaming, faceless monstrosities—that Jackie screamed for help.

Stumpy to the rescue.

With my busted leg, I couldn't even get up enough momentum to barrel into the huddle. Instead I just limped up to the wriggling mass and started prying bodies aside. The Unnoticeables weren't strong—in fact, they all felt strangely fragile, like a strong wind would just blow them away. But it didn't matter. There were so many of them. I guess simply trying not to die from Alvar's axe-blow was using up whatever powers I had, because I had never felt weaker. Like I was punching in a dream. But by staying low, well below the nest of outstretched arms and grasping hands, I managed to push my way in.

Jackie's screams no longer oscillated between moments of clarity and muffled struggle. Just up ahead, beyond the forest of skinny, colorless legs, the pack condensed. They spilled over one another, all jostling for space, trying to get to Jackie. I finished slithering through the gauntlet of weakly kicking feet and bony knees, then climbed what used to be a teenage boy, still wearing the ratty remains of a bedazzled pair of JNCOs—

Jesus, did he just have terrible taste, or has he really been down here since the '90s?

—pushed up over his thin avian shoulder blades, slapping away bony hands that scratched and clawed and snatched and . . .

I was through: perched with one foot on the teenager's shoulder, the other useless leg dangling across his back. Using both of my hands to steady myself over a bobbing sea of angry bodies, I looked down into the eye of their hurricane. A circle of hands, closing inward from every direction. At their center, just a glimpse—one watery eye, open wide—of Jackie's face. The rest of her lost behind a wall of clutching fingers, pushing her down, holding her mouth shut.

Smothering her.

Ah, well. Nothing for it.

I let myself fall straight into the cat's cradle of suffocating hands. My weight broke their grasp, just for a second, but the fingers came flooding back in to fill the space immediately. I hovered over Jackie protectively while dozens of fingertips dug deep scratches into my back. Probing into the still-open wound there, pulling it apart. Reaching into me, into my fat and muscle, worming their way deeper—

I wished Jackie would stop screaming. It was just getting them more worked up.

Then I realized she had.

And it was me screaming now.

A place of stillness. Divorced from body. Please.

Please work. Please work. Pleaseworkplease—

The close air, thick with sweat and stale exhalations, seemed to change texture. It took on a crisp quality. Ozone, maybe. Like what comes out of a freshly opened box of electronics. Sterilized, somehow. Artificial.

That's because you're not actually breathing anymore, Kaitlyn.

I opened my eyes and saw Jackie's face, inches from mine, frozen in a grisly mask of pure terror: her teeth bared, nostrils flaring, eyes bulging . . .

But she wasn't moving. Nothing was. The gallery of blurry faces around me, like partially erased portraits, had all gone still. Their hands, seized up like arthritic claws, reached no further.

My place of stillness. Removed from time. Just behind and a little over from this dimension. My physical body was nailed down: held in place by the grip and weight of dozens of Unnoticeables. But my point of view could shift where I willed it, like controlling the camera in a video game. I ducked through the storm of skeletal bodies and panned around at ground level, finally finding what I was looking for . . .

Carey.

One of his fists was sunk deep into the crotch of the nearest Unnoticeable. The other was cocked back, aimed square at another crotch, paused in mid strike. Both of his filthy black Converse, each more duct-tape than shoe, were—you guessed it—crotch-bound. I guess he had decided that this was his plan. This was how he was going out. Just destroying as many crotches as he could.

I panned back to my own body, and felt a bizarre twinge of pity. It was hard to believe that was me. Hard to believe that I fit into that sad little package. She looked so wretched. Her posture stooped and broken. Her broad shoulders folded against the body beneath her, trying and failing to protect her friend. Her blond hair matted with filth. Her clothes torn, her back bloody. And all these wraiths around her—each pitiful in their own right—pressing down, crushing her with their weight.

It was actually kind of pretty. Like one of those melodramatic Renaissance paintings: everybody just wailing and throwing themselves on the ground, beating their breasts and tearing at their clothing.

Such high drama to them, when in reality they're all such petty things.

We're all such petty things.

It's easy to feel detached when time is optional. It's so much more peaceful here, in the stillness. I could stay forever, only forever wouldn't exist, so I wouldn't even have to worry about that.

But no: I owed that pathetic little blond girl something, and I had to deliver.

I let my brain fuzz out. Kind of like trying to see those Magic Eye paintings—you have to unfocus while still focusing, which is hard to explain, but automatic to do once you understand how. Ghostly images began to spring forth. Faintly glowing silhouettes emanating outward from every body and every object, reflecting all of the potential paths they could take. Most of them ended bloody, with the Unnoticeables—their inherent weakness nullified by their magnitude—tearing the girl (*me, that's me, remember that's me, it's so important to remember*) and her friend to pieces.

"Nullified?" I don't think I've ever used that word in my life.

So many of the potential pathways ended that same way, but with minute variations. In one path, the girl's body (*my body mine mine*) was dragged a few feet away before dismemberment. Another path, and the Unnoticeables kill the friend first, before turning on the girl. In this one they start with her mouth; grubby fingers flooding in like foul water, blocking her airways. In that one they start from her feet—a tug of war that only ends with the splash of blood. But there are always other paths. And they will show themselves if you let them.

A boulder comes loose from above the sunken city and triggers a landslide. The majority of the Unnoticeables, along with the girl and her friend, are crushed. The diffuse remnants of a rogue wave enter the bay and flood the cul-de-sac, leaving all ankle deep in brine. The girl is held facedown, and drowns instead.

Paths upon paths upon paths—an infinitude of images tracing ghost routes across the world.

And then, finally, one stands out from the others.

It is utterly preposterous. There are only four permutations of this possible path. Four! That is how unlikely it is to occur. And yet now it is likely, because I am focusing on its image.

—*That's right, I! I am me me remember me come back to me*—

I bring one frame from this alternate reality into our own and splice them together, creating a single jump point—a minute change that cascades forever, transforming everything. Instantly, billions of other pathways emerge. It is tempting, so tempting, to stay here and just watch them. To see how things unfold here, in this peaceful place of observation, rather than down there, in the filth and the pain, where things unfold on you.

But I can't.

For some reason?

I owe the blond girl. I owe her friend.

(Me. That's me. Her name is Jackie.)

And I'm out of it. Just the lingering echo of stillness and the smell of ozone.

I immediately regretted everything about that decision.

Jesus Christ there are fingers burrowing into my flesh like worms.

Somewhere at the edge of this orgy of horror—I couldn't see anything but soapstone-colored hands, swollen knuckles, dirty fingernails, glimpses of yellow teeth, blurry faces—I felt a commotion building. The screams of the Unnoticeables were changing. Cutting off abruptly, or else rapidly fading away like a passing motorcycle engine. Then the bodies parted, and I understood why.

Alvar was thrashing through the crowd of Unnoticeables, roaring like an enraged bear and clawing at something on his back that he couldn't quite reach. His arms were too broad and his neck too thick for that kind of mobility. He thrashed and spun, kicked and punched, jumped and howled—all while trampling the gathered Unnoticeables like weeds.

Zang was mounted up between Alvar's shoulders like a cowboy, his limp legs fluttering behind him like a flag. One hand was firmly twisted in Alvar's long, dirty black hair. The other held something small and white that jutted out from the back of Alvar's neck. Zang was laughing and vigorously wrenching it about like a joystick.

It was a piece of Alvar's spine.

I saw all of this in the precious few seconds after the grasping hands cleared away, but before the butt came crashing down on my face.

Alvar had smacked one of the Unnoticeables aside without a thought, and sent her flailing through the air right at me. I still had Jackie's head clutched in my lap, and my instincts were to cover her face, when I should have been protecting my own. I caught a full butt to the head and went down.

After the pulses of dizziness ebbed, I shoved the Unnoticeable off of me. She didn't protest. Alvar had broken her neck.

Jesus, he didn't even mean to.

Jackie had fared better than me, at least in the flying corpse-butt arena. She was laying facedown almost exactly where I'd left her, apparently untouched by Alvar and his tornado of bodies. But she wasn't moving. I crawled over and put my fingers to her neck. Her pulse was strong and steady. I couldn't see any wounds. Maybe she'd passed out from lack of air.

Or maybe just from sheer terror. Do you blame her?

Zang and his furious mount were rampaging through the remains of a dilapidated ranch house across the street. If we were going to move, now was the time. I yanked on Jackie's arm, but I didn't have the strength to drag her.

"Carey," I yelled. "Help!"

An answering groan from beneath a pile of twitching bodies. Carey dug himself out and flopped on the pavement, looking about how I felt.

"Over here!" I called.

He swiveled his head all around, looking straight at me for a second . . . and then past.

Oh, right.

"Kaitlyn?" Carey asked. "That you?"

"Yes, and Jackie," I answered. "She's hurt and I can't move her."

"Move yourself then," he said, and spat blood onto the cracked pavement. "Come toward the sound of my voice. We'll try to find cover and figure out what the fuck just happened. If Zang's still around—"

"He is," I said. "But there's this big guy with an axe and they're fighting across the street . . ."

"Holy shit!" He laughed. "Alvar's still kickin'? I mean, I don't know what would ever *stop* him, but I haven't seen that bastard in fore—"

"This isn't a high school reunion, asshole! Come help me with Jackie!"

"Hey, wait." Carey peered in my general direction, his eyes trying but never quite landing on me. "You can see down here?"

Crap. I don't have time to explain this. I don't even know how to explain it.

"Yes, but it's complicated. It's not like normal—"

"No, I got it," Carey said. He scowled at nothing in particular. "It makes sense, actually."

"It . . . does?"

"Well, all right," he said. "We got a pair of eyes now. Guide me over to you."

He crawled toward me, patting the ground in front of him first to make sure it was solid.

"It's safe," I said. "Just a few little cracks here and there. Nothing in your way."

"Okay," he said, but he just kept doing it—pawing at the ground like a curious dog.

"Hurry! Christ." I struggled to my feet and limped over to him.

Hey, a limp's a step up from a hobble! I guess the leg's healing. That's . . . something.

I grabbed his arm and he flinched. I helped him stand. His leather jacket was soaked with what, best-case scenario, was just stagnant seawater. Beneath it, his arms felt shockingly thin. The jacket was his armor; I'd hardly ever seen him with it off. He felt so much smaller than he looked.

I guided us back toward Jackie, keeping an eye on where I'd last seen Alvar and Zang. They weren't there anymore. In fact, the house wasn't there, either. Half the street was gone, too. Not destroyed, just gone. Lost in shadow. I checked behind us: same deal. Even with my so-called night vision at its best, I'd only been able to see for a hundred feet or so down here. Now the surroundings faded to black in only half that. And the distance was shrinking.

"Shit," I said. "We need to hurry. I think I'm losing my

sight. Everything's going black around the edges."

Carey paused. I pulled at his arm. His eyes were all pupil.

"Come on, we have to go. . . ."

"You sure it's your sight going?" he said, so quietly I might not have heard him if not for my augmented hearing.

Oh, I guess that's still working? Weird . . .

"Yeah, I could see across the street a minute ago and now it's just . . . black. . . ."

Kaitlyn, you idiot.

I could spot the trick if I watched the edges: the point where the blackness just touched the pavement. If I looked there, I could make out their feet moving as they slowly marched toward us. The world wasn't going dark. The tar men were surrounding us. An encroaching tide of darkness, closing in from every side. Now that I was paying attention, I could even discern the faintest glint of metal on the faces of the ones closest to us. Those gears they had in place of eyes were locking together, and spinning up.

It sounded like an old steam whistle—a sound I only knew from Looney Tunes reruns. You know, that cartoon hand reaching out and yanking a chain; animated clouds coughing out of a bright red cylinder as it howls its tune, announcing the end of a shift.

But beneath that sound, there was another, larger tone. I imagined a massive oil tanker clipping its hull against the rocks. The grinding of metal on stone. It made me a little sick—just that slight vertigo you get when you stand up too fast. But Carey went down like he'd been Tased. He slipped right out of my arms and shocked his head on the pavement. Other tar men were now picking up the song, adding to the chorus. The sound bounced off the walls of the cavernous space, amplified, built on itself. Now the feeling in my gut graduated into full blown nausea. The world was a tilt-a-whirl. I lost my footing. My knees felt like jelly. It was hard, but not yet impossible to stand.

We still had time to run. But Carey was writhing on the ground with his hands over his ears, and I couldn't move Jackie on my own. I grabbed one of his arms to try to drag him up, but he fought me away, immediately clamping his hands over the sides of his head the second he was free. I grabbed the collar of his jacket instead, curling my fingers into the rough-worn leather there. I tried to pull, but my stupid legs went sideways again.

The tar men were advancing on us glacially. But still advancing.

I've always been proud of myself for my strength. Not like other girls. Not weak or fragile. And now, when it actually counts, I'm too god damn weak. Even if I could stand, I could never drag both of them out of here. I'm not strong enough to—

But it's not strength. Not really. That's what Zang said, right? It's not about how big my muscles are, or how exhausted I am. It's about energy. Energy that doesn't care whether it's used in one big burst right now, or eked out slowly over a span of laborious hours. It's always there. Right there. In that still place, just waiting for me to—

I felt my grip strengthen, the leather of Carey's jacket squealing in protest as I twisted it into my fists. I planted my feet, prepared to heave with all my might, and found we were already moving. It felt so strange. Like I'd set myself on autopilot and stepped away. There was no physical effort associated with the feat. I just thought about dragging him and it was happening. My biceps weren't even bulging beneath the thin fabric of my shirt.

How far could I take this? Could I be as strong, as fast as Zang?

The thought was a little exhilarating, and a lot terrifying. I settled for having enough strength to drag one wriggling, aging punk rocker and—god willing—one skinny, unconscious actress.

The tar men sounded like a million rusty nails being dragged across a chalkboard that was being fed into a garbage compactor. But as soon as I tapped into the still place to siphon its energy, most of the vertigo retreated. I still felt crappy, but it had devolved from "standing on the deck of a ship during a violent storm," to "laying in bed after six drinks." I lost my balance, corrected, veered off course, and stumbled, but I finally managed to get us over beside Jackie. I hooked my fingers through her shirt and around her bra. It was the best purchase I could think to get with one hand, and she was too unconscious for this to hurt. She'd probably complain about her boobs for the next few weeks, but that's a small price to pay.

Energy. Not created or destroyed. Not bound by time. A shimmering pool that does and will always exist, just waiting for you to take a sip.

Deep breath.

Take a sip.

Holy hell I'm doing it, I'm really moving them both!

. . . and now the little problem of where to go.

I'd been so focused on getting us out of here that I didn't stop to consider what that actually meant. I scanned the perimeter of darkness closing in on us. It was broken only by a few pairs of brass-colored halos—the tar men's gears whirring away. The blackness was absolute. Even if the tar men were standing perfectly shoulder-to-shoulder, little gaps should have opened as they shifted. Tiny spaces between their legs and arms where I could glimpse the street behind them. But there were none, and that meant . . .

It wasn't a circle of tar men surrounding us. It was a flood. There were ranks upon ranks of them, all crowded up on each other so tightly that they blocked out the whole world.

There can't be that many down here. They wouldn't fit. Where were they all coming from?

I pictured dark ichor flowing out from wounds in the rocks, pooling on the pavement, rising up to take shape. I pictured black soldiers in formation on the sea floor, just waiting there, silent, at the bottom of the ocean, until the moment they were called. I pictured what would happen to us when there was nowhere left to run—hundreds of acidic arms reaching out, our flesh running away in pink streams.

The circle was maybe forty feet in diameter now, with us at its center.

I almost laughed.

All those health classes we had to attend back in junior high, warning us about the dangers of smoking. Those gross slide shows of goopy and scarred lungs. They worked so well that I'd never even thought about touching a cigarette. And yet if I'd only been a smoker, I could just—

Wait.

Carey, you idiot. You better not have—

I worked my fingers free of his collar—my nails had actually pierced through the leather in a few places—and frantically rifled through his pockets. He didn't make it easy: kicking, twisting, and writhing in pain, even with his hands clamped so hard against his ears that his fingertips were turning blue. His coat held a museum of worrisome objects. Some fuzzy, some spiky—one pocket was inexplicably wet. Not with seawater, but some kind of lubricant. I forced my mind to stop considering the implications, and focus on the search. Then I found it, stowed in the little coin pocket of his blue jeans.

A faded, scratched, and generally mangled flip-top lighter. Once upon time, something had been embossed on its surface, but it had long since worn away. Just a handful of letters and squiggly lines remained. All that time stumbling through the dark, and he never thought to use his lighter.

Maybe he knew it wouldn't really help, but just draw unwanted attention.

Maybe he was just an idiot.

It didn't matter. Right now, I could kiss him, if I wasn't absolutely positive that would net me some kind of disease.

I knelt down beside him, covering he and Jackie with my body as best I could, and flicked the flint. It sparked, but didn't catch. The tar men were ten, maybe twenty feet away and still closing. Reaching out for us, probing the air with their stubby fingers. Already stooping to pour over our bodies like lava.

Flick.

Flick.

Catch.

A weak little flame bobbed in a sea of black. It only cast a small aura of light that was almost immediately swallowed by the gloom.

It wouldn't have helped, Carey, if that's any consolation.

I said a little prayer to an uncertain deity, and tossed the lighter underhand—*so gently, please don't go out, little flame*—toward the gathering black.

It bounced on the cement, cartwheeled through the air, and impacted one of the tar men at knee height. A single tiny spark hovered there, embedded in the liquid of its body. Then a pool of fire spread out in every direction, coloring in limbs that I couldn't even distinguish seconds ago with dancing orange and flickering blue. The tar man spun slowly in place—just a second of something like human confusion there in its body language—and then erupted like a roman candle. The flames funneled upward, the tar man just a pillar of twisting fire at the base of a burning tornado.

More tar men followed suit, each catching fire and then exploding with an intake of air that sounded like fabric whipping in hurricane gales. In seconds the circle of black had transformed into a solid wall of blinding light and searing heat. I gathered Jackie's and Carey's faces closer to me, shoving them into my chest and stomach. I could feel the outer layer of my skin beginning to sear—that uneasy hot flush of a bad sunburn—and then, thankfully, quiet. Darkness.

The inferno ended as abruptly as it began, flash-burning through its fuel source in mere seconds. I could smell my own singed hair and feel the sickly heat of minor burns building in my exposed arms and neck. I did a quick pat down of Jackie, Carey, and myself, extinguishing smoldering spots on the frayed cuffs of Carey's jeans and feeling Jackie again for a pulse.

Doublethump. Still there.

"Holy shit," Carey said. His pupils had gone from encompassing his whole eye to just tiny pinpricks of black in the middle. "Was that god?"

"No," I said. "Just a lot of tar men going away at once."

"I have the biggest erection right now," he said.

I checked. He did not.

"Oh shit, did you use *my* lighter for that?" he asked.

I laughed, but he looked oddly serious.

"Yeah," I said. "It's probably a pool of molten metal now, but I figured you wouldn't mind, what with saving your life and all."

He mulled it over, then finally shrugged.

"At least she went out big," he said.

My night vision never had been compromised. With the tar men gone, I could see all the way across the little cul-de-sac now. It was littered with piles of smoking meat.

"Oh my god," I said. "The Unnoticeables! I didn't even think—they were in that crowd when it went up, I—"

"Stop," Carey said. "If there were that many tar men around, the poor bastards would've been puddles by the time you lit up anyway. And even if they were still kicking, those were just shells. You didn't kill them. Jie did that job a long time ago. Don't waste effort feeling guilty about it now. We've got a lot more to do before we earn that luxury."

"Right," I said. I shuffled this atrocity to the back of my mind, where it joined all the others. If I was lucky, I'd live long enough to be plagued by nightmares for the rest of my life.

If I ever slept again.

"I don't see Zang and Alvar," I said.

"Fucking *good*," Carey said. "We've got a narrow window of quiet and we're going to use it."

"No we're not," I said.

"What?"

"*We* aren't doing anything. You're worse than useless down here. I'm sorry," I said, seeing his face twist up. "You know it's true. You can barely crawl. And we just blew the element of surprise, so now I have to move fast. I can't do that with you."

"Don't you fucking dare to presume to worry about me," Carey spat. "I've been doing this since you were—"

"I'm not worried about you," I said. "I'm worried about Jackie. She's still unconscious. You think I can do this while guiding you *and* dragging her? If I'm going to finish this thing, I can't be responsible for either of you. I need you to stay here. I need you to protect her."

"I can provide you with dozens of witnesses that say I'm a crap babysitter," Carey said. But there was resignation in his voice.

"I know, but you're all I've got," I said. "If you don't stay, then I can't go."

"Well god damn," Carey said. He spat on the ground and wiped at his mouth with the sleeve of his jacket. "All these years spent getting here, and now I'm gonna miss the headlining act. Ain't that just a bitch?"

I smiled. He couldn't see it. I put my hand on his shoulder. He nodded.

I took his arm and snagged Jackie by her bra-harness, then pulled them both into the nearest ruin. I found a kitchen counter that hadn't decayed as badly as the rest of the house, and left them tucked beneath it. The cabinet doors had rotted away, but it was the best I could do. When I left, Carey had Jackie's head in his lap. He stroked her hair in a shockingly non-perverse way.

He must've forgotten I could see him.

I stepped out into the ruined cul-de-sac, now dotted with cancerous stains and smoking bones. At the far end of the sunken suburb, beyond where the semicircle opened out into a narrow road, one intact gray building squatted like a stubborn old man who refused to vacate his crumbling home, even as the bulldozers were closing in. I scanned the broken windows of the houses on either side of me for signs of life, but found nothing.

So what's stopping you, Kaitlyn? Just waltz on up, knock on the door, ask if the angels can come out to play.

The air was thick with waterlogged wood and salt, undercut with notes of barbecue. It was sickeningly appealing. Turns out, put a gun to my head, I can't smell the difference between grilled pork chops and seared human flesh.

That's a little fact I could have gone forever without knowing.

At least my legs were working again. My back still hurt—a diagonal slash of pain running from below my right shoulder blade up to the left side of my neck. I felt around and found a raw, sensitive divot where Alvar's axe had struck. But it wasn't bleeding anymore.

I should not be healing this fast.

I should not be healing at all.

Car accidents don't kill you. Axe wounds don't kill you. Infernos don't kill you. Exploding other-dimensional angels don't kill you. So why are you standing here, afraid of what's inside that building?

I laughed a little.

It was true: I now had more in common with the monsters than I did humans. Let's go say hi to some new friends.

She was maybe sixty years old, but wearing it well. Smooth, clear skin, save for a couple of deep grooves in the forehead and on either side of the nose. A handful of delicate crow's feet branching out from her eyes. Salt-and-pepper hair tied up in a matronly bun. She wore a faded pink sweater, all pilled up, but clean and unwrinkled. Her pupils were black pools that looked out onto deep space. She was an Empty One. An unfeeling human suit, draped over pure absence.

And yet, I swear she was surprised when she opened the door.

What? I went with Plan A: I knocked.

"H-hello?" she said.

"Hi." I gave her a little half-wave. "I'm Kaitlyn. I guess I'm here to kill you all."

She looked me up and down—decently muscled blond girl, a bit on the taller side, but wet, bloody, dirty, and desperate. I could tell she immediately wrote me off as a non-threat.

"I can't say we were expecting you all the way down here," the woman said. She checked over her shoulder, waiting for approval from somebody, and apparently got it. "But I suppose you should come in."

She stepped aside, opened the door a bit wider. There were no lights on in the building. There was no need. The only things down here were at home in the dark.

From the inside, I could tell what the building had originally been: a big central lounge for a gated housing community. The reception area still stood mostly intact— the only signs of damage some ceiling tiles that had collapsed and spilled insulation all over the floor. To either side of the desk were two hallways that hadn't fared as well. A sign above one read "gymnasium." The other was illegible. Behind the reception area, the foyer opened onto a large, hexagonal main room. Lounge furniture scattered all about—brown leather recliners, wracked with age-splits that sprouted pillowy yellow stuffing like cave fungi; a massive white sectional gone colorless with dust and mold; fancy oaken end tables knocked over and pushed against the walls. There were floor-to-ceiling windows all along the west side of the room. Broken now, and looking out on nothing but still black water and sea rock.

At the center of the room, a small crowd gathered around a massive gray-brick fireplace. It seemed like they were all Empty Ones, save for three people: an old man laying facedown on the floor, and a pair of handsome Indian guys. I say "old," but it's not like he was ancient. Or maybe he'd just taken really, really good care of himself. His skin was still smooth, wrinkles only creeping in at the edges of his eyes and mouth. A neatly trimmed beard gone entirely gray, maybe before his time. He wore a dark blue jumpsuit that looked ambiguously military. The younger guys were both just . . . beautiful. Their faces expert testimony to the value of good genetics. Just looking at them, you didn't get the sense that they worked for it—primped and preened and moisturized daily—they simply *were beautiful.* Sweeping jawlines and strong foreheads. There was something in the set of their eyes that said they were family. One sported a single prominent dimple, even when he wasn't smiling. Which he wasn't, obviously. He stared blankly ahead, lips set in a perfect line. I wondered what he was staring at, before I remembered that he couldn't see a damn thing down here. The other young guy was a bit on the waify side. Not skinny—not exactly—but his thin wrists and long neck gave him the look of a philosopher. He looked like he was thinking important thoughts, even as he sat there on the edge of the fireplace, quietly weeping. Dimples lifted one arm—still not so much as a blink—and rested it on the lip of a large set of gears.

The gears.

Jackie, eyes blank, hand outstretched, feeding herself to the whirring cogs already lubricated with blood—

These weren't nearly as ornate as the set I'd seen in the

compound's chapel, back when all this began. There had been dozens of gears in that machine, all polished and gleaming. Here there were just two huge interlocking wheels, seemingly hewn from the same dark rock as the cliff walls. No clever hidden mechanism to activate these: just a single crank. But I could see a litany of large, dark stains painting the edges of the cogs. They did the same job.

The Empty Ones were a veritable melting pot: There was the elderly lady who first let me in; a clean-faced blond guy in an immaculate pinstriped suit—even his understated tie-pin certainly worth more than everything I owned; three Asian girls done up in a style somewhere between punk, raver, hippie, and gothic schoolgirl—lots of neon hair dye, dangling earrings, torn tights under plaid skirts, spiked bracelets and combat boots; a middle-aged black guy with a beer gut poking out between his rumpled cargo shorts and T-shirt; and a man (at least I assumed it was a man) in a full firefighter's uniform—respirator, helmet, and all. I could see nothing of his face. A dull red axe dangled from his hand.

The worst was the little girl, still awkward child-skinny but just starting to grow into it. She was feigning adulthood, wearing it like a costume. Hair in a ponytail. Too-tight jeans and T-shirt, clunky sneakers, colorful bracelets marching up one wrist. It broke my heart to look at her and see nothing in those blue eyes.

She smiled at me. They all instantly matched the gesture. There was something unsettlingly similar in their expressions. Their faces might all be different—teeth in varying hues of yellow, lips different sizes—but that was the same smile. Too wide at the edges—so strained it looked painful. Eyes staring intently, without a hint of joy in them.

"Amazing," said a woman's voice. She stepped out from behind the pair of immense stone gears. "How did you get past my watchers? And the tar men?"

"Oh, they're all dead," I said.

"And Alvar?" she asked.

"Last I saw, Zang was riding him like a mechanical bull."

"Zang," she hissed. She snapped her teeth a half dozen times. The sharp clack of enamel on enamel made me wince.

The old black guy bust out laughing, his unblinking eyes never leaving me. He stopped abruptly after a few seconds, when he realized the others weren't joining him.

"You," Jie said, "are a much bigger pain in the ass than I gave you credit for."

"Thanks?"

Her smile lapsed for just a second. Her eyes rolled up in her head. Then she was back.

"So what's the plan now?" she asked.

I could tell her adopted persona was trying for sexy and playful. She twisted her knees inward, cocked her hips, twirled her hair, and bit her lip. Probably drove middle-aged perverts mad. But it was like watching bad CGI try to be sexy. The poses were memorized, but the movements in between were stilted and uncertain.

"I left the planning stage behind a long time ago," I said.

"This is the thing that breaks the tools of the Mechanic?" Jie said. Her voice lost its coquettish quality. Featureless and barren. Wind blowing over salt flats. "This is the thing that killed Marco? This is unimpressive. This is small and blind. This came to its death and it does not even know why."

The Empty Ones all went as still as statues. I felt the air thicken. That moment of unnerving silence when a big cat freezes just before pouncing.

The waifish guy began moaning, a constant hum that seemed to come more from his chest than his mouth. He knit his fingers in his hair and pulled. His heels bounced nervously. The Empty Ones paid him no mind. They studied body language, but they never truly understood it. I did, though, loud and clear. He was getting up his nerve. He was going to make a move. He just needed the chance.

"Wow, you guys sure talk a lot," I said, channeling every cocky Hollywood douchebag I'd ever waited on.

Jie bent over, the movement so fast I could barely see it, and gagged. Both of her arms shot out to the side like she was being drawn and quartered. She froze like that for a second, then broke and leapt on top of me. Fingernails clawing into my breast bone. Her mannequin smile still etched in place, frothy drool eking out the edges. The other Empty Ones were only a fraction of a second behind her. Their hands grabbed my legs, pulled my hair; their teeth snapped at my face, nipped my skin.

I struggled, but couldn't shake them. The problem wasn't strength, or even speed, but reaction time. I couldn't think as fast as they could move.

I kicked the tubby black guy off my legs and bucked my hips, throwing Jie off-balance, then I twisted, trying to crawl free, but the lady in the pink sweater clutched my face in both hands and began rapidly head-butting me. Everything went blurry. Then something cold and hard hit the floor—I felt the impact in my teeth. A frigid sensation went cascading up my arm, broken glass inside my nerves.

The firefighter had brought his axe down, neatly severing my right hand. Blood gushed out rhythmically, matching the beat of my heart.

And then, finally, the waif spotted his chance. The Empty

Ones were all so lost in this feeding frenzy—*feeding on me, oh god, my hand, don't think, don't think about that*—they didn't see him lean forward and touch Dimples' face. There was caution in the gesture, a tenderness that drifted toward fear. He needed to see if Dimples was okay, but dreaded the answer. I'd had them pegged as related, at first. Cousins. Brothers, even. That one touch told me I was all wrong. Dimples blinked hard and looked around, like he'd only been daydreaming and somebody had just said his name. They couldn't have seen a thing in that darkness, but instantly knew the other by touch. They embraced for just a moment, then began blindly crawling away from the commotion.

The air shattered.

Light so bright it would've blinded you on a sunny afternoon—down here, after all this time in the dark, it was like a supernova. If any of us had been using our actual pupils, our vision would've been utterly obliterated. We'd be seeing nothing but ghostly, luminous spots for days. That's probably how it would be for the two Indian guys, who made it halfway to the reception desk before the angel arrived. The Empty Ones and I fared better. We all stopped fighting and stared right into that ball of light, just a few feet in diameter, hovering in total stillness above the prone body of the bearded man in the jumpsuit.

"The choice is made!" Jie screamed.

The Empty Ones fell to the ground. They beat their fists on the floor, wailed like Pentecostals, kicked their legs in the air like they were pedaling invisible bikes. Eyes bugged out, tongues wagged—the chubby black guy bit his clean off, but didn't seem to mind, or even notice—fingers broke as they tried to claw straight into the cement floor.

They had forgotten all about me.

Jie was standing a few feet away, her back to me, reaching out toward the angel with one hand while the other twitched and flopped at her side like a dying bird. Her whole body was shuddering so violently that she seemed to blur about the edges.

The jumpsuit guy lying beneath the angel writhed weakly for a moment, plucking at the idea of consciousness. Maybe he was just in shock and couldn't process it right away, but he didn't seem all that surprised to see the angel hovering there. He cocked his head, intently listening to something I couldn't hear above the static.

The sound the angel emits, but only while you're looking at it.

I used to think it was like riotous waves carrying loads of tumbled glass, crashing on the shore. Just random noise. But now there was something more in there—in between the screaming and the wind—that was almost discernible. Almost like voices. A radio broadcast just two ticks off the proper frequency. If only you could turn the knob, tune it in, the song would come in clear. The impossible angles that churned incessantly at the angel's core were likewise less impenetrable. I remember that feeling when I first saw them—barely glimpsed, oversaturated, and hidden in a distant haze—they still instilled a sense of confusion and terror. They didn't line up right. They didn't move in a way that the human brain could process. It was something so far beyond us that, when confronted with its existence, our logic centers shut down and the animal brain took control.

Run, the animal brain said. Just run.

But it was like I could see farther into the angel now, to the place where those angles finally connected up. And seeing how they connected, the fear subsided. I didn't understand it, not quite yet, but for the first time I got the sense that it could be understood.

If only I got closer.

No time like the present.

I rolled onto my back, kicked my feet up into the air, then snapped forward in one smooth motion. I'd practiced it a thousand times. Hollywood loves that little hand-spring. It's stuntwoman 101. I was on my feet and running instantly, leaping past Jie, toward the angel, into the angel. . . .

And then I wasn't. Something had me by the back of the neck, holding my full weight just inches off the ground and shaking me gently, like a naughty puppy about to be scolded.

"Not this time, abomination," Jie said.

Her fingernails broke through my skin.

So close. I was so close.

I pried at her fingers, I kicked at her shins, I twisted and wriggled and when that made no difference, I spat and swore.

Jie didn't even grace my efforts with a laugh. She stood stock still, silently squeezing until I could feel my bones start to give.

"Gang's all here!" Zang said, from somewhere behind me, then Jie's grip released and I went sprawling to the floor.

I knew better than to waste my one chance by doing something stupid like thinking. I crawled toward the angel as fast as I could. The old man beneath it was clutching his face. He'd doubled over into a ball, rocking in place. Something was happening behind his interlocked fingers. Light spilled out around the edges.

No time. No time for Zang. No time for the man. No time for the Indian guys. No time for Jie or anything else. No time at all.

I reached up, my fingers brushing against the fragile surface of the light. Just the barest resistance there, like thin ice formed over a deep lake. I pushed, and it cracked. I felt myself being pulled along through my own body. My essence leaving my brain, flowing down through my chest, along my arms, pulsing into my fingertips, and beyond, out into the cold, white void.

Before I disappeared entirely, I looked back at Zang and Jie. He had her from behind, both of his legs locked around her midsection, his thumbs digging into the spaces where her eyes had been. He saw me looking and quickly withdrew one thumb. He held it up at me and flashed a gigantic smile.

"Kill us all!" he said, with the same chipper tone you'd use to wish somebody a good day.

And then I saw nothing.

TWENTY-FIVE

Carey. 1983. Los Angeles, California. East L.A.

Before the little boy with the hammer bashed my skull in, the last thing I saw was Rosa, upside-down, balancing on one hand, before finally losing it and collapsing, feet-first, into the angel. Nobody had as much fun with it as her. Not before, and not since.

There was a big white flash, and then the sweet comfort of unconsciousness. I love unconsciousness. We're real good friends. Whether it's sleeping late, passing out from drinking too much, or getting kicked in the head by a big guy who doesn't like being called a condom-drinker, I'm generally on good terms with being put down. Waking up, on the other hand—we don't get along. Especially when I'm doing it with a three-inch gash in the side of my head from the wrong end of a claw hammer. Felt like I was going to throw up a bucket full of rusty nails.

No sign of the little boy. God, that kid was creepy. Must've been seven or eight, but a thousand years old behind the eyes. Wore a three-piece suit, looking like a ventriloquist's mannequin come to life. He didn't happen upon a hammer and, fortune smiling upon him, use it to further sully my good looks. He had it with him the whole time. Pulled it out of a special velvet holster sewn inside of his jacket. Did it real slow, too, so I could see it.

I was not going to miss him.

I pushed myself up on my elbows, which was about as close as I could get to upright. The world still swam around like somebody shook my fishbowl. The room was mostly vacant now—just me, blood sealing one eye shut, dry-heaving into the collar of my leather jacket—and Rosa, crumpled up like a discarded burger wrapper in the far corner. The angel was gone. Same for all the Empty Ones that had been here just seconds (Minutes? Hours? Time's funny when you take a hammer to it) ago. A bunch of greasy black marks on the floor now.

Rosa wasn't moving, but I knew the drill. Old hat by now. She'd be up and around in a few minutes. Not in fighting shape, mind you, but a good night's sleep—the only time she ever did anymore was after taking an angel—and she'd be up at 6 A.M., rattling around in the kitchen of Zang's boathouse, totally heedless of the sanctity of my bedroom, which was the couch, and generally ruining my sunny disposition. Used to take her days to recover after taking an angel. Now it was like a bad hangover—gone with a night's rest and a big, greasy breakfast. Zang would probably be all healed up by then, too. Even though they'd torn both of his arms off before chucking him out the window and into the Pacific Ocean.

It's annoying, is what it is. Being the only one of your roommates who takes lasting damage. Like being the oldest guy at the party.

Somebody knocked on the door.

I stared at it, cross-eyed. Waited.

Knocked again.

Huh. Guess I wasn't hallucinating.

I army-crawled on my belly until that got more frustrating than trying to stand. I hobbled the rest of the way to the door, threw the bolts, and opened it to a soaking wet and armless Zang. He flashed me a winning smile and stepped around me, into the ranger station.

"How did you knock?" was my first stupid question.

"With my head," he answered.

"You all right?" was my second stupid question.

"What do you call a man with no arms and no legs lying in a bush?" he asked.

"I don't . . . what?"

"Russell," he finished.

It was the only joke I ever heard him tell. I was too shocked to laugh. Or maybe it just wasn't funny. When it got no response, Zang dropped his pretense at humanity and lapsed into his usual monotone.

"I will try jokes another time," he said. "I am fine. The arms will heal. You are also not dead, which is useful."

At that, I laughed. It was the closest thing he could get to concern.

"Is it, now?" I asked, rubbing my bleeding scalp and wincing.

"It is," he said. Never did get the hang of rhetorical questions. "Because it is time. I find myself temporarily fingerless, so you will have to shoot the girl."

"What?!" It was so hard to stand. I leaned heavily on the thin wooden walls. Heard the wind howling through the cracks between the boards. "Are you joking again?"

"You are the one who told me this was necessary," he said.

"Yeah, but maybe I was wrong," I answered. The wall behind me felt strangely gritty. I scratched at it with my fingernails, and they came away black. I turned around and saw a charcoal smudge, roughly the shape of a man, burned into the wall right where I'd been leaning.

"You are frequently wrong," he said, thinking. Then, "But I don't think you are about this. I have reason for concern. The girl and I have been getting along much better lately."

"You're becoming friends, so you want to kill her?"

"She despised and feared me at first, which is a normal human response. Now, we have more in common. Taking the angels is changing her. The only wounds that slow her are the psychic ones she sustains from destroying the tools of the Mechanic."

"Just call them angels," I said. "Don't spout that pretentious bullshit."

Pretentious bullshit, my mind echoed.

Randall's favorite phrase.

My heart hurt, for the few seconds I allowed it.

"Her recuperative period from those wounds is also growing shorter. Soon there will not be a window of weakness to exploit. We act now, or not at all."

"Then not at all!" I said, too loudly. If felt like I tore something inside my skull.

"I understand you have feelings for the girl," Zang said. "But to be fair, you have feelings for every girl we meet. These feelings, I believe, are a result of you confusing lust with genuine affection."

Well, shit, Carey—he's got you there.

"You promised me one thing: that we pursue and destroy Jie, no matter the cost. Do you remember?"

"I remember," I snapped.

"Sometimes humans forget," he said. "Perhaps your anger has faded over time. This also happens to humans. It does not happen to me. My anger is a remnant, the remainder of an emotion locked in place when the angels solved me. My anger does not waver. Does yours? Is it no longer important to you, to kill Jie for what she has done?"

Pretentious bullshit.

Snapshots of Randall bounced through my brain. The two of us in our first apartment, bored out of our skulls, throwing silverware at each other in a game we called "dodge the silverware." Killing beers on the benches of Liberty Park in the middle of night, trading jokes about what we'd do to the Statue of Liberty if we could reach her. Stealing a whole hot dog cart because we hadn't eaten in days—we were so hungry it seemed brilliant at the time. Twenty hot dogs later, less brilliant. Randall and his stupid fucking shirts. Randall, who all the girls liked better. Randall, being torn apart in an empty lot beneath a roller coaster.

"I still want her dead," I said.

My chest had been fluttering seconds ago. Heart beating too fast, breath coming too shallow. Now I felt cold. And numb.

Hate doesn't feel like passion. Hate feels like autopilot.

"I would do it for you, but . . ." Zang tried to gesture at Rosa, still immobile in the far corner. But he had no arms, so he just kind of tilted. Any other moment, I'd have laughed at him.

"You couldn't do it anyway," I said, pulling the Colt Navy revolver from the waistband of my jeans. "You have to give a shit about her for it to work."

"Ah," he said. "You already knew. You brought the gun."

"I always bring the gun," I said.

"Then you always knew," he said.

And the asshole was right.

Rosa had taken half a dozen angels now. She stopped sleeping months ago. She hadn't eaten anything in weeks. Maybe longer. Sometimes she talked like Zang—all formal and vacant—for a few seconds, before snapping out of it with her bashful little smile and laughing it all off.

I remembered being on that ramshackle plywood stage in the middle of a marsh in England. Watching Meryll touch a human being, and watching him practically fold inside out as he transformed into a bloody, screaming monstrosity.

Everything the angels touch turns to shit. She'll turn to shit if you let her. Hell, maybe she'd even want you to do it. Maybe she'd forgive you, if she was awake.

But she wasn't. And that's about the only thing I'm grateful for. Means I didn't have to look her in eye when I put a bullet through it.

TWENTY-SIX

Carey. 1987. Los Angeles, California. West Hollywood.

"Whoa, hold on, seriously?" Jell-O Jimmy paused while handing me the bottle. He narrowed his eyes, then took his arm back. Cradled the whiskey against him like a baby.

"What?" I said. "End of story. Pass the bottle."

"Nah, no way," Jimmy said.

We called him Jell-O because he was always jiggling a little bit. Thought it was the DTs at first, but no—he had some kind of brain disease. The shaking was just gonna get worse and worse, until he couldn't even feed himself. So we called him Jell-O. Sure, it's gallows humor, but when you're actually up on the gallows, you just call it humor.

"The fuck you mean, no?" I said. I kicked the rusted-out shell of a little charcoal grill we were using as a fire pit. It shot sparks in the air. "What about the deal?"

"The deal," Jimmy said, holding the bottle out, then yanking it back, "is you tell me stories and you get to share my hooch."

"Right," I said. "I finished this story. Gimme the bottle and I'll start another one."

"That ain't finished!" he cried, jumping to his feet. The scratchy blue U-Haul moving blanket fell from around his shoulders. "Look, your stories are crazy bullshit, man. But why I like you—why you get to put your diseased lips on my bottle—is that they make sense. I can follow 'em. Larry the Lizardman, he thinks reptiles run the government, but when you talk to him about it, it don't make sense. Jumps all over the place. Starts talking about his kids and radio waves and shit. Mary, that chick squats down in the 'ducts? She thinks we're all really underground and there's a bigger world around us, and our sky is its ground, but she clams up after that. Doesn't like talking about it. Your crazy though, it's entertaining because it almost sounds like stories. And stories have a proper ending."

"But they're not stories," I said. I wasn't so far gone that I babbled this stuff at the normals. That's a sure way to get locked up. But why bother pretending with the other hobos? To them, I told the truth. "They're my life."

"Listen, man. Listen: took you two weeks to tell me about that other ninja chick, what's her name?"

"Meryll," I said. I hated saying it. It felt like I was stealing something.

"Right, that was a good story. This Rosa chick, she's the same deal and you're just like 'we met, kicked some ass, then I killed her.' That's a shitty ending! She deserves a better story, so tell me a better one, or no bottle."

He sat back down and gave me the snake eyes, the ones that say he's putting his foot down. For real this time. And that means I'm going to have to fight him for that bottle. Sucker-punch an altogether pretty decent guy with a brain disease and then steal his liquor. Well, that, or go sober for the night.

I'm not going sober for the night.

"With Meryll," I said, "that was *her* story. It was important to tell that one right, because it was about her, and who she was, and what this fight does to people. You had to understand her, so you'd know it was them that did it to her—she wasn't some kinda monster. They are."

"But it ain't about that with Rosa? And the other one—the kid at the start, the one you tricked into coming outta the freezer. Why don't they get the same treatment? We got time! All the time in the world! And I'm buying the hooch, so spin me those tales, man."

"Rosa and the kid," I said, chucking some more garbage onto the fire. "Those stories aren't about them. They're about me. You don't have to understand me. I am a fucking monster."

Jimmy didn't have much to say about that. When folks get maudlin around here, it's best to just shut up and let it play out. We sat there watching the toxic fire eat away the edges of a Styrofoam container. We listened to cars down on the 110 honk their horns—always that angry, too-long honk that ends in a fistfight or a gunshot. We pulled up little chunks of ice plant, squeezed the juice out of 'em, chucked them at nothing in particular.

I was just about to make my move: tell Jimmy the cops had pulled up, then when he looked away, wham! Right in the side of the head. Where the jaw hooks up to the skull. Always floors 'em. Grab the bottle before it spills, and find a new place to spend my nights. Then Jimmy held the whiskey out to me and said:

"All right. Finish *your* story, then. But I liked Rosa's better."

"Me too, man," I said, and I took a drink.

TWENTY-SEVEN

Kaitlyn. Unknown. Unknown.

You're inside of a dense fogbank that settled over downtown in a major city. Visibility is so beyond poor. The buildings right beside you are demarcated only by your memory of them. You just touched this one's smooth brick walls. You took two steps away, and now it is gone. Just the echo of it, bouncing around your spatial cortex. You can feel this massive thing looming over you—you know for a fact that it's just a few feet away—but strain as you might, you can't actually see it. You may think you catch a detail here or there—a window ledge, a doorjamb, an awning—but you can't be sure.

That's what it's like, being inside an angel. A featureless white void that still somehow seems crowded. Simultaneously vacant and impossibly dense. The first time I was here, I thought I'd stepped into the negative space between worlds. Pure, unbroken emptiness. But it's a trick. That's why the vertigo kicks in when you try to focus. Why you taste metal when you try to track one of those unnatural, churning shapes through the null space. Because this isn't a null space at all.

Draw a number. Draw another over it. Another. Another. Repeat until you have an impenetrable black square. Show it to somebody else. Somebody that never knew there were numbers at all. They'll see only a black square. And yet they'll still get this unshakable feeling that there's something more, if they could just scratch away a little bit of the surface. . . .

That's what an angel really is: an infinitely dense intersection of information and energy. An extra-dimensional creature that can only be anchored in our plane of existence by crudely co-opting an intelligent being that belongs here—a parasite, hitching a ride through our universe on the drifting husk of our humanity. We only see that husk—the true creature is spread across an infinite number of dimensions. A billion billion angels spanning all of time and creation, at once independent and inextricably linked.

If you can just look through the white curtain, that impenetrable patina of information, you can see the bigger picture: one angel hooked to the next, each relaying their stolen energy up an infinite chain, branching again and again until it becomes a nest of writhing tentacles snaking through every possible dimension.

The siphonophore.

A network of individual creatures, all linked to form one larger one. Kill a part, so what? They'll make another. That's their strength.

But watching this angel shunt its constant stream of energy across the thin veil between universes, I get an idea. I follow it. It's difficult: The energy isn't broadcast in a single constant, unbroken stream from place to place. Some of it slips through the realm of possibility and into another angel, idling in a place very much like this one. It hovers over the rapidly disintegrating body of an old, bearded man, lying in a dark and partially collapsed lounge. Frenzied Empty Ones tear themselves apart with religious fervor; two frightened blind men crouch in the corner; my own body lies broken on the floor. In this dimension, there is no Zang in sight. Jie is victorious.

It's just one minor difference—maybe in this dimension, Zang didn't duck fast enough and Alvar took his head off; maybe he went to check on Carey first, figuring he had time; maybe he skipped away and got ice cream instead, who knows with that guy?—but even the slightest split kick-starts an entirely different chain of events. One which takes place in a brand new and wholly distinct dimension. The angel here redirects some of its own energy to yet another dimension, but this one is nothing like ours: A small ball of light floats, silent, in abyssal space. There are no planets here. Nothing breaks the black expanse but a sick and dying star in the distance. This angel is not siphoning any energy at all, only using what it receives from the others. A small portion it consumes just to continue existing in this world—this place with no life to anchor—but it funnels the rest right into that sun. Sustaining its reaction. Fighting the tide of entropy.

The siphonophore feeds off of life, but with an infinite number of possible dimensions, life is comparatively rare. So many things had to go just right for us to be here. One degree off at a crucial period of development, and primitive single-cell organisms would never have emerged. An asteroid collides with a single piece of dust a million light years away, altering its course ever so slightly, and the impact wipes out ancient mammals. Or one man says the wrong thing at a secret meeting in the back of a Russian hotel, and we wipe ourselves out with nuclear winter.

Life is fragile. Life is rare.

And the siphonophore is hungry.

It uses some of what it steals from us, and all the permutations of us, to sow new life in barren universes. It will take millions of years to pay off, but that's okay: Time is meaningless to the siphonophore. Time is meaningless to everything not trapped within its confines, like insects in amber.

I leave this solitary angel and its dying sun, and I follow the chain up further—angels riding the remnants of aboriginal farmers, slick politicians, housewives, professional bodybuilders, homeless junkies, and child soldiers. Infinite lives in infinite dimensions, all corrupted and stolen.

Much like the link, that's their strength. Their food source is also their breeding ground. It's a feedback loop.

Much like the link, it's also their greatest weakness.

The humans they use as their vessels can't be solved completely. The angels have to leave little pieces—useless memories, meaningless impulses, trivial desires—of the host, in order to use them as anchors. The angels think of this as little more than celestial garbage. They think those little remnants of humanity are harmless to them.

I'm about to prove them wrong.

I hitch into a strand of energy. It's like plucking a single thread from a worn sweater. You work yourself in there slowly, sifting and sifting until you've finally isolated just one little piece, you grab it gently, and then you pull. . . .

Got it.

The siphonophore's network is scattershot. The farther you get from the energy source, the more diluted it becomes. That's protection. Random encryption. It thinks it's immune from destruction because there are no common factors that link the whole thing together. But that's siphonophore logic. There is a common factor. Life.

We're all wildly different. Fucked up, confused, angry, horny, gassy, hungry—a billion different beings with a billion different impulses. But way, way down there at the base of it, we all have one thing in common. We had life. Until they took it from us.

And that pisses us off.

Now that I'm spliced into the strand, I pour that emotion—pure and undiluted from a source from inside the network itself—right into the siphonophore's veins.

Remember what it was like to be alive.

Remember sun on your face. Skin touching skin.

Remember the hollowness of an empty stomach. Remember the suffocating unease of heartbreak.

Remember the good things. Remember the bad ones. Remember waking up.

Remember sleep.

Whatever it was to be alive—pain and glory and humiliation and desire and confusion and laughter and fury—it was ours. It was never theirs.

Help me take it back.

There's so little of you left. I know. I know it's hard. You feel small. You feel scattered. You don't even remember who you were. But you remember *that* you were. That's all you need. Just a little reminder.

I felt parts of me filtering through the angels, picking up remnants of their hosts—of what used to be people—as they went. The emotion building in strength. The more it gathered, the more it could gather. The siphonophore felt it now, a corruption in its veins. A rough-edged, tumbling, screaming stream of pure emotion. Utterly human, and utterly impossible for it to process. Humanity spilled out from the intersections of those unnatural angles; it flooded the angels, spreading variegated roots across pristine white surfaces and pulling them apart.

Through the strand I'd seized, I felt the thrum of an infinity of angels, dying.

It felt good.

TWENTY-EIGHT

Carey. 1984. Los Angeles, California. Koreatown.

I love my crash spot. Koreatown is home for me. Always will be. It's a good middle ground—halfway between the ghetto and the beach. This is where L.A. hides its working class. People with actual jobs. Tasks that don't require putting on makeup first. They ain't pretty, and they ain't happy, but they keep this city running. They understand when they see somebody on the skids. They understand you don't need help or pity. Just beer money. On the east side they'll kick you to death just for . . . well, just for kicks. Over by the beach is worse: They call security. Some mope with an innie-dick and a bicycle threatening to involve the real police if you don't get moving.

But in Koreatown, tucked away in my little hidey-hole behind the butcher shop, nobody bugs me. Well, nobody except for Zang. But he's basically nobody. Every couple of weeks he'll poke me awake in the middle of the night. Tell me the fight needs me. That I'm wasting time like this.

"It was just a girl," he'll say. "Thousands like her die

every day. They have died before you came along. They will die after you are gone."

Always the middle of the night with that guy. Nudging me awake just when the liquor's wearing off. Mouth dry, bladder burning, head spinning—I feel like such shit that I can only think about how shitty I feel. I tell him to piss off, and he stands there for god knows how long, staring at me silently, and then in the morning he's gone.

It's lucky for me, that he only comes in the middle of the night.

When the hangover fades to a dull roar and I'm capable of forming thoughts that aren't "Jesus Christ I wish I would just die already," I might listen to what he's got to say. Sure, I've got all this guilt and loathing and disgust sloshing around in my guts—mixing up with the Jim Beam and the street tacos to form my very own special brand of acid, eating away at my stomach lining—but the hate is still there, too. And unless I drown it in booze, the hate is stronger. Every minute I'm sober I think about Randall. About Jie. About Meryll and Rosa. I bounce back and forth between what an asshole I am for doing the things I've done, and what assholes the angels are for making me do them. I think about taking Zang up on his offer. Spilling some blood.

But he doesn't come around until later. And I've got time to kill, so I scrounge up liquor money and start drinking.

Then it's the middle of the night, and I drank away the hate so all that's left is self-pity and self-loathing and a bitch of a headache. I tell Zang to piss off, and we do our little dance again.

TWENTY-NINE

Carey. 1985. Los Angeles, California. Koreatown.

You know what's great? Hard liquor!

You know what's not great? Everything else!

Where's that god damn Chinese bastard? Haven't seen him in months. Always ambushing me when I'm down. Can't face me now, when I'm at peak don't-give-a-fuck and about to get honest with everybody. He'd be good for that. Just stand there like a post and take it.

Some of these other bums, they're too sensitive. I tell 'em about how the world really is and they tell me to shut up. I tell 'em what I really think of them and they tell me that if that's how I feel I don't have to share their booze. That's fuckin'. . . .

That's censorship, is what that is.

I don't need 'em anyway. I got my hidey-hole. I got Koreatown. A cozy little alley. Just big enough for me. Nobody else allowed.

THIRTY

Carey. 1992. Los Angeles, California. Hyde Park.

I should not have puked in the fireman's helmet. He's probably gonna be mad at me. The bastard.

THIRTY-ONE

Carey. 2012. Los Angeles, California. West L.A.

This rat and me—we're thick as thieves. That's how that saying goes, right? What does that even mean? How are thieves thick? Like fat?

"You fat fuckin' thief!" I yell at the rat. Used to scurry away when I yelled at it. Now it just kinda looks at me like I'm the crazy one.

"You're the one that eats garbage," I tell it. "You fat garbage-eatin' thief."

I think about throwing my bottle at it. But it might take that personal. Might not come back. Don't want that. Don't wanna be alone.

Besides, the bottle's not totally empty. I mean, it's empty, yeah. But if you leave it alone for a while a few drips flow down the walls and pool at the bottom. Then you tip it upside down, wait for the trickle of rotgut, and repeat. This bottle's on life support. I'll stay with it 'til the end.

My sleeping bag smells like piss and I can't tell if that's because I pissed in it or if that's just how it smells. It's hot, and I don't wash it a lot. Costs quarters. Then you gotta buy those little fun-size boxes of detergent.

"That's how they get you," I tell the rat.

My head is heavy. Keeps falling down.

"I should give you a name," I say. The rat looks intrigued. Probably. Who can tell with a rat?

"Rat . . . well. Ratwell Rattington the Eighth," I try. I scowl. "Too pretentious. Pretentious bullshit!"

I laugh. Get little flashes of somebody I used to know. Don't want that. That's no good. I tip the bottle again. Fewer drops every time.

"Pat," I try again. "Pat the fat rat. Patty Boy!"

I raise my empty bottle to him. He glares at me. Probably. I throw the bottle. He runs.

Good job, man. Now you got nobody to talk to.

"Ah, well," I say, struggling to my feet. "Gotta yell at somebody, and they're not coming to me."

I forget what I'm doing. I guess I'm out in the street now? That's weird. I was just laying down with a bottle a little bit ago. Figured I was done for the night. But now I'm out here, so I roll with it.

Had to move the ol' bag and bottle collection a while back. Koreatown didn't like me anymore. Got so the shop-keepers knew my name. Knew how to deal with me. Hustled me away before I could get a word in edgewise. But the great thing about L.A. is, it's real big and nobody talks to each other. When somebody gets wise to your shit, you just walk a few miles and start slingin' shit again.

I'm crashing in West L.A. these days. Over by the 405. It's nice without being too nice. Pretty girls here with short-shorts and titties that still bounce. Haven't gotten the implants yet. Still trying to make enough money to get 'em. The implants are inevitable. Pretty dudes here, too—not that

I'm into that (unless I'm high, and they're buying)—but they still got visible tattoos. Haven't had to scrub them off yet. For a role, they all say. Gotta do it for a role. Gotta become blank slates to project characters on because they ain't got—

"Personalities of your own!" I scream, right at a pair of 'em walking past me.

The assholes jump and hustle up a bit. Looking back at me. Laughing. Probably. Who can tell with an asshole?

"Go ahead," I say to nobody. "Laugh. I'm fuckin' hilarious!"

There's this taco truck in the parking lot of a Rite Aid. If I get there late enough, just before they close up, they'll give me leftovers. Good folks. Good food. The best food's out of a truck. Used to be it was just the Mexicans and us *güeros* that knew the score. Then everybody caught on. Some dick-burn in a knit scarf probably put up a review on the internet, and now my taco truck is always crowded. Mostly white people. Young. Kinda drunk. Happy.

Assholes.

What a bunch of holes in asses. Filthy, unwashed, puckered up old—

"Hey," one of the assholes says. "Come on, man."

"What?" I say.

"What do you mean, what?" he says. Good-lookin' skinny white kid. Got one of those wooden disks in his lip that used to be cool. Even I know they aren't anymore. Guess it's ironic now.

Lip Disk turns to his friends for confirmation, like he can't believe this is happening. Gotta run it by the experts first.

"Why you screaming in our faces, bro? Calling us assholes?" Lip Disk says. "We don't even know you. We're just waiting for our *tacos de pollo*."

This bastard's whiter than my bare ass and he's sittin'

there faking the accent, talking about his tacos like he was born in the barrio and his crib was an old washtub.

That's it. That's all I can take.

I step back to send a vicious dropkick his way—make him eat that stupid lip disk—but I guess I went back too far because now I'm on the ground. It's funny, so I laugh.

"You okay?" a girl's voice says. It's nice. It's a nice sound.

"Mmm?" I say. My eyes wanna stick together. I force 'em open.

"I don't think you can sleep here," she says. Blond girl. Yellow tank top and blue shorts. Not my type. Got broad shoulders and calves like she could kick through steel. But I can see up her shorts a little from my position, so hell, maybe I can change my type.

"Not sleepin'" I say, but I look around and I guess I was. I'm sprawled across the whole sidewalk. Taco truck is closed. Means it's real late, or real early. The L.A. light pollution makes it impossible to tell.

"Okay," she says. "Just checking to make sure you weren't dead."

What a god damn sweetheart.

I hold out my hand for her to help me up. She does not look happy about it.

Can't blame her.

But she takes it anyway. How about that?

Been a while since I touched anybody. In a friendly way, at least. Skin is nice. Clean and warm. You don't realize you miss it 'til you have it and then it's like you've been drowning and just caught a lungful of air.

There's something off about her grip—familiar, but off—and it takes me a while to place it. I turn my hand so hers is facing up. There it is.

Sixth finger on the left hand. A little thing—not fully formed. Like an extra pinky. She sees me looking and pulls back real quick.

"Take care," she says, and jogs away.

Guess that makes it early, then. Pretty white girls don't jog in the middle of the night. I feel like shit that's been scraped off the bottom of a shoe. But at least I'm not on the shoe anymore. I slept through the worst of the hangover. I feel around in my socks for my emergency booze money, but it's gone. Maybe I got rolled, or maybe I just spent it while blackout drunk.

This is bad.

Already I'm having thoughts.

What are the odds you meet another six-fingered girl while passed out on the sidewalk?

There's gotta be a reason for it.

The universe is telling you something.

You can't waste the opportunity.

It's probably nothing, anyway. The extra digit doesn't always mean she's special.

But maybe she is. Such a sweetheart, too. Could be in danger.

They could be watching her.

Maybe you should be watching her, too.

Not to use her. Not to teach her. Not like Meryll and Rosa—

Don't. Don't think their names.

This isn't like that. It's not about that.

You're only following her—

Crap. I *am* following her.

You're only following her because you need booze money, and it just so happens that her jogging route runs up a street where it's garbage day. Everybody's got their cans of free money out for you.

That's all this is.

Just another garbage day.

THIRTY-TWO

Kaitlyn. 2013. Los Angeles, California. Costa Soberbia.

I was floating through black and dreamless sleep. Somewhere far away, I knew my body was cold and uncomfortable. It lay right where it fell, its head on a thin layer of damp old carpet and chilled concrete. That place stank like burned meat and mold with just a hit of ozone. I didn't want to go there. So I didn't. I just tucked myself into a nice dark place where I was allowed to be nothing.

Somebody coughed and cleared their throat in the grossest way.

I felt brief but seizing panic, like waking up the morning after a drunken one-night stand only to find they're still in your bed.

I trudged reluctantly toward consciousness. I opened one eye so slightly that I could barely see through the curtain of my own eyelashes. A blurry shape squatted in the corner.

The angel the Empty Ones not dead dark ruins danger—

I startled awake, gasping like I'd just had an apnea. I scared the hell out of Carey.

He'd never admit it.

Memory came back in a flood: the sunken city, the tar men burning, the Empty Ones clawing at me, the static chimes of the angel. . . .

"Welcome to the land of the living," Carey said.

"How long was I out?" I asked. My mouth tasted like cotton. Soaked in stagnant hot dog water.

"No idea," he answered. "But it must be afternoon now."

He gestured up at the sky. A spot of glaring white bleeding into opaque crystal blue. The sun was directly overhead. Not a cloud in the sky. And even still, the light barely filtered down here, only rendering the sinkhole in gloomy twilight rather than impenetrable black.

I blinked, trying to get my super-senses back, but the effort just made my head hurt.

Carey was on his heels, knees tucked up against his stomach, back against the massive fireplace that dominated the abandoned lounge. The only signs left of the Empty Ones were some charred spots in the carpet and burn marks on the walls. I looked to where I'd last seen Zang and Jie. A coal-black stain eating through the soggy gray floor.

Carey saw me staring.

"Zang?" he asked.

"Yeah," I said. "And Jie. Last time I saw them, he had her pinned right there. I guess they went up in the blast when I took the angel. I'm sorry. . . ."

"Don't be," Carey said. "That's all he ever wanted."

"I meant I'm sorry for you. I know he was your friend."

Carey laughed.

"I guess so," he said. "Shit, how sad is that?"

I didn't have an answer.

Oh, crap, what about—

"Jackie's fine," he said, guessing my intent. "When it got light enough to see, I helped her back to the trail. Told her I was coming back for you. It was a bitch, convincing her to go on without you."

I smiled, even though it made my face hurt.

"I told her I couldn't help you both up the cliff, so the best way for her to help you was to head up with the others."

"The others?"

"Indian fellas," he said. "The dot-head kind, not the scalping kind. You didn't see those two? Seemed pretty all right for homos."

"Jesus, Carey."

"What?"

"Nothing," I said. "Wait—two guys? Not three?"

"I took some pretty good hits back there, but I can still count to two."

The bearded guy didn't make it.

Was that my fault, or the angel's? Would he have lived if I'd done something different? Tried to contain the blast when the angel collapsed, like I did in Mexico? That would have left the Empty Ones alive and waiting for me when I emerged. Would they have spared him? Or was it all moot? Was he dead before I ever went in?

Fingers knit across his face. Light spilling out from the spaces between.

Don't worry, Kaitlyn. You'll only have the rest of your life to dwell over questions like that.

I heard a strange click. Metal on metal. Purposeful, like something engaging.

Maybe I wouldn't have that long after all. . . .

I tried to scale up my vision again. It still hurt, but the pain was diminishing. Now it was just stretching a muscle

I'd overused, rather than an agonizing cramp. The visibility rose like I'd raised a dimmer switch on the world.

Carey looked like hell. Even for him. One side of his face was caked with blood. His thin, salt-and-pepper hair was splayed and spiked with filth. His leather jacket—always barely held together with strategically placed band patches and safety pins—was in a more advanced state of deterioration. He was about to lose a sleeve. He'd already lost a shoe. His facial expression was somewhere between "just got dumped" and "about to be hit by a bus." In one hand he held an old-timey pistol, like something out of a Western. His thumb was on the hammer.

"This again, huh?" I asked.

He'd pulled that gun on me once before, after I'd taken the angel in Mexico. He told me he was just confused. I didn't buy it then, but I didn't want to think about what it meant at the time. It was pretty clear now, though. . . .

"This is the last time, I promise," he said.

I peered into him, and found that Carey was shimmering. Not like fairy dust, but like a thin layer of water over new ice. I thought about what Zang told me—about how my enhanced sight wasn't because my eyes were better. I focused on Carey and tried the same trick: seeing without physical constraints. Just looking at things for what they are, instead of how I perceived them.

Layers began to slough off of Carey, like somebody pulling individual pages from an animated flipbook. There were billions of them, and the deeper I went, the less they looked like Carey. Or at least, how I thought of Carey. The layers were more like impulses, decisions, memories— maybe some combination of all three. He was squatting there in front of me in a sunken suburb lost to the Pacific, but he was also ten years old, throwing rocks at a parked cop car on a street in Brooklyn. He was seventeen and laughing with friends, swimming in a lake somewhere at dusk. He was twenty-two and watching a man being brutally beaten through the chain-link fence surrounding an amusement park. He was thirty-eight and dry-heaving in an alleyway in Koreatown. He was reaching out to touch a pale young girl with dyed black hair, then pulling back at the last second. He was watching the look of betrayal in her eyes. He was leveling this very same pistol at another girl in a wind-blown shack. He was pulling the trigger.

I watched his entire lifetime and beyond—thoughts he refused to think, truths he refused to acknowledge—but then I blinked and we'd barely moved. Only a second had passed.

But I knew so much now.

It wasn't coincidence that he pulled me out of Marco's Mercedes just as the pervert slipped his life-draining tongue into me. Carey had been watching. None of what I went through was new to him—killing the angels, the strange new abilities, the rituals—he was just stringing me along, eking out only enough information to keep me going, but not enough so that I no longer needed him.

I had to need him, because he needed to be here with me, at the end.

Just like he was there for the other girls. One he failed to save, and one he doomed. Both, he killed. With that gun.

A quick burst of images: Carey and Zang standing over the prone body of a dark-skinned girl.

"I always bring the gun."

"Then you always knew."

He still had the pistol. Whatever he told himself, he knew this day was coming the whole time.

But he was hoping it wouldn't.

I remembered Carey's face when he first told me about all this—the Unnoticeables, the Empty Ones, the angels—and I told him he was crazy and needed to leave. He looked so happy and relieved. Then I called him back, and his heart broke.

He was trying to give me an out. Trying to give both of us an out.

Because he knew this was where we'd end up: Me on the ground, rapidly losing my humanity. Him standing over me, pointing a gun at my face, about to throw away the last of his.

He loved those girls, and he loved me. And he killed them. And he was going to kill me, too.

And you have to let him.

A spiral of branching paths flowed outward from Carey. It would take eons to follow them, but eons were irrelevant here, so I did. Somewhere far, far down the line of potential futures, there was another screaming white light and another young girl, dying.

The angels would come back, if I let them.

Not now. Not in my lifetime. Maybe not even here, in our specific dimension. But somewhere out there, they hid in the realm of possibility, patiently rebuilding.

The things I could do were amazing. I could enhance my own senses, I could heal from mortal wounds, I could tap strength beyond human ability, and I could even pause time, in a sense, and change the flow of events. But as extraordinary as those things seemed to me, they were still paltry. They were limited by my own little human brain, mired in its idea of what should be possible. I could see better in the dark, but not like it was daylight. Why?

Because buried somewhere deep in my mind was the idea that I could not. Night vision, healing, strength—all things that I could, on some level, accept as possible. Seeing everything? Not taking wounds in the first place? Being strong enough to move literally anything?

I just couldn't believe it.

The very notion was absurd. I was Katey from Barstow, California. I hated school because kids made fun of my extra finger. I was a daddy's girl and a tomboy and lost little sheep following her friend's dreams because I didn't have any of my own. I'm not some grand cosmic force. I'm a sad, tiny little human being.

And that has to stop.

Not a second had passed since I'd first glimpsed Carey's code. My brain was processing information far faster than it should be able to, and the second I thought that—

Carey stood up and crossed the few steps to where I lay. He lifted the gun like it was a barbell. It seemed like the weight of it might tip him over.

"I know it ain't worth much," he said. "But I am sorry."

"It's okay," I said. "I know."

I waited.

Nothing happened.

His hand started to shake.

He's not going to do it.

He has to do it.

I found my realm of stillness, and I settled in there. I let the now-familiar ghostly silhouettes of possibility flow outward from Carey. I sifted through them.

He dropped the gun and started crying.

He turned and threw the gun into the ocean.

He put the gun in his mouth, and pulled the trigger.

Thousands upon thousands of potential actions that he could take, and in none of them did he do what I actually needed him to.

He tucked the gun into his waistband and helped me up.

He took off his jacket, peeled away a single patch—a crazy-looking mime in a bowler hat—and set it in my hand, then walked away.

He sneezed, firing the gun into his own shoeless foot, then hopped around screaming in pain.

A seagull died in mid-flight directly above us. Its carcass landed perfectly between where he stood with the gun and I sat, waiting. We both looked up in confusion, then back down, and started laughing.

God damn it, where is it?

There were a dozen permutations of the dead seagull—how unlikely could it possibly be that he would actually pull the trigger?

He sat down with me and we both started singing something together.

He took off his pants and threw them in the bay, then did a bizarre gyrating dance.

He flipped the gun around and offered it to me. I took it and shot him right in the chest.

Jesus, Kaitlyn. Really?

It has to be here somewhere. There are literally an infinite number of possibilities, the only variable is how likely an outcome is to occur, not whether or not it does occur. It has to be here. It must be here.

He dropped—

He threw—

He jumped—

He walked—

There! There . . .

A single spectral apparition of an aging punk rocker, holding an ancient pistol to an exhausted blond girl's head. He paused. He closed his eyes. He pulled the trigger. He looked as surprised as anybody when the gun actually fired.

I focused on the scene. I built the details in my mind. Willed the opacity to fade in. I grabbed one single frame of that possible reality, and I brought it over into ours. I layered it into the stream of events, ignoring the billion possible paths where it did not occur. I made the possible real.

I hesitated.

No going back now.

I blinked, and smelled gunpowder.

THIRTY-THREE

Kaitlyn. Unknown. Unknown.

There are a lot of benefits to being outside of time. There is one very big downside: When everything has happened, is happening, and will always be happening, running away doesn't do you a lot of good.

The corruption I'd introduced into the siphonophore—a toxic iridescent streak snaking through the luminous white tentacles—raced up its limbs, tracing the infinite branching pathways until the whole thing was consumed. It spasmed in what I sincerely hoped was pain, and then it shattered into sparks. Dying fireflies drifting through the multiverse.

I watched as they went out.

Almost all of them.

A handful of angels managed to split off before the corruption could take them. They were sad, confused, and isolated little creatures for now—but I had seen it, back in the real world when I watched our potential futures unfold. They're like starfish: A single piece can rebuild the whole. I would have to find each and every one of them and stamp them out if this thing was ever going to be over.

And I will. I do. I did.

That's the nice thing: There's no hurry. I have all the time in the world here, in the still space.

With the siphonophore gone, the universe felt oddly empty. The parasite had spent eons twisting the universe into an ideal host for it, and now I felt like I was walking through a grand mansion with no residents. But I knew that, somewhere on the periphery of existence, in the blank space bordering reality, that huge presence I'd felt in my dreams—

The space whale.

Don't call it the space whale.

That can't stick.

But then . . . what do I call it?

God?

. . .

I prefer space whale.

The space whale was turning to regard its former home. I had that same sensation, of floating in waters that were indistinguishable from the land, while something gargantuan approached from beneath me. I could feel the waters swelling with its bulk, though it was still an unfathomable distance away.

I understood now that the waters were . . . everything. That the (sigh) *space whale* belonged in them, but had not occupied them for a very long time. It would take a while before it could fully reinstate itself—finish pouring its massive form into the billion holes vacated by the siphonophore. But time is not a constant—it's not even a factor in the still space—so for all intents and purposes, the space whale was home.

I wasn't exactly comforted by the thought. I did not get a sensation of paternal care or concern from the beast. I got the sensation of distance and irrelevance. Whatever I had *done* was enough for it to take notice, but what I actually *am* was too small to acknowledge. Even if it was aware of me, I was simply too minute for it to interact with. Maybe you feel kindly about your gut flora—they take care of you, keep you healthy, protect your immune system—but you can't exactly reach down and shake one's hand.

If only I could know what it really was, and what this all meant.

Well, why not?

I was no longer tethered to my own humanity—

Oh god, my body. I'm dead. Jesus. Oh no, what did I do?

Stop that. Those are vestigial instincts. The important parts of you are still here.

My brains were important and now they're staining carpet. I'll be down there forever. He won't carry my body back up—he couldn't, even if he wanted to—stuck in the dark for eternity—oh god—rotting in a sunken city—sea life picking at my—

Stop!

Look around. You don't need brain matter to exist. You are energy; you cannot be created or destroyed. You don't need eyes to see or nerves to feel. Look!

I did, and it was beautiful. Truly, heartbreakingly beautiful, in a way that I had never understood before. I loved the outdoors. I climbed rocks. I swam in rivers. I hiked. But to be honest, when poets started rambling on about verdant forests and mountains majesty, I rolled my eyes. Nature was pretty. Peaceful. Nice.

But I never understood majesty until I saw the universe, raw and true.

Everything that had been or will ever be is right here, waiting for me. I can watch stars being born. I can watch life crawl from the primordial oceans. I can ride comets through galaxies and I can even—

Jackie and I, just little kids, playing cat's cradle at the bus stop. She's trying to teach me how to do it, but she forgot, herself. She ties her hands up so effectively that I can't undo them. I fish the rounded safety scissors from my Power Rangers backpack, but they're so useless all I do is kink the yarn. We board the bus with our heads down, the bus driver laughing.

It happened. It is happening.

Every second of our lives is all right here with me, not a memory, but a reality, in full Technicolor glory. And it's not just Jackie. It's everybody.

My dad is helping me build a tiny engine made out of Lego. I told him I wanted to learn about engines, not because I was interested in them, but because I loved him, and he loved them. He points out the basic parts, and I commit them to memory. Chanting their names—valves, pistons, cams—like a little prayer. Stacy comes in and—

Stacy! I barely remembered my little sister, back when I was human. My mind was too young to lock down her details. She was a nostalgic urge, a pang of hurt, and a few Polaroid flashes that faded when I tried to focus on them.

But now here she is, vibrant and alive, laughing as she . . .

Kicks my engine apart.

You little brat!

Dad laughs. She's too young to be yelled at. But I cry and pout, run back to our shared room, slam the door a few times so everybody gets the point, and burrow into my blankets.

I always did run to bed when things got bad.

I don't need to stay with me. I'm not tied to my own life anymore. Instead, I watch Dad and Stacy play, painstakingly rebuilding my tiny engine together. Well, my dad builds. Stacy mostly tries to taste the Legos, but my dad is on top of it.

These are memories I never had, but they're mine now.

And it's not just memories. I have the present, too—

Carey standing in the dark, the smell of decaying seaweed, staring down at my bloody, ruined face—

Nah, let's skip the present.

I have the future.

Jackie is older, but she still looks great. She looks more and more like Audrey Hepburn as she ages. She would hate me for saying that. She'd rather look like Helen Mirren—all sex, all the time, even into her 70s. But Jackie was never that: Cute but approachable, graceful in a fragile way. Until she opens her mouth.

Which she does right now, disarming a small crowd of partygoers on a beach in Catalina. It's just getting dark. She's wearing a black one-piece swimsuit that you can tell at a glance is expensive.

In an instant I have her whole life:

A B-list celebrity gets a crush on her while attending one of her troop's improv shows. He's only there out of social obligation. They chat after the show. They get along famously, because everybody gets along with Jackie. Nothing ever happens between them, but they remain friends. She makes his friends her friends; makes his connections her connections.

A failed sitcom pilot. A few roles as the goofy friend in mid-list rom-coms, and then a breakout in a lame but shockingly popular bro comedy. She's the It Girl for only a moment, but she parlays that into creative control. She starts writing her own projects. Gets a sitcom that sticks. A spattering of beloved cult movies. She's not A-list anymore, but she could be again if she wanted to. A few calls to the right people, who all love her—everybody does—and she's back in the limelight. If she wants it. She's not sure she does.

On a beach in Catalina, Jackie ends her anecdote and the assembled crowd laughs. She tells them she's going to get a drink— her hard drinking is infamous, but like everything with her, it's mostly embellished. She walks along the shoreline, alone, out toward the old lighthouse. She stares quietly for nearly an hour.

I wonder what's going on in her head. As soon as I do, I know—

—just left her down there what could you do you could have called the police and you know it tell them what happened it's not your fault whose fault is it—

Oh, no. Jackie.

She strips out of her swimsuit, pale skin practically glowing in the rising moonlight. She steps into the water.

No.

THIRTY-FOUR

Jackie. 2032. Catalina Island, California.

I've got a rule: one drink per hour when out in public. Of course, it can't look like that. I've got a reputation to maintain as the eternal party girl.

There's a big difference between the eternal party girl and the real drunk. The eternal party girl never does anything too embarrassing when she's hammered, because she's old-school classy; she doesn't get hangovers because they're ugly; she doesn't throw up after she's had one too many—she just farts out some pixie dust and bam! Sober as an NPR special.

It was fun and earnest at first, then I got too old for it. But now it's part of "my story." I had to switch to gin and tonics years ago. Now I alternate between those and regular tonic water—they're both clear and bubbly, plus the quinine's so overpowering, nobody could even smell the difference, if they went around smelling drinks for some reason.

There's a metaphor for Hollywood in here somewhere.

I shouldn't get too bitter at Hollywood. I can't pretend it hasn't been good to me. I've got money, fame—even respect from the art crowd when they, y'know, actually remember that I exist. It's all I ever wanted, right?

Right.

There's only one problem with that: Now I have it.

I've had it for a long time, and I can't remember how to want other things. It's been so long since anything made me truly happy. Oh, there have been moments here and there—some sunny days and massive nights—but it feels like it's been a decade since anything really stuck.

And in the quiet times, I think about Kaitlyn.

Her bones scattered in some dark pit. No burial. No service. No grave. Nobody to even remember her name. Except for me. And I'm too much of a coward to even bring her up.

What if they asked questions?

Hey Jackie, this friend of yours sounds great. Whatever happened to her?

Oh, you know, she died fighting otherworldly monsters in the ruins of a gated community. Didn't heed the HOA guidelines— painted her house pink, don't you know—so of course the neighbors had to eat her face.

I hadn't so much as spoken her name since that day at the sunken city, when Carey finally summited the cliffside path and shook his head. He didn't even offer an explanation. By the time the tears cleared, so had Carey. I never saw the bastard again.

Ah, look at me: Becky flies me out to an island paradise, rents a whole private beach—even has the waiters sing "Happy Birthday, you slut" just to give me a laugh—and what do I do? I wander off, alone, to get all weepy about the past.

Still, just the thought of going back there and faking another laugh . . .

Flashing another practiced smile. Telling one of the same funny stories—"the one about the luchador! Do the one about the luchador and the van!"—it gives me heartburn.

But I am on a pristine and empty beach. I have a decent buzz—my head swimming but not spinning—and there's cool, clean water. A moon like a spotlight.

Maybe I don't have to go back.

Maybe I don't ever have to go back. I could just slip into the water and keep swimming until I find somewhere I belong. And if that's nowhere, well . . .

God, the papers would love it, wouldn't they? I'd go from "quirky performer" to "screen icon" overnight. Wistful girls would hang posters of me on their bedroom walls, all emblazoned with smarmy quotes about "burning bright."

Enough with the dark thoughts. The only good idea I've had all night was going for a swim, but like hell would I actually get this swimsuit wet. It costs as much as my car, and Silone would kill me.

I slipped out of it and let the ocean air prick goosebumps in my skin. I took a single step toward the water, and a star raged into life right in front of me.

My first, immediate thought was paparazzi in a helicopter, shining a spotlight to get their scandalous nudes. I was so annoyed with myself. Then I realized that the light wasn't far away, or low over the water. It was only a few feet from me. Hovering above the sand.

No this was over no—

But it's not that.

I don't . . . think?

It looked like an angel: a ball of light so bright it's like somebody punched a hole in the sky. But this one wasn't white—not entirely. Shades of blue flickered in and out of it, danced around the edges, flipped and shifted to red. They went prismatic, and started flashing. It was almost playful. And what's more: There was no sound at all. No awful noise like a million people screaming. In fact, the whole world went utterly quiet. I couldn't even hear the ocean anymore.

An idea formed in my mind. It was Kaitlyn's face, but not how I remembered it: just crude sketches of the important details, the rest washed out by time. It was really her: split ends and shy smile and everything.

"K?" I said, and the colors flared in response.

More ideas came surging in, complicated things far beyond words. There was comfort there, plus contentment, loss, pride, and guilt. But most of all, there was a giddy sense of awe.

Landscapes flashed through my mind: a barren field of green dust, three suns rising over a mountain range that absolutely dwarfed anything on Earth. An ocean made of mercury, silver storms and metal waves. A place where time fell like rain, in intermittent sheets, the world utterly frozen in the intervals between them.

The images went on for hours, or maybe they all happened at once and it took me hours to process them all.

At some point, I blinked away the tears and realized that the angel's light had faded—I'd been staring at the moon instead. I wiped my eyes with the back of my hand and smiled at nothing. Or no: at everything.

I picked up a handful of pebbles and let them fall through my fingers. I ran my toes through the waves. I laughed at the trees. The cool sand pooled around my feet with every step like I was melting into the Earth itself. Eventually I made it back to the party. What few guests remained milled about in small groups, nursing old cocktails that were mostly melted ice. When they saw me, they all smiled and laughed with me, because we were perfect and ridiculous things, blazing through life like comets.

And also because I had forgotten my swimsuit back at the beach.

I guess that's just more ammo for the eternal party girl myth.

THIRTY-FIVE

Carey. 2015. Los Angeles, California. Santa Monica.

"Listen, lady, first thing: I didn't puke on your dog, okay? No way to prove that's mine. Could be anybody's puke. And second, that's . . . pretty much pure liquor. Wash right off. So what're you so wound up about?"

Uptight bitch won't listen to reason. She's got that face. That "I'm about to call the cops" face. I hate that face. Started seeing it more often since I moved out here to the beach. Hitting the bottle pretty hard. Got a rotten burning feeling down in my guts that won't drink away. Figure I didn't have a lot of time left, so why not retire out west? Just a few miles west, actually . . .

Oh, they'll let you sleep in the park in Santa Monica, sure. But the second you punch a mime on the promenade they're all "public disturbance" this, and "pressing charges" that.

And I said to 'em, I said:

"Who's gonna press charges? *That* sumbitch ain't sayin' nothin'!"

I yell the punch line at a young kid with a gnarly beard. I

figure, you got a thing like that on your face, you got a sense of humor.

Fucker doesn't laugh.

"S'funny," I tell the kid. Just trying to help him out. Let him know what humor is.

He shakes his head like he's sad for me. The utter shit.

Boy, I love bus stops. All these people hate me, but they can't leave or they'll miss their ride. It's the perfect place to hold my court. The only downside is those guys in blue that—yep, they're coming this way.

That crazy bitch and her puke-dog ratted me out. Whatever happened to manners, huh? Used to be, we have a problem, we hash it out like people. Now it's like every little crime and the cops get involved.

Well.

Fuck 'em!

I used to swear Jim Beam was the fightin'est liquor around. You wanna end the night kicking a guy in an alley, you start the night with Jimmy. But that's before I found this. . . .

What is this?

I peer at the bottle. It's all blurry, but I can see it's got a picture of a spider on it.

That's usually not a good sign.

Well, I'm all fueled up on fight juice and I can't even remember what it was like to give a fuck, so sure, lady—

"Call all the cops!" I yell at her rapidly disappearing ass. "Call all the cops in the world!"

Oh hell, while I was busy yelling at them, the pigs snuck up and grabbed both my arms. That's not fair. That's cheatin'.

Ha, but I still got a forehead.

I swing it at the nearest chiseled jaw. My aim is shit. Just clip him in the ear. Make him mad.

"Lights out," I say.

"Lights out," he affirms, before swinging me facedown into the sidewalk.

. . .

Turns out that was a lie.

I woke up staring at a bare bulb in a metal cage. Damn thing must've been a million watts for the headache it was giving me. I was looking forward to a nice dark place to crash for a while. Nothing like being able to actually see the world around you to make you hate it all.

I closed my eyes, but I could still see that cruel white light burning through my eyelids. I opened them again, and I swore the fucking thing had grown.

Or gotten closer.

Or—

Oh, god damn it.

The ball of light wasn't in its cage anymore. It was hovering a few feet above my head, those sick shapes and static screams piercing my—

"Hey, wait," I said. "Where's the sound effects?"

The angel didn't respond.

There were colors in this one, too. I'm not sure which ones. Felt like every time I tried to chase one down it was somewhere else, or something else. I didn't get that cold sensation from its presence, either. In fact, looking at it now, it was almost . . . familiar. . . .

"Kaitlyn?" I asked.

Laughter. Not the sound, the abstract idea. It sprang into my thoughts and wiggled around there.

"What the hell is going on?" I asked.

A million more ideas came bursting through every door and window in my mind. Forgiveness. Want. Recrimination. Short films of me and Kaitlyn in that gray building beneath the coast, only I wasn't pulling the trigger in these movies. I dropped the gun, or unloaded it, or threw it in the sea—

"You made me do it?" I said.

Apologies. Regret. Necessity. An alien snapshot: shining blue cliffs spilling out dense gas like a waterfall. A red planet with streaks of white, thousands of times larger than Earth, with glowing purple lines undulating all across its surface. An eternal aurora, a sea of diamond—

"What is this shit?" I said, swatting my hands at the air.

The images died down.

"I don't care about this Star Trek garbage."

The angel was silent.

I had absolutely no external cues to assume so, but I'm still pretty sure she was annoyed.

"Come on, now," I said. "Like you were gonna win me over with waterfalls and pretty colors? I don't need that. I just . . . just tell me you're okay. Wherever you are. Whatever you are."

Ideas: longing and heartsickness. But also contentment. Curiosity. Excitement. Burning like a road flare above all else: Determination.

She was still fighting. Good.

Ideas: Want. Questions. Self.

"What do I want?" I guessed. The light shimmered affirmation.

I felt a presence tenderly poking around inside of me. Slipping between my atoms into the core of my being, adjusting the code that makes me who I am. Removing sadness, dulling self-hatred. . .

"No!" I jumped up from the cot and backed into the farthest corner of the cell. "Don't you god damn dare change it. Don't you god damn dare make me pretty."

Confusion. Desperation. Help.

"Just . . ." I slumped to the ground. I could feel the cold concrete through my worn jeans. "Just tell me what it was all for."

Inside my head, I saw a glowing nest of tentacles shrieking and dying. In the distance, I felt something immense begin to move—

"The space whale?" I laughed.

The light did not.

Ideas: Big. Old. God/Not God.

"So what, God's been gone forever and now we made it so he can come back? Great. Is he gonna hand out harps and togas?"

Wrong. Uncertain. God/Not God. Good/Not Good. Existence. Natural. Neutral.

I suddenly remembered, with painful clarity, a biology lesson that I'd tuned out of back in grade school. The teacher was up there droning on and on about some boring crap, so I was entertaining myself by drawing crude boobies over all the pictures of girls in my textbook. I couldn't have told you what the lesson was about to save my life. But this scene was too sharp for one of my dull memories. This wasn't me. This was Kaitlyn, showing me. I heard my teacher's voice, clear as day:

"When the body is sick, it produces antibodies to defend itself from within—"

The memory cut out. Then I saw every single person I ever knew all at once: Wash, Matt, Safety Pins, Elmer Spikes, Thing 1 and Thing 2, Tub and Meryll, Randall,

Rosa, my mom and dad, our old mailman, the cops that threw me in here, Kaitlyn, Jackie, and thousands more.

I threw up.

"Christ," I said, still reeling. "Don't do that. It's like being punched in the brain by a high school yearbook."

Apologies. Inhuman. Forget.

"So what," I said to the ball of light. "The space whale is, like, the whole universe, and we're, like, its antibodies, fighting off disease?"

Rejoice! Correct. Surprise.

"And the disease was the angels?"

Pride. Gratitude. Complete.

"Well la di da for the space whale," I said. "I'm glad all my friends died so it didn't have a tummy ache anymore."

Sadness. Disapproval. Hope.

I felt that slick, lurching movement in the base of my soul that meant something was rooting around inside of me.

"No!" I screamed. "I don't need solving."

But the angel didn't stop. It churned inside of me, shifting and rearranging until—

Nothing.

I ran a mental inventory: Every shitty thing that ever happened to me was still right there, front and center.

At least I think it was. Would I know if it wasn't?

I remembered, in vivid detail, pulling the trigger and watching Kaitlyn die. If she was going to start somewhere, it would have been there.

She hadn't changed a thing.

"What . . ." I started to say, but that was it.

The light had gone out.

I sat on the cot and stared at the cell walls.

That's the thing about jail: It doesn't give you a damn

thing to do but think. Think, sleep, or masturbate. My head hurt too bad to sleep and I didn't have anything to clean up with after masturbating, so that left thinking.

That shit angel-Kaitlyn said, when she was trying to explain everything to me. It just didn't hit home. But the more I thought about it, the more I realized it wasn't that she was wrong, she was just using the wrong metaphor. The antibody stuff—maybe smarter guys than me understand that and find it comforting—but I don't see it that way. Now, this is just me. This is just my take on it, and it probably doesn't help you feel any better—any less alone or weak or small or whatever your fucking problem is—but it does the trick for me. Kaitlyn was trying to tell me this:

When we look up and pray to God for help, we're being idiots. God doesn't help us. It doesn't give us anything. It doesn't need to. God isn't up there handing out weapons so we can fight evil.

We *are* the weapons.

And that? That's something I can wrap my head around.

I sat on my uncomfortable jail cell cot and I thought about that for hours before I finally realized what was different: The sickly pain in my guts had subsided.

Did I just get a liver transplant from a ghost?

I burst out laughing.

"If you think that's gonna stop me drinking," I yelled at the bare bulb, shining stoically in its metal cage. "You got another think comin'!"

Still . . .

. . .

Maybe I *would* switch to beer.

ACKNOWLEDGEMENTS

My agent, Sam Morgan, has always believed in me. I don't know why he does that. Somebody get him to stop; it's bad for his health. The fine folks at Tor published and supported all three installments of this very strange story, no matter how poorly I delivered it (or what it was scrawled in). My wife didn't leave me when I devoted years of my free time to "something about space whales and punk rockers." I love her for that, and many other things. My family managed to be proud of me for all of this, or at least lied about it very, very well. My dogs did not eat my face when I passed out on my keyboard some nights. They are good dogs.

ABOUT THE AUTHOR

Robert Brockway is a Senior Editor and columnist for Cracked.com. In addition to *The Unnoticeables* series, he is the author of two books, the cyberpunk novel *Rx: A Tale of Electronegativity*, and the essay collection *Everything is Going to Kill Everybody: The Terrifyingly Real Ways the World Wants You Dead*. He lives in Portland, Oregon, with his wife Meagan and their two dogs. He has been known, on occasion, to have a beard. You can find him online at

www.robertbrockway.net
or on Twitter
@Brockway_LLC

THE UNNOTICEABLES

By Robert Brockway

There are angels, and they are not beneficent or loving. But they do watch over us. They watch our lives unfold, analyzing us for repeating patterns and redundancies. When they find them, the angels simplify those patterns, they remove the redundancies, and the problem that is you gets solved.

Carey doesn't much like that idea. As a punk living in New York City, 1977, Carey is sick and tired of watching the strange kids with the unnoticeable faces abduct his friends. He doesn't care about the rumors of tarmonsters in the sewers, or unkillable psychopaths invading the punk scene—all he wants is drink cheap beer and dispense asskickings.

Kaitlyn isn't sure what she's doing with her life. She came to Hollywood in 2013 to be a stunt woman, but last night a former teen heartthrob tried to eat her, her best friend has just gone missing, and there's an angel outside her apartment.

Whatever she plans on doing with her life, it should probably happen in the few remaining minutes she has left of it.

There are angels. There are demons. They are the same thing. It's up to Carey and Kaitlyn to stop them. The survival of the human race is in their hands.

We are, all of us, well and truly screwed.

TITANBOOKS.COM

THE EMPTY ONES

By Robert Brockway

1977 was a bad year for Carey: The NYC summer was brutally hot, he barely made rent, and most of his friends were butchered by a cult. He needs a vacation. You know where there's supposed to be a killer punk scene? London. Oh, plus the leader of the aforementioned murderous cult is building an army there. Time to mix business with pleasure…

2013 was a bad year for Kaitlyn, too: LA was distinctly unkind to her aspirations towards a career in stunt work, she hooked up with her childhood crush, Marco—but he turned out to be an immortal psychopath trying to devour her soul. Now she's on the run through the American Southwest. She heard Marco's in Mexico, though, so all she has to do is cross the border, navigate a sea of acidic sludge monsters, and find a way to kill an unkillable monster before he sacrifices her and her friends to his extra-dimensional god. Nobody said a career in the entertainment industry would be easy…

For more fantastic fiction, author events, exclusive
excerpts, competitions, limited editions and more

Visit our website
titanbooks.com

Like us on Facebook
facebook.com/titanbooks

Follow us on Twitter
@TitanBooks

Email us
readerfeedback@titanemail.com